TOKYO EVER AFTER

TOKYO EVER AFTER

EMIKO JEAN

MACMILLAN

First published in the US 2021 by Flatiron Books, 120 Fifth Avenue, New York, NY 10271

First published in the UK 2021 by Macmillan Children's Books
an imprint of Pan Macmillan
The Smithson, 6 Briset Street, London EC1M 5NR
EU representative: Macmillan Publishers Ireland Limited,
Mallard Lodge, Lansdowne Village, Dublin 4
Associated companies throughout the world
www.panmacmillan.com

ISBN 978-1-5098-9999-9

1 3 5 7 9 8 6 4 2

A CIP catalogue record for this book is available from the British Library.

Printed and bound by CPI Group (UK) Ltd, Croydon CR0 4YY

MIX
Paper from
responsible sources
FSC® C116313

For all the girls who lead with their hearts

THE IMPERIAL FAMILY*

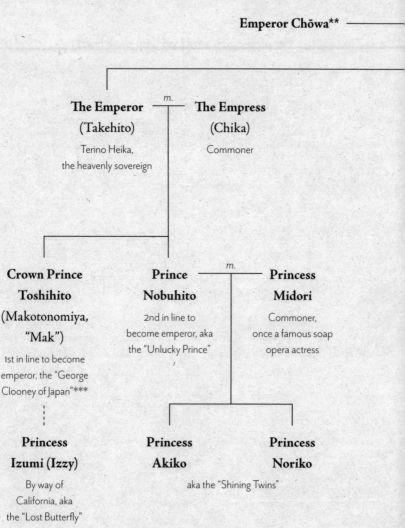

Emperor Chōwa**

The Emperor
(Takehito)

Tennō Heika,
the heavenly sovereign

m.

The Empress
(Chika)

Commoner

**Crown Prince
Toshihito**
(Makotonomiya,
"Mak")

1st in line to become
emperor, the "George
Clooney of Japan"***

**Prince
Nobuhito**

2nd in line to
become emperor, aka
the "Unlucky Prince"

m.

**Princess
Midori**

Commoner,
once a famous soap
opera actress

**Princess
Izumi (Izzy)**

By way of
California, aka
the "Lost Butterfly"

**Princess
Akiko**

**Princess
Noriko**

aka the "Shining Twins"

* an annotated, unofficial genealogy
** deceased
*** pre–Amal and twins

m. **Empress Aimi****

~~**Princess**~~ **Kuniko****

Abdicated, left everything to her tennis partner, Sei

Princess Tamako —— *m.* —— **Prince Yukihito**

3rd in line to become emperor

~~**Princess**~~ **Yumiko**

Left royal house, married a commoner, couldn't be happier

Princess Asako —— *m.* —— **Prince Yasuhito**

Commoner, keeps a secret residence for her cats

4th in line to become emperor, sleeps with a teddy bear

Princess Sachiko

Engaged to a commoner

Prince Masahito

Succession doesn't matter at this point, insists his room be cleaned 3x a day

Prince Yoshihito

Spends most of his time in Tokyo's red-light district

THE TOKYO TATTLER

The Lost Butterfly gets her wings clipped

April 4, 2021

A timeless elegance imbued Prime Minister Adachi's wedding to shipping heiress Haya Tajima at the luxurious New Otani Hotel. Though this is the PM's second marriage (his first wife passed away several years ago), no expense was spared. Men wore coattails. Women dressed in silks. Glasses bubbled over with Dom Pérignon. Black-and-white swans, imported from Australia, swam in the garden pools. Attendees were a veritable feast of Japan's upper-crust society, including the imperial family. Even His Imperial Highness Crown Prince Toshihito was present, despite ongoing disagreements with the PM.

But the focus wasn't on the feud, or even the bride and groom, for that matter. All eyes were turned to the newly minted princess, Her Imperial Highness Princess Izumi, aka the Lost Butterfly. The wedding marked her first formal entrance into Japan society. Would she fly—or fall?

HIH Princess Izumi certainly dressed the part in a jade silk gown and Mikimoto pearls, pulled from the imperial vaults and gifted by the empress. Press wasn't allowed inside the actual celebration, but by all accounts, the affair was flawless.

So why was the Lost Butterfly spied boarding a train to Kyoto this morning? The Imperial Household Agency insists it was a planned, scheduled trip to the countryside. But we all know the Kyoto imperial villa is where royals go to repent. Last year, His Imperial Highness Prince Yoshihito stayed there while he recovered from an unauthorized trip to Sweden.

It appears this butterfly's wings have been clipped. What could HIH Princess Izumi have possibly done to warrant an expulsion from the Tokyo imperial estate? No one has a clue. But somebody is definitely in *trouble* . . .

1

It is the sacred duty of best friends to convince you to do the things you should not do.

"You're never going to finish this. You tried. You really tried," Noora, aforementioned best friend, says. "You gave it a shot."

A shot consisted of one five-minute attempt at an essay on the theme of personal growth in *Huckleberry Finn*. Noora is supposed to be helping me. I called her over for moral support. "Better we just give up and move on." She flops onto my bed, arms across her eyes—the literal definition of a swoon. So dramatic.

Her argument is compelling. I've had four weeks to work on the journal. Today is Monday. It is due Tuesday. I don't know enough about math to approximate the statistics of finishing on time, but I bet they're low. Hello, consequences of my own actions. We meet again, old friend.

Noora's head pops up from my pillow. "Good Lord, your dog stinks."

I cuddle Tamagotchi close to my chest. "It's not his fault." My terrier mix has a rare glandular condition for which there is no cure or medication. He also has a you're-so-ugly-you're-cute face and a gross fetish for his own feet. He sucks his toes.

Pretty sure I was put on this earth to love this canine.

"I can't ditch the assignment. I need it to pass the class,"

I say, surprising myself. I am seldom the voice of reason. Confession: there is no voice of reason in our friendship. Conversations usually go:

Noora: *suggests bad idea*

Me: *hesitates*

Noora: *disappointed face*

Me: *comes up with worse idea*

Noora: *delighted face*

Basically, she instigates and I double down. She's the Timberlake to my Biel, the Edward to my Bella, the Pauly D to my Jersey Shore. My bestie from another teste. My ride or die. It's been this way since second grade when we bonded over our skin color—a shade darker than the white kids in Mount Shasta—and a shared inability to follow simple instructions. "Draw a flower?" *Scoff.* How about an entire ocean landscape with starfish criminals and an I-don't-play-by-the-rules dolphin detective instead?

Together, we're one half of an Asian Girl Gang—AGG, for short. Think less organized crime, more *Golden Girls*. Hansani and Glory are the other two parts. Membership dues are strict and paid in some claim to Asian ancestry. Meaning: we're pan-Asian. In a town strung together with tie-dyes and confederate flags, one cannot afford to discriminate.

Noora levels me with her eyes. "It's time to give up. Adapt. Overcome. Be at peace with your failure. Let's go to the Emporium. I wonder if that cute guy still works behind the counter. Remember when Glory got all flustered and ordered Reese's penises ice cream? C'mon, Zoom Zoom," she cajoles.

"I wish you'd never heard my mother call me that." I shift, and Tamagotchi scrambles from my arms. It is no secret: I love him more than he loves me. He circles and lays down, tucking his chin into his butt. So. Cute.

Noora shrugs. "I did, though, and it's amazing. Now I cannot *not* use it."

"I prefer Izzy."

"You prefer Izumi," she volleys back.

Correct. But by the third grade, I'd heard those three syllables butchered enough to want to simplify my name. It's easier this way.

"If white people can learn Klingon, they can learn to pronounce your name."

When someone is right, they're right. "True," I admit.

My bestie taps her fingers against her stomach, a clear sign of boredom. She sits up, and her smile is catlike—secretive, smug. Another reason I'm a dog person. Never trust a cat, they'll eat your face if you die. (I have no proof of this. Only a strong gut feeling.) "Forget the Emporium, then. I'm feeling pale and unattractive."

Now I'm grinning. We've been down this road before. I am happy to follow. "Maybe we should just freshen up and try again?" I ever so helpfully suggest. Tamagotchi's ears perk up.

Noora nods sagely. "Great minds think alike." She flashes me another smile and dashes out the door toward Mom's master bathroom, otherwise known as the Rodeo Drive of cosmetics. It's hard to think about what's on the chipped vinyl counter and *not* salivate—shiny lacquered cases of Chanel eye shadow palettes, a La Prairie caviar sleep mask, Yves Saint Laurent Couture eyeliner. Oh, and Korean skincare products, anyone? Yes, please. Each decadent little indulgence holds a promise of better tomorrows. Like, things are super bad right now, but I really think this bronzer in Golden Goddess is going to turn it all around.

Irony is, the pricey makeup is the diametric opposite of mom's no-fuss practicality. She drives a Prius, next-level recycles (sometimes I think she had a child just to help her turn the compost pile), and reuses her pantyhose. Got leftover soap slivers? Shove them in the toe of an old stocking and get every last bit of suds out of them. When I point out this hypocrisy to Mom, she is flat-out dismissive. "Whatever," she says. "It's all part of my feminine mystique." I don't disagree. We ladies contain multitudes. What it comes down to is, the glosses and highlighters are Mom's guilty pleasure. And it's purely Noora's and my pleasure to paint our faces while Mom is teaching at the local community college.

I find Noora applying a Dior gloss and peeking through the blinds. "Jones is in your backyard again."

I cross the carpet and join Noora to peer out the window. Yep, that's him. Our next-door neighbor wears a floppy pink sun hat, white T-shirt, yellow Crocs, and a sarong so colorful it's offensive—I mean, who created such an unholy thing?

He carries two jars of dark liquid and places them on our back porch. Probably kombucha. The bearded wonder is sweet on my mom, brews his own tea, keeps bees, and his favorite T-shirt says Love Sees No Color. This, of course, is a lie. Love definitely sees color. Example: when I mustered up the courage to tell my seventh grade crush I liked him, he replied, "Sorry, I just don't find Asian chicks attractive." Since then, my love life has followed the same cursed path. My last relationship ended in a dumpster fire. His name was Forest and he cheated on me during homecoming. We consciously uncoupled. I rub my side where there is a sudden sharp pain—probably gas, definitely not the memory.

"It's a little creepy that he brings your mom stuff all the time. Kind of like a feral cat that leaves dead mice on your porch." Noora re-caps the gloss and smooths her lips together. The deep red color matches her personality. Subtle is not in her vocabulary.

I cross my arms. "Two weeks ago, he brought her a book of pressed flowers." Mom may be a bio professor, but botany is her real jam. What Jones lacks in fashion, he makes up for in game. I'll give that to him.

Noora moves from the window and pitches the gloss onto Mom's flea market quilt. Mom's a fan of old things. "Is this the book he made her? *Rare Orchids of North America?*" She's at Mom's nightstand now, rifling through her stuff. Such a snoop.

"No," I say. "That's different." I've never paid much attention to the book. Because, rare orchids and all.

Noora flips open the cover. "Ruh-roh, Scooby Doo. What's this?" She taps a finger against the title page and begins reading. "My dearest Hanako—"

It takes a moment for me to catch up. *Dearest? Hanako?* I lunge, snatching the book from her hands.

"Grabby," she mumbles, resting a chin on my shoulder.

The handwriting is neat but slanted, the pencil nearly faded.

My dearest Hanako,

Please let these words say what I cannot speak:

I wish I were close
To you as the wet skirt of
A salt girl to her body.
I think of you always.
—Yamabe no Akahito

Yours,
Makoto "Mak"
2003

Noora whistles low. "Guess Jones isn't your mom's only not-so-secret admirer."

I sit down on the bed. "Mom never mentioned a Makoto." I don't know how to feel about that fact. It's strange to think about your parent's life before you. Call me narcissistic, but it's a teen's prerogative to believe everything started the moment you were born. Like: *Izzy's here now. Earth, you may begin spinning.* I don't know, maybe it's an only child thing. Or maybe my mom loved me so much she made it seem that way.

I'm still processing this when Noora carefully says, "So, hey. You were born in 2003."

"Yeah." I swallow, staring at the page. Our thoughts have turned in the same improbable, yet intuitively correct direction. Mom said she got pregnant with me in her final year of college. My parents were in the same senior class. Harvard, 2003. My father was another student, visiting from Japan. A one-night stand. *But not a mistake*, she always insisted. *Never a mistake.*

I stare at the name. *Makoto. Mak.* What are the chances Mom had separate affairs with two different Japanese men in the year I was born? I glance at Noora. "This could be my father." Saying it out loud feels weird, heavy. Taboo.

The topic of my father has always been a biographical footnote. *Izzy was conceived in 2003 by Hanako Tanaka and an unknown Japanese male.* It isn't the knowledge of my origins that makes me feel bad. I am a daughter of the twenty-first century; no way I'd be ashamed of my mom's sexual liberation. I respect her decisions, even though the word *mom* and the word *sex* makes me want to set something on fire.

It's the *not* knowing that makes my soul ache. Walking down the street, examining people, and wondering: Are you my father? Could you know my father? Could you know something about me I don't?

Noora looks me over. "I know that look. You're getting your hopes up."

I hug the book to my chest. Sometimes it's hard not to be jealous of my bestie. She's got so much I don't—two parents and an enormous extended family. I've been to Thanksgiving at her house. It's a real Norman Rockwell painting except with a tipsy uncle, Farsi flying around, pomegranate gravy, and persimmon tarts in lieu of apple pie. She knows exactly where she comes from, who she is, what she's all about.

"Seriously," I say finally.

Noora sits down and nudges me. "Seriously? This could be your dad. This could not be your dad. No need to jump to conclusions." *Too late.*

As a kid, I thought lots about my father. Sometimes, I fantasized he was a dentist or an astronaut—and once, though I'll never admit it out loud, I wished he was white. Actually, I wished both my parents were white. White was beautiful. White was the color of my dolls and the models and families I saw on TV. Like shortening my name, a paler skin color and a rounder eye shape would have made my life so much easier, the world so much more accessible.

I glance at the page. "Harvard must have records of who attended." It comes out wobbly. I've never dared search for my father. I don't even really talk about him. For one, Mom hasn't really encouraged it. In fact, her unwillingness to speak about him *discouraged* it. So I kept quiet, not wanting to rock the mother-daughter boat. I still don't. But I shouldn't have to do this alone, either. Isn't that what best friends are for? To share the weight?

Click. Flash. Noora takes a picture of the page with her phone. "We'll get to the bottom of this," she promises. God, I wish I could bottle her confidence, her self-assuredness. If I only had half as much as she does. "You okay?" she asks.

My lips twitch. There's a skittery feeling in my chest. This could be big. Really big. "Yeah. It's just a lot to process."

Noora flings her arms around me, squeezing me tight. We hug it out. "Don't worry," she says earnestly. "We'll find him."

"You really think so?" I let all the hope shine in my eyes.

The catlike smile returns. "Is Cinnabon my downfall?"

"Based on past consumption, I'd say yes."

Her nod is swift and confident. "We'll find him."

See? Ride or die.

2

School. Noon. Tuesday. I barrel through the hallways of Mount Shasta High. Eighteen hours have passed since a book about rare orchids and a semiracy poem teetered my world off its axis.

It was a rough evening and morning. There were so many questions bouncing around in my mind—did Mom lie about not knowing my father? If so, why? Could my dad know about me? Then, why didn't he want me? The struggle is real. I've been careful to contain my hopes while simultaneously dodging my mother. It's good that I'm excellent at subterfuge. Under my bed, there is half a bottle of peach schnapps and a handful of romance novels (impoverished duke plus lower class heiress equals true love forever). Mom doesn't know any of this. Acting casual is key—just a girl going about her business, nothing to see here.

The library entrance is in view. I bear down, pushing past a group of cowboys and two girls named Harmony. Double doors slam behind me.

Ah, quiet at last. If only my thoughts were as easy to turn off. Deep in the stacks, Noora is waiting for me on pins and needles. I'm on tenterhooks, too. In the last hour, a flurry of texts passed between the AGG.

Noora

OMG. OMG. OMG.

Noora

Big news. Emergency AGG meeting
in the library during lunch.

Glory

We eat there every day.

Me

?

Noora

Be on time. You're not going to
want to miss this.

Glory

If this is about Denny Masterson's
third nipple again . . .

Noora

YOU WISH!

Hansani

How about a little hint?

Me

??

Noora

Puh-lease. And ruin my big reveal?

Noah fence, but you're just going to
have to wait.

I push down the hope-filled balloon in my chest. It is very likely Noora's big news isn't about my alleged father anyway. She lives to call emergency meetings.

"Finally." Noora latches on to me, pulling me through the shelves. We emerge in the northeast corner. Hansani, a svelte Sri Lankan, and Glory, a half-Filipino with eyebrows I'd die and/or kill for, are already waiting at our usual table. These girls. *My* girls. We have the unique ability to stare at one another and know exactly what the other is feeling. Our connection was born in elementary school, where we learned our biggest "flaw" was our appearance.

For me, it was Emily Billings. She cornered me on the school bus with her eyes taped up at an exaggerated slant. I knew I was different, but I didn't know different was bad until someone pointed it out. Of course, I laughed with the other kids. After all, humor is always the best defense. I pretended it didn't hurt. Just like I pretended it didn't hurt when some kid asked me if my family celebrated the bombing of Pearl Harbor like Christmas. Or when students requested my help on their math homework. Joke's on them, I'm terrible with numbers. Still, each time, something inside of me shrivels up, ashamed and silent.

Anyway, we get it. We all know what it's like to roll with the cultural punches. Noora gets questioned about why she doesn't wear a hijab. People wonder if Glory was adopted when she's with her white dad. Hansani endures Mr. Apu accents—wrong country, for starters. And of course, there's the universal *no, but where are you* really *from?*

The girls have already cracked into their lunches—pita and hummus for Hansani, egg salad for Glory. There's a No Eating sign above our table. Meh, rules are meant to be broken.

I dump my backpack and water bottle onto the table and smile at the other two. Noora falls into the chair beside me. She snaps her fingers at Glory. "Laptop."

Glory's eyes flick to Noora and narrow. "Say 'please,'" she says, even as she pulls out a shiny Chromebook.

Noora pokes her with a pencil. "You know I adore you, even if your name doesn't suit you." This is true. Though I'd never say it. Glory is the type of person to poke her finger in someone's mouth while they're yawning to establish dominance. Noora, on the other hand, is not afraid to say it. Their relationship is best described as love-hate. The two are so alike, and they don't even know it.

Glory hands over the laptop. "Stick me again with that pencil and I'll throat punch you."

So today, more hate than love.

"Can we get on with it?" I chime in.

Noora takes the laptop and types away. "Yes. Yes we can." She pauses, laces her hands together and cracks her knuckles. "Drumroll, please!"

Hansani obliges, tapping her fingers against the table.

Glory takes out a file and starts shaping her nails into talons.

I close my eyes. Brace myself. Allow the hope balloon in my chest to expand. *Let it be about him. And if it is him, let him not be a serial killer who collects skin suits.*

"I found him! I found Makoto. Mak. Your father!" Noora exclaims.

I open my eyes. Blink. Her words dig under my skin, grow roots, leaves. *Bloom*. So many feelings. Above them all, discomfort. So I do what I do best. I crack a joke. I deflect. "This isn't about Denny's third nipple?"

Noora flicks a hand. "God, no. That's so two and a half months ago. Now, before I show you what I found, I need to tell you something." She seems unsure, serious.

Blood rushes in my ears. Hansani reaches across the table and lays her hand over mine. She has a sixth sense of sorts where she can detect emotional frequencies. It's her superpower.

I glance at Glory and Hansani. Do they know what Noora has found? Both shake their heads. It's one of our things, communicating by looks alone. We operate on the same wavelength. We're all in the dark right now. "Okay," I say. Deep breath. "Lay it on me." *Prepare for the worst. Hope for the best.*

Noora inhales gustily. "I am very attracted to your father."

Hansani giggles.

Glory rolls her eyes.

The wind is knocked out of my nervous sails. "Yuck," I say. "Plus, we don't even know if he's my father yet."

"Oh, he's your dad."

Dad. In my mind I've always referred to him as my father, never *Dad*. The former is a title given at birth, the latter earned over time—after scraped knees and sleepless nights and graduations. I don't have a *dad*. But I could. The promise of that scoots me to the edge of my seat.

Noora says, "You're a dead ringer for him. Check it out." She turns the laptop to face the group. Images fill the screen.

Glory slams her nail file on the table. "Fothermucker."

Hansani whistles low. "Shut your face."

"Meet Makotonomiya Toshihito. Who's your daddy, Zoom Zoom?" Noora exclaims. She moves the cursor and clicks, enlarging a photo. It's even more eerie up close. He's posing in front of a brick building. Harvard, I presume. He's young in the photo. His smile full of promise and foolish hope. The kind of grin before the world knocks your teeth out. The resemblance is impossible to ignore. Uncanny. There I am in his full lips, in his straight nose, even in the spaces between his teeth.

My mouth opens, closes, then opens again.

"Noora was right. Holy hot-dad," Glory says.

Fist bumps go around the table. My pulse is racing. I remind myself heart attacks are rare in eighteen-year-olds. "How'd you . . ." I pause. Gather myself. Gather my thoughts. "How'd you find him?"

"Harvard didn't have a student register available online, but they do have an order form along with a phone number. I called this morning. Spoke to a super cool chick named Olivia. Funny story, she grew up in Ashland." Ashland is close to Mount Shasta. "We got along like a house on fire. We're friends now. She'll probably name her first child after me."

"Ugh, get to the point," Glory grinds out.

As for me, I can't stop staring at him. At Makoto. My father. At all our similarities. We have the same eyebrows, though I've plucked mine into submission. I brush my fingers against the screen, then withdraw them. No need to get emotionally attached.

Noora goes on. "Anyway, she couldn't tell me very much.

Something about confidentiality. So that was kind of a dead end."

"Oh my God," Glory says.

Noora frowns at Glory. "So then I did a Google search of the words: Makoto, Mak, Harvard 2003. And there he was. Easy peasy Japanese-y." Noora waves a hand in front of my face. "All right?"

Words form and die in my throat. "Yes. No. Maybe?"

"I'm going to take that as a yes, because there's more."

More? How could there be more?

"Stay with me."

Noora is quiet for a moment. She clears her throat. *Ahem.* I'm drawn from the screen.

"He's royalty." Pause. Her smile grows brighter. "A prince." Another pause. Smile brighter still. "*The* Crown Prince of Japan, to be exact. His real name is Makotonomiya Toshihito."

Seconds tick by on the clock above our heads. Noora's grin brittles. I snort. I have the distinct feeling of standing at the end of a very long and dark tunnel.

"I don't think she's okay," Hansani whispers, concerned. "Maybe we should call the nurse."

"We don't have a nurse anymore. Budget cuts," Glory states.

Hysteria swells in my throat. It's got nowhere to go but up and out. I laugh sharply, uncontrollably. Yeah, I'm losing it.

Noora says, "Seriously, Zoom Zoom, this isn't funny. You're a prince's love child. The fruit of his loins."

"The words *fruit* and *loins* should never be said together," Glory remarks, mouth full of egg salad.

Noora's grin flattens into one unhappy line. "You don't

believe me. None of you believe me. Fine. Proof, meet pudding." She minimizes the photo and brings up an article from a newspaper.

THE TOKYO TATTLER

Oldest unmarried heir in the history of the Chrysanthemum throne has no plans to marry

May 23, 2018

At thirty-nine years old, His Imperial Highness Crown Prince Toshihito remains a confirmed bachelor and has no plans to marry, a palace insider reports. Despite plenty of eligible candidates, the Crown Prince refuses to settle down. The Imperial Household Agency is extremely distressed, though they won't come out and say it . . .

The article goes on to speculate on the Crown Prince's eligible brides: a distant royal relative, the niece of an official at the Ise Grand Shrine, the granddaughter of the former prime minister of Japan, or the daughter of a wealthy industrialist. Pictures accompany the article of the women. They appear on my father's arm, beautiful show ponies basking in the limelight and his attention. He is opposite in demeanor—stoic, stance rigid, frown firmly in place. Nothing like his Harvard photo. There are criticisms of the women in the article, too.

Not the right hat for a garden party; not the right gloves for a state dinner; not enough family money—or worse, too much *new* family money.

The girls have gathered behind me. We stare at the laptop screen.

Hansani says, "He's like the Asian George Clooney."

"Pre–Amal and twins," Glory amends.

I close out of the article and spend the next five minutes clicking through more photos. There he is sharing the Covent Garden Royal Box with Prince Charles and Camilla for a performance of *La Traviata*. In another, brunching with the Grand Duke of Luxembourg at Betzdorf Castle. In another, sailing the Mediterranean with the King of Spain. On it goes: skiing in Liechtenstein with Prince Hans, attending a state dinner with President Sheikh bin Zayed al-Nahyan in the UAE . . . To top it all off, there's an *actual* photo of him with George Clooney! I slam the laptop closed and push away from the table, needing space.

Noora, Glory, and Hansani smile hesitantly. They radiate anxiety. "My father is the Crown Prince of Japan." Perhaps speaking it out loud will make it more real.

Nope.

It's hard to believe, but the pictures don't lie. I'm his spitting image. The fruit of his loins. Yeah, still don't like that term.

"Holy childhood-dreams-come-true! You're a princess," says Noora.

Princess. Most little girls dream about this. I didn't. My mom bought me building blocks with Ruth Bader Ginsburg and Hilary Clinton on them. I just dreamed of having a father, knowing where I come from, and being able to speak proudly about who I am.

"If you're royalty, then I've got to be something, too," Noora barrels on. "I'm going to pay for that genealogy thing when I get home. Fingers crossed it shows I'm fifty percent Targaryen, thirty percent British royals, and one hundred percent Oprah's long-lost sister."

"I'm pretty sure that's not how it works," says Hansani. At Noora's stink eye, she holds up both hands. "Just saying."

Noora dismisses her and turns to me. "This is the greatest thing ever to happen to me. My best friend is royalty!" She squeezes her clenched fists under her chin and bats her eyes at me. "I'm going to ride your coattails so hard."

My head spins. This is more than I could ever want. More than I could ever dream up. What I've been waiting eighteen years for. And yet . . . something gets stuck in my throat. It's inescapable, unpalatable. "My whole life is a lie. Why would my mom hide this from me?"

Glory snaps her fingers. "That's the million-dollar question, my friend."

3

Messages

5:26 PM

Me

Legit, the thought of confronting
my mother is the best laxative ever.

Noora

You can do it.

Noora

Go in and *Law and Order* it up. It's
time she pays for her crimes. You
be the plucky DA who brings her to
justice.

Me

I'd much rather be Mariska
Hargitay. She's badass. Plus,
Ice-T is her partner.

Me

Gotta go. Mom's home.

Remember. Hammer of justice!

With a sigh, I silence my phone. My shoulders square. My heart resolves. The pit in my stomach remains. I carry it with me as I head down the hallway and into the kitchen. Mom is already banging around, opening and closing cupboards, pouring oil into a giant wok. Stir-fry night. I flex a tremor from my hands. *Play it cool.* Act natural. This shouldn't be hard to do. It's practically my job to hang around the kitchen starting at six o'clock and ask every ten minutes when dinner will be ready.

I belly up to the bar and sit on one of the stools. Mugs hang from hooks under the cabinet. Mom collects them. Her favorites have quirky sayings. Geology Rocks is in my direct line of vision. Mom places a cutting board, knife, and multi-colored bell peppers in front of me. "Chop, chop," she says.

I do as I'm told, slicing into an orange bell pepper. "Mom?"

"Hm?" She wraps tofu in a cloth. She's removed her suit jacket, but still wears the rest of her "school uniform": button-up shirt with sleeves rolled to her elbows and a tasteful pencil skirt.

"Tell me again about my father, the sperm donor."

Our relationship used to be so straightforward. I could distill it into one sentence—single mom with daughter, two against the world. Now, it all seems so complicated. Everything has changed. But she doesn't realize it yet. Kind of like when Glory's parents got divorced. Her mom fell out of love and started dating their dentist while her dad planned their twentieth anniversary. Lies taint everything.

Mom closes her eyes. Ah, she's in one of her I've-had-a-long-day-and-don't-have time-for-this moods. "I've asked you not to use that term."

"Sorry. I go to public school. We have sex education. I know too much."

She unwraps the tofu, cubes it, and throws it into the wok. It sizzles and the sound is oddly satisfying, like coming home. "Can this wait? I'm in the middle of making dinner."

I grip the knife harder, a rush of determination courses through me. Her answer doesn't make me feel stabby. Not at all. "It can't wait. Just tell me again."

She stops and stares at me over her shoulder, a suspicious gleam in her eyes. "What is this about? Are you missing something not having a father?"

Gah, the look on her face—heartbreaking. My determination goes on the defensive. What can I say? *Yes. I miss having a dad. Even more, I miss having a past.* There isn't any family on Mom's side. She's sansei, third generation Japanese. Her grandparents emigrated in the thirties. They didn't speak the language and only had a whisper of a better life when they boarded a ship bound for America. After World War II, they slipped their heirloom kimono under the bed, put up Christmas trees in December, and exclusively spoke English.

But some traditions refuse to fade. They seep through the cracks and cling to the walls—remove your shoes before entering the house, always bring a gift when visiting someone for the first time, celebrate the New Year by eating Toshikoshi soba and mochi. The promise of that ghost life makes me yearn. I want to understand myself. I want to put my hands in the earth and pull up roots.

But I can't tell my mother any of this. I can't tell her that when people ask me about my story—who I am, where I come from—I tell it like it's an apology. *No, I don't speak Japanese. No, I've never been to Japan. No, I don't like sushi.* It's always clear in their disappointed gazes. I am not enough.

All of this would hurt her.

So instead I let my silence do the talking.

Her sigh is long and suffering. She looks to the ceiling. Lord, give her patience. "I met him my senior year of college at a party. We slept together. I found out I was pregnant with you after I graduated. By then, it was too late to find him."

"You never knew his name?"

She won't make eye contact. "That's right."

"Didn't know where he lived?"

"Nope."

"What about one of his friends? Did you try tracking him down through them?"

"We didn't have any mutual acquaintances."

"Huh."

"Are we done with this now? Did you finish your English project, the journal on *Huckleberry Finn*?"

I take her question as a personal insult. "Of course I finished it." Truth: I didn't finish it. But I did get a week extension. All hail the period excuse. What Mom doesn't know won't hurt her. "And no, we're not done talking about this."

Tofu crisps in the wok. She dumps in onion. "Izumi." I love the way my mom says my name. Elongating the *I*, softening around the *zumi*, an ounce of love behind it all. But today, there is an extra helping of annoyance.

"So he never told you his name was Makotonomiya

Toshihito?" I say his name softly, but it drops like a boulder onto our linoleum floor. This is the moment I know for sure Mom has lied about everything. She swallows, her lips part. Her dark eyes dart to mine. *Guilty. Guilty. Guilty.*

"How do you know that name?" Her voice is tinny.

I set the knife and bell pepper down. "I saw his name in that book on your nightstand. Well, part of it—the name Makoto. Noora and I figured out the rest."

"You went through my things?" Wisps of hair have escaped her low ponytail.

"No." A technicality. *Noora* went through her things. "I wasn't snooping. I came across it by accident."

Her eyebrows dart inward. She doesn't believe me. That's not the point. The point is . . . "You lied to me. You told me you didn't know his name. You told me he wasn't anybody. He's very much *somebody*." Her dishonesty is exposed. It feels as if the ground is shaking. A chasm forms between us. I cross my arms. Two bell peppers remain uncut. Vegetables and dinner be damned.

Mom's face shutters closed. She turns. I watch her profile. "So what? I knew who he was." She says, jabbing at the tofu and onion with a wooden spoon. "It was so trite. A poor girl falls in love with a prince. Things like that don't happen in real life. And if they do, they don't end in a happily ever after."

"Mom?" Her motions are mechanical. Stir. Season. Toss. "Mom!" This gets her attention. We stare at each other. Many unsaid things pass between us. "Why did you lie to me?"

She shrugs, rinses broccoli, and sets to it with a butcher knife. "His whole life had been planned. Mine was just beginning. When I learned I was pregnant, I confided in a friend.

I was somewhat familiar with court life, but she educated me even more. It would have been constricting. You should have seen him at Harvard. There was always someone with him—a chamberlain, a valet, an imperial guard, or police. We stole kisses in the hallways and snuck away to hotels. He lived in a fishbowl." She pauses, wiping her hands on a dish towel. Her focus returns to me. "Women royals are especially scrutinized. Everything is done under a magnifying glass. You're picked apart for the causes you support, the dresses you wear, and what sort of child you bear. I witnessed your father given choices like he was a toddler. You can have this or that, but never all of it. Your life would have been determined by the family you were born into—I didn't want that for you. For us."

"And he agreed with all that?"

Her eyes dart away from mine. "I didn't tell him."

I ball my hand into a fist. Eighteen years old and my father doesn't know I exist. "You should've told him. He . . . maybe he would've stayed in the States."

Her smile holds all the sadness in the world. "He said more than once if he stayed in America, he'd be like a tree without sunlight. How could I ask that of him?"

"You should've told me. I deserved to know the truth."

"You're right." She flicks the burner off and removes the wok from the heat. She leans over the counter and cups my cheeks. Her fingers are cold. "We've had a good life together though, right? I guess all I can say is, I had your best interests at heart."

It is a mother's instinct to protect, I suppose. But her good intentions are eclipsed by my anger and her betrayal—a dangerous combination. I lash out. "And yours," I say.

She pulls away. "What?"

"You had your best interests at heart, too." I point out my mother's selfishness. I have no excuse for my awful behavior. But sometimes when you're down, you can't help but try to pull others into the gutter with you. It's lonely at the bottom. "You didn't want a life with my father so you chose something else, but I never got to choose."

Mom inhales sharply. I've hit her where it hurts the most. "Izumi—"

I slide from the stool. I let my guard down with my mom. Big mistake. I'd never have guessed she'd be someone who could hurt me. The world is a cruel and unfriendly place. Things are about to get ugly. A messy emotional breakdown looms on the horizon.

Ever so slowly I walk to my room, off to lick my wounds in private.

Mom gives me space. While I cry, Tamagotchi sleeps. He's not much of an emotional support animal. Our relationship is distinctly one-sided. I feed him treats and he burps in my face. Such is life.

Noora texts me a gif of a Chihuahua dancing on two legs.

Noora
Dying. What did your mom say?

I turn the phone over. I'm still sorting through my emotions, picking at the scab of my anger. Stewing.

There's a knock on the door. "Zoom Zoom?" Mom enters,

carrying a bowl of rice and stir-fry. She places dinner on my dresser and sits next to me on the bed. Since I'm still in a snit, I gaze out the window. She takes my hand. Warm and dry, her touch brings me comfort, despite everything.

"This is what I should have done years ago," she says. Her voice is calm, collected, easy, the lie no longer weighing it down. "Your father's name is Makotonomiya Toshihito. He is the Crown Prince of Japan. Someday, he will be emperor. People bowed to him, but he never asked me to. I called him Mak. And for one season, he was mine."

The sun shifts, descending. The tall grass in our backyard sways.

Soon, I know everything. My parents met at a party. It wasn't love at first sight, but there was a connection. The connection led to phone calls, then to meetings, then to overnights. They agreed to keep their relationship a secret. Mom didn't want the attention. "I worked so hard to get where I was. I couldn't risk it for a boy," she explains. "He respected my wishes. We had fun. But we both knew it wasn't meant to last. Our worlds were too different." She laughs. "He didn't know how to iron a shirt, do laundry, or make a cup of soup. He drank like a fish, loved microbeers. And he was funny. He had this dry sense of humor and a wicked wit. You wouldn't know you were at the receiving end of one of his barbs until you were bleeding and he was gone."

My eyes crinkle at the corners. "You kept the book he gave you all these years?"

She gazes at her lap. "It's a rare edition. I forgot the poem was in there." We both know she's lying. My mom still totally holds a candle for my father. The secret is hers to keep.

Mom stands and withdraws a slip of paper from her pocket. "I have no idea how to get hold of him now, but we did have mutual friends. David Meier is a chemistry professor at the University of Stockholm. He and your father were close. They might keep in touch." She places the slip of paper next to my hip and touches my shoulder, then my cheek. "Try to eat something."

As she goes to close the door I say, "I'm sorry . . . for what I said before."

"I'm sorry, too," she says. "For what I never said." A bridge forms over the gap between us—rickety, but passable. Everything will be okay.

I'm itching to grab the paper. "One more thing," I say. "You really don't mind if I try to get in touch with him?" If we connect, we'd be diving headfirst into the fishbowl. Our lives might never be the same.

She hesitates. Apprehension sits heavy on her shoulders. A single headshake, and her spine straightens. It's a signature Mom move, bracing for the hard stuff. I've seen it before, like on my first day of kindergarten, when I clung to her ankles and cried as she pried my fingers from her body. Or the time she cut her hand making me a sandwich. Blood was everywhere. She wrapped it in a towel and we drove to the emergency room, but not before she packed my lunch and some books. She's always put me first.

"No, I don't mind." Her voice is so gentle, so understanding I want to spontaneously burst into tears again. "I've accomplished what I wanted to and more. Our life is small in comparison to his. But I'm happy."

She leaves and I pick up the slip of paper. On it is an email address, davidmeier@stockholm.uni. I press the envelope icon on my phone.

Dear Mr. Meier,

My name is Izumi Tanaka. My mother, Hanako, graduated Harvard in 2003 and she believes you may have kept in touch with my father, Makotonomiya Toshihito. It is my hope you will be able to connect me with him. Below, I've included a note that you may forward to him.

Thanks,
Izumi

I take a deep breath and start a letter to my father.

Dear Mak,

You don't know me but I know you.

Ugh. Too creepy. Too casual. I delete and start again.

Dear Crown Prince Toshihito,

I think I'm your daughter . . .

4

"Nothing?" Glory asks, balling up a bit of napkin.

I lean back in the red vinyl booth and rub my overfull stomach. Black Bear Diner is a Mount Shasta institution. It is known for its newspaper menus, kitschy black-bear-slash-lumberjack decor, and dinner plate–sized biscuits. We frequent here on the regular. We come. We eat. We conquer. This is where we live our best lives. "Nope."

Hansani's smile is gentle. She pats my hand. "Give it some more time. It's only been a week or so."

Actually, it's been thirteen days, two hours, and five minutes since I sent the email to David Meier. Not that I'm counting or anything. I stopped compulsively checking my email every five minutes yesterday. Now I only check it every hour. Progress.

I pull my hand back and shoot Hansani an appreciative glance. I have a special place in my heart for Hansani. She has a resting happy face and a total America's Sweetheart vibe. To boot, she's the size of an Ewok. I mean, if she'd let me, I'd carry her around in my pocket. Sometimes, our opinions differ. Like half of Mount Shasta's residents, she loves The Grateful Dead. I think their music is self-indulgent guitar noodling. There, I said it—fight me.

Noora says, "Maybe his email went to junk mail?"

Hansani makes a low humming noise of agreement.

"Already checked. Nothing."

Up until now, I hadn't considered the possibility my father might not want to know me. *Ouch.* The thought hurts. I care much more than I should. After all, he's nothing but a biological stranger.

Maybe if I say it enough times, I'll believe it.

Our bill arrives and we dig through our pockets and bags. We pay in crumpled ones and tip in change. I offer the waitress a shy, apologetic smile as we leave. *Sorry about the twenty percent in pennies.*

We load into Noora's hatchback, complete with peeling paint and a rock chip in the window shield. I claim shotgun and we head on to Lake Street toward Glory's house. Mount Shasta looms in the distance, a lonely white pyramid. Behind us is Main Street—one stoplight, half a dozen crystal shops, one indie bookstore, and one coffee shop. "We're dropping you off first." Noora peers at Glory in the rearview mirror. We pass a family on horseback. "And I need you to never wear those pants again."

Glory's leggings are bright purple with eyes all over them. "Fine by me," she says. "As long as you stop wearing two testicles on top of your head." Noora's hair is done up in twin buns.

I glance back and share a grin with Hansani. The two bicker the rest of the ride.

Fifteen minutes later, we pull up to Glory's cedar shingle house.

"Ugh." Glory slumps back in her seat, hugging her purse to her chest. We all know what this is about. A Mazda Miata is parked in front and coming down the driveway is her mom's new boyfriend. The dentist. He wears a thick gold chain and uses the term "cool beans" way too often. Glory despises him and would rather catch vomit in her bare hands than speak to him. It's no wonder, really. He's a total home-wrecker and has major yellow fever. Plus, he and her mom met each other on Facebook Marketplace. So yeah. "I'm going to have to talk to him." Already, he's waving.

"I got you." Noora's phone is out and she's ringing Glory on speaker.

Glory picks up and climbs out of the car. "Hi, do you have something important to tell me?" She bypasses the dentist without saying a word, doesn't even make eye contact. I silently root her on.

"I do. So important," Noora says. Glory is halfway up the drive. The dentist is in his car. "Those pants are worse from the back."

Glory opens her front door. "Fuck off," she says, but there's no heat in it.

The door closes. "Safe and sound?" Noora asks.

"Safe and sound. Love you."

"Love you, too." They hang up.

Hansani's house is next, a craftsman with a wraparound porch. "You have a kind, beautiful soul, Noora," she says, car door opened.

Noora makes a show of examining her nails. "I wouldn't attempt to tell anyone. I'll deny it. Then everyone will call you a liar and I'll be so embarrassed for you."

Hansani giggles and skips up her driveway.

We're off. Noora zips through the streets of Mount Shasta. Her driving is a cross between *Mario Kart* and *Grand Theft*

Auto. On this lazy Sunday, I've grabbed the oh-shit bar three times already. She pats my knee. "I haven't seen you this quiet since you and He-Who-Shall-Not-Be-Named broke up."

She's talking about Forest. After I found out he cheated, he called me emotionally unavailable. I called him a bag of rats disguised as a person. I'm not bitter. We wouldn't have worked out long-term anyway. He likes girls who don't wear makeup. I like guys who don't tell girls what to do with their bodies.

Forest is definitely not the reason I'm so glum. I'm trying to convince myself the letter didn't reach my father. It's not the first time I've made excuses for him. My mantra for the last eighteen years has been *If he knew about you, he'd love you.* I could tell this all to Noora, but instead I say, "Just focusing on surviving the drive." I give her a fake smile. "No offense."

Her mouth flattens. She casually extends her middle finger in my direction. "Some offense. But I'd be more offended if I didn't know you were deflecting."

Because misery loves company, I blurt the truth out. "He hasn't emailed me, Noora," I yell, crestfallen. "I've made a colossal mistake. This feels worse than never knowing my father. I should've just left it alone." New rule: never take risks. Risks are for the bold, the hard-hearted. I mean, what was I thinking? I literally eat the same thing for lunch every day. God, I'm dying. Dying.

Noora changes lanes and I jerk to the side. While she excels in school, I know for a fact she barely passed her driver's test.

My phone chimes with a text.

Mom

Where are you?

Me

With Noora. Almost home.

There are a few missed calls from Mom, too. We pull on to my street and Noora slows the car. *Thank goodness.* Cars are parked on the grass. *Hmm.*

"Jones must be having people over again," I say absently. Jones hosts a range of events, from farm-to-table dinners to an annual pseudo-bacchanalia with the Rainbow Gatherers, a seasonal group that congregates in Mount Shasta promoting peace, freedom, respect, and so on. They enjoy dancing, bongo music, and nudity. I've seen enough saggy buns to make my eyes bleed.

We park in my gravel driveway behind Mom's red Prius. Another text chimes.

Mom

Don't get out of the car.

Too late. Gravel crunches under my feet. Car doors slam. Lights flash. Then I hear it. My name.

"Princess Izumi, over here."

Like an idiot, I turn. Another flash. I'm temporarily blinded. I blink. My vision clears. In front of me is a pack of reporters. Most are Asian. A few are white. I focus on one of their badges. Press, it says. *Tokyo Tattler.*

"Oh my God," Noora exclaims. She's in a similar frozen state. Keys dangle from her hands, her mouth is open, and her jaw totally unhinged. I've never seen her struck speechless. It's glorious—but no time to appreciate the novelty. I am under siege.

"Will you be traveling to Japan?"

"How was it growing up without your father?"

"Have you known who your father is your whole life?"

An arm snakes around my shoulder. "Izumi," Mom says. Noora snaps out of it, too. Her arm joins Mom's. Together, they force my wooden body to turn, guiding me to step onto our porch. More flashes. A barrage of endless questions. My name, over and over—except they're calling me "princess."

Princess Izumi. Princess Izumi. Princess Izumi.

The door slams shut. We're inside. I am momentarily deaf, kind of like after you go to a concert and your eardrums are numb. All my synapses are firing in different directions. I struggle to form words, thoughts. It doesn't help that Tamagotchi won't stop barking. A fine time for my stinky, sleepy dog to find his backbone. I pluck him off the ground, shushing him.

"I told you not to get out of the car," Mom says.

Know what I don't like? When my mother tells me *I told you so.* I hit her with my most withering look.

Noora slumps in a chair close to the window. "That was intense." The blinds are closed, but through the slats, I spy shadows. They're still out there.

I don't swear often but now seems the appropriate time to say, "What a shitshow."

A throat clears.

Oh, we're not alone. Mom shuffles to the side. A group of Japanese men sit at our kitchen table. All three are dressed in navy suits. You know, the standard uniform for fifty-and-over politicians. They stand and execute fluid deep bows. Their leather shoes are polished to a high shine. And wow. I never noticed how yellow our linoleum floor is or how worn the cabinets are—and not in the trendy, shabby-chic way, either.

One of the men steps forward. He's slight and wears round glasses. "Hajimemashite, Your Highness." He bows again.

Mom's smile walks an apprehensive tightrope. She extends a hand by way of introduction. "Izumi, this is His Excellency Ambassador Saito from the Japan Embassy. He's flown all the way from Washington, DC."

It's too late, but now I remember seeing a black town car parked outside with little flags. I didn't pay much attention. Note to self: stop being so self-obsessed.

"I tried calling you," Mom says.

"You know my preferred method of communication is through the written word," I reply through my teeth. Texting. I mean texting.

Mom seems pretty frazzled. It could be because she's entertaining a foreign dignitary in her cat house slippers and a T-shirt that reads Woman Up. I'm not wearing much better. Black Bear Diner calls for elastic waistbands and big T-shirts. I'd barely managed to throw my hair into a bun this morning. I did put on a bra, though, so that's a win. Go me.

Noora is rapid-fire scrolling through her phone. "You're all over the foreign press."

Ambassador Saito says, "We apologize for the media. We'd hoped to get here first, but our flight was delayed."

"How did they even find out? How did they get our address?"

Ambassador Saito steps forward. "An unfortunate turn of events, but not entirely unexpected. The press in Japan is similar to America's. They have ways of obtaining information. The Crown Prince regrets this situation could not be handled with discretion, and he sends his sincerest apologies he could not be here himself. In addition, he apologizes for any undue stress this has caused you or your mother. He wishes circumstances were different." All right, then. So I'm a dirty little secret. "He also wishes for you to join him in Japan."

One of the men at the table produces a large envelope from inside his jacket and passes it to Ambassador Saito. The move is very cool, very smooth. I'm sure I've seen something similar in spy movies when agents exchange sensitive information.

Ambassador Saito presents it to me with both hands and a bow. Mom and Noora are watching me. I take the envelope. It's heavy, white, and crisp. My name is written on the outside in an elegant script.

Her Imperial Highness Princess Izumi

泉内親王殿下

The moment seems too big for our humble two-bedroom home. Noora and Mom peer over my shoulder, their breaths brushing against my neck. Personal space isn't a thing between best friends and mothers. I slide my finger under the wax seal, a golden chrysanthemum. A single card is inside. The calligraphy is loopy and black, clearly inked by hand.

Another golden chrysanthemum stamps the top.

> *On behalf of the Empire of Japan,*
> *His Imperial Highness the Crown Prince Toshihito*
> *requests the honor of his daughter, the Princess Izumi,*
> *to visit and stay at his personal lodgings, Tōgū Palace.*

The Ambassador cuts in. "The Crown Prince wishes to explain that this invitation is open. He is happy to receive you upon your convenience."

My eyes connect with Mom's—hers are dark fathomless pools. It's impossible to decipher her thoughts. Is she remembering Harvard nights with my father, this stoic man? Or is she concerned about the press on our lawn, that our veil of privacy has been ripped away? But there's no going back now. Only forward. All she says is, "What about school?"

I swallow.

Noora grins. Her thoughts are much more transparent. *Go. Go. Go.* "Spring break is soon. Zoom Zoom could go then and the week after?" she helpfully chimes in. Then adds, "Last semester of senior year is basically a wash, anyway." Noora elbows my mom. *"Amiright?"*

Mom sighs, rubbing her forehead. "I guess it's not the worst thing in the world if you miss a week or two of school. It's your choice, honey. Give it some thought. I'm sure Ambassador Saito doesn't need an answer right this minute."

Ambassador Saito is utterly serene. "Of course. Take all the time you need."

All eyes are on me again. *All the time I need* suddenly feels like *within the next sixty seconds.*

I look at the invitation, chew my lower lip, and contemplate. Allow myself to entertain the idea of Japan, of a father.

It's definitely risky business.

The upsides: a dad and a country where I might belong, blend in, turn on the television and see someone who looks like me. It would be so nice to walk into a restaurant and not be in the minority. The downside: failure to meet both my father's expectations and mine. So basically, shrivel and collapse into myself like a dying star. No biggie.

I glance up. Take in everyone's varying expressions. Mom is wary. Ambassador Saito is hopefully expectant. Noora scowls, whispering, "If you don't go, I don't think I ever really knew you."

Join the club. I've never felt like I've known myself.

"Do you want some time alone?" Mom asks. She's already moving toward Ambassador Saito and his team, ready to usher them out the door.

"No," I say. Mom stops. I look to Ambassador Saito. "I'd like to accept my father's offer." Fortune favors the bold. That's a saying, isn't it?

"Excellent," he purrs, then rattles off how excited the Crown Prince will be to hear of my RSVP.

My fingers tap a rhythm against my thighs. Noora hugs the breath out of me. "You won't regret this."

I hope not. This must be what standing at the edge of a cliff is like, unsure waters raging below. I'm unsteady and scared and excited—alive and on the verge. I might be destroyed. I might be recreated.

Holy shit. I'm going to Japan.

THE TOKYO TATTLER

The imperial scandal of the century

March 21, 2021

All attention should be on Prime Minister Adachi's upcoming nuptials, but the bride's thunder has officially been stolen. Weeks ago, the world's oldest and most private monarchy was rocked with shocking news: His Imperial Highness Crown Prince Toshihito has fathered an illegitimate child. Even better? She's been raised in America with no knowledge of her royal roots.

The Imperial Household Agency has remained mum on the matter, only issuing a brief press release after the news broke. When asked about the newest addition, the twin princesses, their Imperial Highnesses Akiko and Noriko (pictured here on a Goodwill Ambassador trip to Peru) refused to comment. They've been media-shy since our March 1 article covering the adjustment disorder of their mother, Her Imperial Highness Princess Midori. But everyone is wondering how the twins will handle this new interloper. The two aren't used to sharing the spotlight.

On the other hand, His Imperial Highness Prince Yoshihito was spotted at the kickoff of Mori Art Museum's newest exhibit. There, he toasted the new princess and said he was looking forward to meeting her. Three months ago, the prince famously severed ties with the imperial family and moved off their estate. Recently, he returned to the nest after The Imperial Household Agency reportedly cut off his allowance—the Mori event marks his first official duty back.

Now, Her Imperial Highness Princess Izumi is on her way to Japan (pictured here with her mother at the San Francisco International Airport). The Lost Butterfly is coming home at last, which has everyone wondering . . . just who *is* this American upstart? How will this girl from small-town America adapt to the glitz and glamour of the imperial family? Is she ready for the royal treatment? Only time will tell . . .

5

"Did you pack enough underwear?"

"Mom."

The cute porter loading my luggage onto a cart smirks. We're outside the San Francisco airport. Yesterday, I kissed Tamagotchi's smelly face one last time and said goodbye to Noora and the girls. Then, Mom and I drove to the Bay Area to spend the night.

It's 7 a.m. The skyline is pink and hazy. My flight departs in one hundred and twenty minutes. In less than fourteen hours, I'll be in Japan, meeting my father. I thought I'd be exhilarated, but now I'm just kind of terrified. At Mom's continued stare, I whisper furiously, "Yes."

"What about your mouth guard?"

I hold up my backpack. "In my carry-on."

"What about the binder Ambassador Saito sent?"

Ah, the binder. Before he returned to Washington, Ambassador Saito hand-delivered a mound of paperwork. Contents included:

1. A very personal and in-depth questionnaire covering everything from height and weight to future dreams and aspirations. It only hurt a little bit to bypass the Japanese box and check the English box for Only Language Spoken. ("No worries," Ambassador Saito said placidly when I expressed concerns about the language barrier. "The imperial family

and their staff are fluent in several languages, English among them. A tutor will also be provided to help assimilate you to all things Japanese, language included.")

2. A twenty-page NDA prohibiting me from disclosing financial, personal, private, *and* any architectural information regarding the royal family and its residences—so basically, *Fight Club* rules.

3. A dossier (the alleged binder) with a flight itinerary and family history, including: a who's who of the current line, assorted genealogies, personal profiles, official duties, public activities, estates, foreign relations, and the role of the Imperial Household Agency, plus various important staff members. I've got big plans to review it in the air. Of course, I've procrastinated reading it. Some things never change. It's not like I'm avoiding it or anything because I'm secretly intimidated by my royal cousins' pedigrees or the fact I'm about to join the oldest monarchy in the world. Not at all.

I tap my bag. "In here, too." A police car idles nearby. Since the news broke, I've had a 24-7 escort, all provided on behalf of the United States government for their friend Japan. I am trying hard not to think about the expense. How someone is getting paid to basically follow my mom and me around and watch us eat pastries in Little Italy. Of course, I bought each officer a cannoli. Figured it was the least I could do.

I note the porter is standing and watching us now. Glad he's enjoying the show. For the record, I am still mortified.

Mom bites her lip. "Didn't Ambassador Saito say someone was supposed to meet us here?" She makes a show of canvassing the area. There's a couple paparazzi about a hundred feet away—Japan foreign press. My outrage over being followed has settled to a low simmer. I'm still not sure what I think about people believing they're entitled to my life. It's a little disconcerting, like when I shopped for bras online and for two weeks after my entire ad feed was boob-related. I've somehow become public property.

"Zoom Zoom."

"Huh?" I glance at Mom.

"Someone was supposed to meet us here."

Right. Ambassador Saito did mention I'd have an imperial security detail meet me at the airport. But did he mean the airport here or the airport in Tokyo? I'm not sure, and I didn't clarify. Mom won't appreciate this lack of attention to detail, so all I say is, "Mom. It's going to be fine. I'm going to be fine."

She grips my upper arms. "I wish you didn't have to go." She hiccups on the last word.

A lump forms in my throat. "I won't go," I say. Then, she pushes me, kind of hard. "Mom. Ow."

"No. This is me kicking you out of the nest." She wraps me in a hug.

I fall apart. I knew things would change starting senior year, but I thought it would be more in the traditional sense. Prom. Graduation. College.

I pull away and wipe my eyes. There's definitely some snot, too, and I use the back of my sleeve on that. I don't even care the porter is still hanging around. Mom seizes my arms in another death grip. "Try to stay out of trouble."

Hmph. As if I'm the troublemaking type. "I'll be back soon," I assure her. "Two weeks."

"Two weeks," she repeats. Mom's face is a mask of apprehension, so I turn up my smile a notch. Someone has to put on a brave front. "This is going to be good for you, I think," she says finally, forcing a smile. "You're putting yourself out there. I'm proud of you."

Why can moms always see into the dark recesses of your soul? I'll admit it. In my own life, I've never been the leading role. I just don't have that star power. Wasn't born with it. I've always been a sidekick. My singular purpose is to bolster heroes, stay in the background, and maybe, in one big on-screen moment, sacrifice my life for the greater good. So far it's served me well. If you don't fly too high, you don't have too far to fall. But now, somehow, I've been thrust into the limelight. All this makes me squirmy. Slightly unbalanced.

Another long hug. Mom and I say goodbye. Double doors slide open and I walk through them toward the Japan Airlines ticketing counter. I don't turn around, but I know she watches me until I disappear.

Ding.

Overhead lights flicker on throughout the cabin. Ever had the sensation where time goes so slow, but when it's all said and done, you can't believe the event is already here? That's where I am right now. Coasting the tarmac in Tokyo, my overall state is dreamlike.

I gaze out the window. My first glimpse of Japan is gray and cold. Reality comes crashing in and butterflies hatch in my stomach. I'm alone and on the other side of the world. I breathe in. Breathe out. I can do this. Navigate a foreign country, live in a palace, and meet my father for the first time—no problem. A piece of cake—*mochi* cake.

The front section of the Triple Seven resembles a luxury yacht. There are eight seats, and each is its own suite. Brown leather armchairs convert into beds. A mahogany wooden console with gold inlay hides all sorts of techy stuff—seat controls with massage functions, power and USB plugs, a gaming system, and even complementary Bose noise-canceling headphones. The toilets in the two private bathrooms automatically flush and are equipped with bidets—a hard pass, but I appreciate the touch. Even the bathrooms smell luxurious, a mix of cashmere and lavender.

Seats are divided by partitions—unnecessary, since I am only one of two passengers occupying the space. For the last ten hours, it's just been me and a stuffy but kind of hot Japanese guy in a suit up here. Between meals (a three-course lunch starting with an amuse-bouche of soft yuba and fresh sea urchin), naps, and binge-watching television, I've observed him. He's barely moved. He hasn't loosened his tie or put up his feet, but he did eat. A tray was delivered to his seat and carried away empty moments later. That's some kind of witchcraft.

A flight attendant makes an announcement in Japanese. She repeats it in English. "Ladies and gentlemen, welcome to Narita International Airport. The current temperature is fourteen degrees Celsius, and the time is 3:32 p.m. Our captain asks you stay in your seats and allow our first-class cabin passengers to deplane first. This is for security purposes. Thank you, and welcome again to Tokyo. Please enjoy your stay."

My cheeks burn. Good thing a heavy curtain separates the first-class cabin from the rest of the airplane. Nobody can see me. Hot Guy stands, buttons his suit jacket, and does a quick sweep of the interior. He speaks with the two attendants and fits a tiny earpiece into his ear. They bow and stand in front of the blue velvet curtains. There's a *whoosh* of the plane door opening. Two men board, both in black suits similar to Hot Guy's. I sit up a little straighter. Hot Guy is beside me. Sweeping into a low bow, he says, "Your Highness, please come with me."

I focus on his shoes, black and shiny, then move up—dark suit, dark tie, then the face. He's younger than I thought—a couple years older than me, maybe. And, oh my God, kill me now, he's even better up close. So good-looking it's borderline offensive—pouty lower lip, hooded eyes, straight nose. I've been on permanent relationship hiatus since Forest, but now I'm rethinking my anything-with-a-penis ban. My mouth opens and closes. He's waiting, eyes cool and assessing. "And you are . . . ?" My voice cracks in the middle.

"Kobayashi. Akio," he says. That's all. Guess he's more of the strong, silent type. Okay, totally on board with that.

I stare at him, unsure what to do. My brain is fuzzy. Definitely jet lag, but combined with adrenaline. There's not a word for my current state. It's an I'm-in-a-new-country-and-about-to-meet-my-father kind of high.

He shifts on his feet, clears his throat. "Pardon, Your Highness. We really must be going."

I smile. "What did you say your name was again?"

"Akio." He's a bit impatient now. "I should be in the dossier you received."

"Riiight." *The dossier.* Japan Airlines had the first two seasons of *Downton Abbey.* I'd chosen the historical drama over my own family history. I've made my bed and now I have to lie in it. "I haven't had much time to look at it," I explain to Akio.

His dark eyes gleam. "Yes. I'm sure you had more pressing matters."

Huh. I crane my neck to look behind me. From his seat, he had a perfect view of mine. No doubt he watched me watching *Downton Abbey.* So it's going to be like that.

"Perhaps you'd like to check the dossier now," he suggests, impatience level rising to a ten. The other suits aren't quite as hostile, but they are just as serious. No help there at all.

"Yes. Um. I would," I say. My face is on fire, and not in the sexy way from my romance novels, but in the bad, hivey kind of way. I jammed the binder into the cubbyhole beneath the television earlier. Akio's eyes stay on me as I wriggle it out, my motions the opposite of elegant. Also, the leather makes an unfortunate squeaking sound. I can practically hear the pitter-patter of his heart's discontent.

I flip the binder open. His photograph is on page five, followed by his contact information and a list of qualifications. *Imperial guard Akio Kobayashi will meet you in San Francisco and personally escort you.* Twenty years old. Two years with the Imperial Guard, the highest dan in a variety of martial arts, expert marksmanship credentials, and on it goes. It all leads me to believe he could kill a man with his bare hands. How chilling. I say, "I'm sorry about not recognizing you." I stand and gather my carry-on. "You know girls, strangers and all . . ."

He flicks two fingers and a suit springs into action, relieving me of my carry-on. "It's of no consequence." I should've read the dossier. I can't imagine what he thinks of me now.

Actually, I can. He probably spent the entire plane ride mentally writing bad reviews about me. *Stuck-up. Didn't recognize me on the flight. Thought no one could see when she smelled underneath her arms. Twice. So far, unimpressed. This is supposed to be a princess? I don't get paid enough for this.*

"The press knows you are arriving today," Akio says as he and the other suits usher me off the plane. His tone is short, but his stride is long. I have to take two steps for every one of his. There's already a stitch in my side from trying to keep up. I should exercise more. But alas, I like cake more than I like running. "They don't know which flight, but I'm sure they'll find out soon. Tabloids have bought tickets to gain access to the main airport. We've arranged access through the employee areas."

More suits join us. The theme of our walk is less talk, more hurry. I glimpse the airport—pretty standard as these things go. Clean shiny white floors. Signs and escalators backlit with neon colors. Some differences, though, like a hotel advertising sleeping capsules and showers.

"My luggage?" I ask as I'm guided through a metal door.

"Is being delivered to the palace separately. It should be there before you arrive," Akio informs me without breaking stride.

The hall is concrete, empty and windowless. Overhead, fluorescent lights flicker. We make our way through, passing doors with signs or numbers. Everything is in Japanese. Finally, the hall widens—we've reached the heart of the airport, I'm guessing. The hallways smell of soy sauce and curry and branch off like arteries.

Sweat dots my forehead. I didn't drink the champagne

on the flight, but I did have three cappuccinos—mostly because they came with these super delicious chocolate sticks. A flight attendant noticed and brought me a dozen of them, so I pretty much love her now. Problem is, that dip into caffeinated heaven is coming back to haunt me.

In layman's terms: I have to pee.

"Um, Akio," I say softly.

He either doesn't hear me or chooses to ignore me. I'm going with the latter. Someone in his position probably has better than average hearing.

"Akio," I repeat more loudly.

He keeps going. Time for drastic measures. My bladder is about to burst. I can't meet my father doing a pee-pee dance. Not a good look. I stop. Everyone halts. All eyes are on me.

"I need to use the ladies' room," I explain. Then I add, "Please," because manners and everything.

Akio is in front of me. "Sorry?" He pretends to misunderstand, but the look on his face says: *I can't believe you'd possibly ask to use the restroom. What kind of demon are you, really?*

"Is there a ladies' room nearby?" I squint, waiting for flames to shoot out of his ears.

He stares down at me for one more blazing second. I really resent the extra foot of height he has over me. "A restroom. You need a restroom?"

I shrug, palms up. "Too many cappuccinos on the airplane."

"There is no plan for that." His voice is a bit strained around the edges.

"Using the restroom?"

A single nod.

"Okay." I shift from one foot to the other.

He scrutinizes me for a moment. Then he barks something in Japanese. A suit checks his phone and points to a door, then half the suits go through. Pots bang, voices get louder. Based on tone and inflection, I can tell someone is not very happy. Once things calm down, a suit holds the door open.

Akio extends an arm. "Restroom."

"Thank you."

It's a kitchen. The staff, a server, and janitor all stand in a corner. A murmur runs through the group when they see me. The air is heavy, laden with the hot greasy smell of woks and miso. A few feet away, a suit holds a bathroom door open.

I flutter my fingers, sending the staff an apologetic wave. A dozen indulgent smiles answer me.

When I emerge, the chef is having some sort of disagreement with one of the suits. After much discussion, including what appears asking Akio for permission, the chef picks up a knife and then his movements are a whir. He moves closer to me and bows, presenting a radish cut into a chrysanthemum.

"A gift," Akio explains stiffly.

I take the vegetable with a wide smile. Water drips from my hands. "There weren't any towels. Sorry."

Akio clips out something in Japanese, and a flurry of handkerchiefs are waved near my face. Even Akio has withdrawn a white square from his pocket. He's closest, but I ignore him. Enemy, remember?

The handkerchief the janitor holds is clean and creased as if it's been lovingly pressed. I take it and dab my hands, still managing to keep hold of the radish. "Thank you," I say to the chef and janitor. Then, I wave to the staff. "Arigatō."

Both bow and reply, "Dōitashimashite."

"I apologize if anyone's lunch was delayed. Will you translate that for me?" I ask Akio.

Akio huffs. "We should be on our way." I add *mulish* to Akio's list of qualifications. I might let this go, but I'm big on being nice to people. I cross my arms and stare up at him. I don't like to brag, but I've won my fair share of staring contests.

One second.

Two seconds.

Three seconds.

Aaand . . . I win. Akio clasps his hands behind his back, clears his throat, and speaks Japanese. No way to tell if his translation is verbatim, though Akio strikes me as honest. You know, the I'd-die-for-my-principles type. Side note: this has been the downfall of many great men.

When Akio finishes speaking, the kitchen staff erupt in approving smiles. Forget the palace and my father. I might just live here.

Akio ushers me back into the concrete hall, and this time, I'm happy to follow. His rain isn't going to ruin my parade—my steps and bladder are light. Daylight peeks through the cracks of a set of double doors, and two suits open them. Fresh air spiced with rain and wet earth floods the hallway.

Lights flash. I am momentarily blinded. A sea of people waits outside for me, chanting my name. Some are press with official badges and long-focus lens cameras. Security guards in blue hold back the royal watchers. It couldn't be any louder if someone grabbed me by the lapels and yelled in my ears.

I press a hand to my pounding heart.

A sleek, black Rolls-Royce idles at the curb. On the

hood, a flag waves—white with a red border and a golden chrysanthemum.

My lips part. I freeze. My father is in that car. Just on the other side of the glass. I turn on my best pageant-winning smile.

Akio's truffle-colored eyes flicker to me. "The crowds were smaller when we landed."

I choose to ignore him. The car door opens and another suit alights. My skin tingles, but he's not my father. This older man wears a black bowler hat and sports a dark blue tie. His jowls remind me of a sad basset hound.

Another suit pops open a black umbrella and holds it over the man. He walks forward and bows, shouting over the hustle and bustle. "Yōkoso, Your Highness. I am Mr. Fuchigami, East Palace Chamberlain. On behalf of your father, His Imperial Highness the Crown Prince, and the Empire of Japan, I welcome you home." Rain slices a path down the nylon and drips from the umbrella's ribs.

Cameras click. I blink, trying to peer into the cabin of the Rolls-Royce. "My father isn't here?" Major letdown.

My name is called, but I keep my focus on Mr. Fuchigami. More photos are snapped. Lights flash, the imprint emblazoned on the back of my eyelids. I wonder if they've captured my disappointment. Perhaps the headline will read "Princess Stood Up by Her Father."

Mr. Fuchigami's smile is commiserative. "The Crown Prince is waiting for you at the palace. We thought it might be best for your reunion to be private." That makes sense. I guess. Still, my stomach clenches like a fist. "Please," he says, sweeping his arm out and creating a line he expects me to follow.

Akio's presence beside me is darker than the clouds in the sky as he glowers at the crowd. The imperial guard can stand down now. He's no doubt going to enjoy this handoff. Probably can't wait to be free and do something he finds relaxing, like winding clocks or frightening little children at a schoolyard or (one can only hope) playing in traffic.

I glance left, then right. The car door is still open. Rain pelts the interior. Mr. Fuchigami is waiting. My father is waiting. Japan is waiting. I brace myself and find the silver lining. My father might not be here, but Tokyo is. I will my nerves to be like the concrete under my feet, hard and impenetrable. I am brave. I am magnificent. I can do anything. (As long as I am gently handled, have ten hours of sleep a night, and a hearty, protein-packed breakfast, of course.)

Ready.

Steady.

Go.

6

I settle into a buttery-soft leather seat the color of fine scotch. Mr. Fuchigami sits across from me, bowler hat in his lap. His hair is shot through with gray and slicked back. Car doors slam. It's just my luck Akio climbs in the front. His posture is ramrod straight. Words like *stick* and *ass* come to mind. Raindrops slide down the back of his neck. He pats them away with a neatly folded handkerchief. I kind of hate him. I hate him more because he's so attractive.

A chauffeur in a brass-buttoned jacket and white gloves drives us. "Who's in the other car?" I ask when I notice a second Rolls-Royce following us. It's a bit stuffy in the car, and the windows fog.

"No one." Mr. Fuchigami pulls black leather gloves from his hands. "It is empty, in case this car breaks down."

The wood of the interior gleams. The engine purrs. "Has this car ever broken down?"

Mr. Fuchigami's face is blank. "No, it is brand new."

"That makes sense." But not really.

Police on white motorcycles flank us. We're speeding down a highway now. Cars pull over to the side of the road and let us pass.

"Your itinerary for this evening and the rest of your stay." Mr. Fuchigami places a sheaf of papers in my lap, his tone all business.

Her Imperial Highness Princess Izumi's Itinerary
3/22/2021

3:32 p.m.—Arrive at Narita International Airport
3:45 p.m.—Depart Narita International Airport,
motorcade tour of Tokyo and imperial grounds

I check my phone. 4:01 p.m. Sixteen minutes behind schedule. It's really not my fault. I was even born late—three weeks overdue and ten pounds to boot, roughly the size of an adult Maltese dog. Mom was so big that everyone thought she was having two, which lead to the nurse joking I devoured my twin in utero. I smile at the thought. Mr. Fuchigami watches me warily, his lips twitching. I turn my attention back to the schedule.

5:01 p.m.—Dress for dinner
5:22 p.m.—Private meeting with Crown Prince
8:00 p.m.—Welcome reception and dinner

"The schedule will need to be adjusted. I understand there was an unanticipated stop in the airport," Mr. Fuchigami continues. His gaze lingers on the radish, which I've placed on the seat next to me. It's kind of my friend now. I've named it Tamagotchi 2.0.

I flip through the pages and bite my cheek. Well, this might be a challenge. Adhering to my school schedule is a minor miracle. My two weeks here are filled with activities. Private lessons in Japanese history, language, and art. Tours of shrines, temples, and tombs. A visit to the imperial stock farm and wild duck preserves. Assorted banquets. Outings with my father—a baseball game, public art exhibit opening. There's even . . . "A wedding?"

Mr. Fuchigami nods. "The prime minister will be married in ten days."

I audibly gulp. "I didn't bring anything to wear to a wedding." My wardrobe consists of leggings and sweatshirts—think Lululemon's sloppy sister—all perfectly acceptable in Mount Shasta. But then again, ax-throwing and cow-tipping are also perfectly acceptable in Mount Shasta.

"A wardrobe has been provided for you. The imperial family works with a number of designers to produce acceptable clothing." I can read the underlying message in his statement, in his tone, in his inscrutable smile. *You represent the imperial family now.*

"Of course," I reply. I have an inkling I may be in a little over my head. No matter.

"Your first cousins, the twin princesses Akiko and Noriko, travel extensively," he adds, tone warming. "Last week, Akiko returned from Scotland. She's planning to study English and medieval transportation at university there next year. She wore home a very charming dress and blazer."

Oh, I think. "Oh," I say. Mentally, I catalog my outfit: leggings and a faded Mount Shasta High sweatshirt. "Sorry, I didn't know . . ." I trail off. Shout out to all the girls who apologize too much. I feel you.

"Yes. You must be aware the press is always watching. But it's of no consequence," Mr. Fuchigami says. "We've assembled a small team to assist you, starting with Mr. Kobayashi. He will be your personal security. His family has worked for the

Imperial House for decades. He is a wealth of knowledge. You may rely on him for his discretion." Ah, the dagger twists a little deeper. My sworn enemy is to be my closest confidant? *Never.* "Please be sure to add his contact information to your phone," Mr. Fuchigami says. You bet I will. I'll file it under Satan's Handmaiden, devil horns emoji, double poop emoji.

My mouth opens to ask Mr. Fuchigami about the rest of the schedule, but my words and breath are stolen. Now, my mouth hangs open for a totally different reason. Surprise. Wonder. *Awe.*

We've crested a hill. Sunbeams filter through a break in the clouds, and the jagged line of high-rises stretches up. Like a mirage, it beckons me. I lean against the window, clear the condensation with the palm of my hand, and tip my chin up, positively struck giddy. Raindrops slice down the window, cutting up my reflection.

"Tokyo." Mr. Fuchigami's voice inflates with pride. "Formerly Edo, almost destroyed by the 1923 Great Kantō earthquake, then again in 1944 by nighttime firebombing raids. Tens of thousands were killed." The chamberlain grows silent. "Kishikaisei."

"What does that mean?" There's a skip in my chest. We've entered the city now. The high-rises are no longer cut out shapes against the skyline, but looming gray giants. Every possible surface is covered in signs—neon and plastic or painted banners—they all scream for attention. It's noisy, too. There is a cacophony of pop tunes, car horns, advertising jingles, and trains coasting over rails. Nothing is understated.

"Roughly translated, 'wake from death and return to life.' Against hopeless circumstances, Tokyo has risen. It is home to more than thirty-five million people." He pauses. "And, in addition, the oldest monarchy in the world."

The awe returns tenfold. I clutch the windowsill and press my nose to the glass. There are verdant parks, tidy residential buildings, upmarket shops, galleries, and restaurants. For each sleek, new modern construction, there is one low-slung wooden building with a blue tiled roof and glowing lanterns. It's all so dense. Houses lean against one another like drunk uncles.

Mr. Fuchigami narrates Tokyo's history. A city built and rebuilt, born and reborn. I imagine cutting into it like a slice of cake, dissecting the layers. I can almost see it. Ash from the Edo fires with remnants of samurai armor, calligraphy pens, and chipped tea porcelain. Bones from when the shogunate fell. Dust from the Great Earthquake and more debris from the World War II air raids.

Still, the city thrives. It is alive and sprawling with neon-colored veins. Children in plaid skirts and little red ties dash between business personnel in staid suits. Two women in crimson kimonos and matching parasols duck into a teahouse. All of the people look like me. Of course there are variations, different eye and face shapes, but there is more dark hair than I've ever seen in my entire lifetime. It hits me: I'm not a novelty here. I am not a sore thumb. What a privilege it is to *blend in*.

But it also still seems like a hallucination, like I'm peering through a keyhole. I can't take it all in. The car hasn't slowed once.

That's when I notice. "We're not stopping at any lights."

Mr. Fuchigami taps his fingers against the leather seat. "Yes. The traffic lights are programmed to switch from red to blue for the royal cavalcade. It is of the upmost importance to adhere to schedules." Another dig. I don't care. My body is humming. It wants to tangle itself up in Tokyo and get lost in all of the city's limbs. This is where I should have been born, should have *lived*. Here, words like *accept* and *tolerate* wouldn't have been part of my early vocabulary. I'd be commonplace, another face in the crowd. Well, aside from the Rolls-Royce and flashing lights of the police escort.

I sit back, overwhelmed and elated, listening to the gentle plinking of rain against the car's metal roof. Mind officially blown.

We cross water. "One of the many moats enclosing the imperial grounds," Mr. Fuchigami explains. This is where my grandparents, the emperor and empress, live—smack-dab in the middle of Tokyo on four-point-six million square feet of private forest.

The car darkens as we enter a tunnel. We're moving away from the imperial grounds. "My father doesn't live there?" There's a moment of panic. I remember watching a movie about an unwanted royal child who was sequestered in the country, hidden away.

"The Crown Prince lives in Tōgū Palace on the Akasaka Estate, east of the Imperial Palace. It is also where the rest of the family resides—your uncles and aunts, assorted cousins. The twins, Princesses Akiko and Noriko, are around your age. Prince Yoshihito is, too. He moved away but recently returned home. You'll have plenty of company." He smiles, as if giving me a gift.

My unease settles as the tunnel ends. We pass an ethereal white and gold gate. Guards in bright blue uniforms stand at attention. A sprawling, manicured lawn culminates in a grand fountain and frames an imposing marble building. "Akasaka Palace is modeled after both Versailles and Buckingham Palace," Mr. Fuchigami says. I see, I see. It does have a whole let-them-eat-cake vibe. "The palace is unoccupied, but it is used for visiting dignitaries."

We round a corner. Walls rise up. We're still skirting the Akasaka Estate. Gnarled oaks line the streets, and the walls give way to a simple bamboo fence wrapped in a hedge. All pretty innocuous, but security cameras are discreetly mounted every couple of feet, and imperial guards patrol the perimeter.

The cavalcade slows.

Ahead, imperial guards in immaculate blue uniforms and hats with shiny emblems stand at attention. The golden tassels on their uniforms wink at me. A black metal gate is pulled open. The police outriders split away, blocking the street and entrance as we glide through.

"Ah, we've arrived. This is Tōgū Palace," Mr. Fuchigami announces evenly, warmly. "Welcome home."

Time stands still, and my brain creates snapshots of each moment. No doubt this will be filed away in my hippocampus, the place where indelible memories are stored. Like when I had strep throat and could only eat bananas. I'll forever associate the fruit with soreness and sickness. But this is the opposite. *This* is beauty and brightness.

A snapshot: driving down a gravel road flanked by maple trees, magenta azaleas weeping at their feet. Stretching in all directions is parkland, swaths of gingko, silver birch, black pine, and cedar. The air smells loamy and of fresh-cut grass.

A snapshot: alighting from the car and craning my neck. The rain clears for a moment. Even though the sun hides behind clouds, it's as if the building creates its own light. It's shining. *Glowing.* The perfect home for a man once believed to be a god descended from the sun. Tōgū Palace is a modern wonder. The sprawling eighteen-bedroom, two-story structure blends into its natural surroundings. A bronze roof rusted to a jade patina mirrors the trees.

A snapshot: walking to the entrance, passing a line of staff. They introduce themselves one by one. More chamberlains. A doctor. Three chefs (because three is better than one), who specialize in Japanese dishes, Western cuisine, and bread and desserts. Equerries. Maids. My father's valet. My lady-in-waiting, Mariko. She bows.

I tug my bottom lip with my teeth. "Lady-in-waiting?" I ask Mr. Fuchigami.

"Personal companion," he says archly, bowler hat back in place. "She will assist you in daily tasks and will tutor you in language, culture, and etiquette. Your father handpicked her. He thought you might enjoy company around your age. Mariko will graduate from Gakushūin soon. Her father is poet laureate Shoji Abe and her mother was a lady-in-waiting for Princess Asako. Her English is excellent and she is an expert in court manners."

Butlers hold glass doors open. I step inside to the genkan and exchange my shoes for house slippers. The floors are mirror-finished and the chandeliers are chrome. Our pace is brisk, and I only catch glimpses of the rest of the house: Silk screens behind plexiglass in the hallway. Living room furniture arranged at perfect ninety-degree angles. The color palettes soft and soothing, woods and beiges with blush accents. Near-translucent paper screens on wooden tracks dividing spaces. It's uncluttered. Airy.

In my suite, there is a wall of clear glass and below it, a pond. It's as if we're suspended, floating over a deep blue expanse. Swans glide on the water, and koi dart under the surface. In the distance, I spy Akio. Hair artfully tousled from the rain, he speaks with the other security personnel. No doubt, directing them. Mentally, I list Akio's preferences:

Likes
- *Bossing people around*
- *Schedules*
- *Tom Ford suits*
- *Earpieces*
- *Glowering* and *more bossing people around*

Dislikes
- *Tardiness*
- *A joie de vivre approach to life*
- *Princesses who pee, watch* Downton Abbey, *or accept radishes from chefs*

Speaking of radishes, I still have it. I held it during the staff introductions and the palace tour. Now it rests on a gold foil chest, next to a single iris in a fluted vase. Something about the flower beckons me to study it.

The arrangement is perfectly framed against the silk

tapestry behind it. The purple petals are simple but elegant. Its placement here seems deliberate, almost ceremonial. I can only take note because it feels as if my circuits are going haywire.

Mariko taps her lips. "The big question is, what dress should you wear?" She's laid out the options on the four-poster bed: a pink silk-printed dress with a floral motif or a yellow cap sleeve with beading. "Princess Akiko wore pink yesterday to the morning tea party for notable persons," Mariko says. She is small, her features sharp and unforgiving, with two slashes for eyebrows and a pointed chin. "We wouldn't want to appear as if we're copying her. But the yellow is so pale. I'm afraid it may have unwanted consequences complexion-wise." Mariko holds up the dress against my cheek. The label is silk and reads Oscar de la Renta.

Me: Meh, designer labels don't impress me.

Also me: Can't wait to secretly snap a picture and send it to Noora. I already know her reaction. Bitch, you lie.

"What do you think, Izumi-sama?" asks Mariko.

"Oh, um." I pretend not to be insulted and consider the options. Cap sleeves? *Pshh.* Baby pink? Double *pshh.* Neither option appeals to me. "Yellow and pink aren't really my colors. Do you have anything darker? Black, maybe?" Preferably with one percent cotton and a million percent spandex. Don't get me wrong, I love my body. I just love it most in black. It would also help with my little spilling problem. I'm a messy eater. Right now, there is a small stain on my sweatshirt— chocolate, and most likely from the Snickers family. If I were with the AGG, I'd have no problem licking it.

Mariko glances at the walk-in closet, complete with a

marble island. Dresses hang. It is a pastel massacre. "No black," she says, then sighs. "The yellow will have to do." She nods as if reassuring herself. Sallow complexion is a risk we must take.

In less than ten minutes, I am outfitted in the pale yellow dress that actually fits rather well and I'm herded to a vanity. Bright lights are flicked on. Mariko laments I don't have bangs.

"What should we do with it?" Mariko asks, lifting my hair and studying the thick strands in the mirror.

"I like it down," I offer, thinking she wants my actual opinion.

Mariko's mouth thins. She sweeps my hair back and pins the mass into a bun. My scalp is screaming by the time she's finished. So she likes it rough, got it. To counteract the buttercup dress, a bit of rouge is applied to my lips and cheeks.

She mumbles something about the color of my nail polish—kinky pink—being too bright, but there's no time for a manicure. She places Mikimoto pearl studs in my ears, and a matching strand around my neck.

"Welcome gifts from the empress. She regrets she cannot be here to greet her newest granddaughter in person." Mariko secures the clasp.

In the mirror, I see a different person. It's me, yet it's not. A royal avatar. I'm not sure what to think, how to feel about it.

There is a knock on the suite doors. Mariko lets Mr. Fuchigami in. He's here to escort me to my father. "Ready?" he asks, eyes appraising, then approving.

I want to say yes, but whole galaxies of words die on my tongue. I am minutes away from meeting my father, who I've waited to meet my entire life. The urge to breathe into a paper bag is strong. But I keep my cool, at least on the outside. On the inside, insecurities rise up. I want my father to like me. I want to like my father. *Is that too much to ask, Universe?*

All I can do is nod. All roads lead to this. No more wandering down streets and wondering if strangers could be related to me. The answers to my questions are a few steps away. Who is my father? Does he want me here? Is this just a political stunt? Shoulders straight, steps sure, I follow Mr. Fuchigami out the door and into a new life.

7

The walls in my father's office are cedar and lacquered to a high shine, every vein in the wood highlighted. For the moment, I am alone. Mr. Fuchigami deposited me here and slid the doors closed. I understand. The Crown Prince doesn't wait for anyone. This is fine; it gives me free rein to snoop.

Like my room here, this one is sparsely furnished. I know why. There's money, and then there's *wealth*. I'm pretty sure I've stepped into the dark heart of the latter. Each item on the bookshelf is given a wide berth from the others. Built-in lights, personal bolts of sunlight, highlight the pieces—a porcelain cobalt blue China vase, a Spanish silver tobacco box, some type of sword with a golden dragon winding around the handle. Each item is old, rare. *Priceless*. Here, families aren't measured by dollar signs but in historical pieces and provenance. And, what's mine? Everything about my life suddenly seems cheap.

There are photographs, too. Simply framed between two sheets of glass are images of my father, all in black-and-white. There he is as a young boy against a shoji screen backdrop, piano keys beneath his fingertips. In another, he is older, dashing and very militant in a brass-buttoned uniform. Then there are the candids. He cuddles a koala in front of a eucalyptus tree. He drinks beer with his brother at a pub. There is a photograph of the empress and emperor on their wedding day, in full imperial regalia, kimono and hakama.

The doors slide open and I straighten, smoothing out the skirt of my dress. My heart pounds. *He* is framed in the doorway, cutting an imposing figure in a white shirt with mother-of-pearl buttons and black slacks.

He inclines his head and speaks in Japanese to the men behind him. The doors are closed. We're alone. We can

(a) hug;
(b) shake hands; or
(c) smile genuinely.

But then, we choose

(d) none of the above—stare awkwardly at each other.

Outside, the gray clouds have moved on, and the sun is setting. The light is different here—burnt oranges and golds, colors I thought could only be mixed by a master artist. Shadows play in the room and cast the hard planes of my father's face into sharp relief. He is aloof. I am adrift.

"You look like your mother," he finally blurts out.

I have the distinct sense of whiplash. Am I reading his tone correctly? Was that *accusatory?* I clench and unclench my hands. My worst fears might be coming true. He doesn't want me. This was a mistake. I'm ready to burn the whole thing down. "I thought I looked a lot like you when I finally saw pictures."

"You do. It's the nose. The imperial family is known for passing down a small bump."

I reach and trace the tiny ridge along the spine of my nose.

"You also look like the empress, my mother." His tone warms. "An elfin chin and wide-set eyes. She was a great beauty in her time. It's good you don't look too much like me. Your mother once told me I often appeared as if I'd just eaten sour grapes."

I laugh. Cancel the fire for now, I guess.

His jaw flexes. "I never cared for her colloquialisms."

I sober.

We lapse into awkward silence. What had I pictured? That we'd run into each other's arms? That our shared DNA would act as opposite ends of a magnet pulling us together? He is not a dad returning from deployment. I am not a child eagerly awaiting his arrival. There are no memories to anchor our relationship. He did not tuck me in at night, hold me while I raged with a fever, or cheer me on when I stole home playing softball. All those missed moments build up between us. I don't want to blame him for his absence, but I kind of do. All of this is so unfair.

"I—" he begins to say, but catches himself. He's got nothing. Neither do I. Time stretches on. We are strangers. Why did I think it might be different?

He smiles, unsure. "I've stared down bulls in Spain and haven't felt as frightened as I do in this moment. My hands are shaking." He shows me. There is a slight tremor in his blunt fingers.

Relieved, I manage a light laugh. "Never ran with the bulls, but I did glue Tommy Steven's butt to a chair in the second grade after he stole my crayons. I was so scared of getting caught I confessed right after."

His eyes flash with pride. "You have a strong sense of justice."

My knees unlock and I answer with a blinding smile.

"Perhaps we should start over." He sticks out a hand. "I'm so glad you're here. I look forward to getting to know you."

I place my palm in his. His grip is firm and reassuring, but not familiar. We erase (d) and choose (c), a handshake.

It's not much, but it's a start, helps me remember why I'm here. To meet my father. To make sense of who I am, the shape of my face, the origins of my stubborn attitude.

"The gardens are beautiful this time of year," he says as we disengage.

I brighten. "Yeah?"

"Would you like to see them?"

I think for a moment. Fresh air makes everything better. "That sounds great. Lead the way."

The air is cool and wet against my cheeks. Pea-sized gravel crunches under my feet. My father saunters next to me, head low, shoulders relaxed—a portrait of a prince, deconstructed. Gooseflesh breaks out on my arms.

"You're cold," he says. He fixes his gaze somewhere, and by silent command, a royal attendant materializes. A trick I'd like to master.

My father speaks in Japanese, and the attendant bows low and disappears. Broad-shouldered black shapes shift in the trees—security. I even spy Akio. This is something that will take getting used to. Even when you're alone, you're never *really* alone. The attendant reappears, and it's staggering how fast he moves. Sweat dots his brow, but he keeps his breaths even. He bows and offers my father an ivory cashmere wrap. My father takes it and drapes it around my shoulders. "Better?"

"Much. Thank you." I hug the shawl around me. Never saw myself as a fine wool kind of gal, but I could get used to this.

"Shall we continue?" He motions ahead.

We fall into amicable silence. The sound of the wind and traffic of Tokyo settles between us. My father points out species of trees. The white birch is his personal emblem. The path opens, expands, and circles around a pond. We pause near a sculpted black pine. Across the water, Mr. Fuchigami and a handful of chamberlains stand, making a big deal of watching us by not watching us.

My father's smile is rueful. "Mr. Fuchigami is probably upset we've gone outside. Not on the itinerary."

I tighten the shawl around me. "Seems to be a recurring theme. I thought Akio's head was going to explode when I asked to use the restroom at the airport."

The sun dips lower. Attendants light stone lanterns. The garden is cast in a hazy, yellow glow. My father hums. "Ah, Mr. Kobayashi. I chose him myself. I thought you'd be more comfortable with someone younger." I nod, not wanting to appear ungrateful.

Boom. I startle. Fireworks sparkle against the night sky like sprinkled sugar. Shimmering pinks, deep purples, wild blues. In the distance, the lights of Tokyo wink at me.

My father shifts, tipping his head to the sky.

"They're beautiful," I marvel.

The sparks reflect in his dark eyes. "It's for you. Tokyo

is welcoming its new princess."

For *me?* I gulp and do my best not to let it go to my head.

An attendant approaches carrying a silver tray, laden with drinks in heavy crystal. My father plucks up the shorter glass filled with amber liquid. I take the flute with something bubbly in it. I sip and grin. It's sparkling cider. Delicious.

He arches an imperial brow at me (pun intended). I explain. "It's the sparkling cider. The way to my heart is anything coated in sugar." The second way is by hugs. Lots and lots of hugs.

He sips the amber liquid. "I don't believe that was on your preference sheet." True. But I did list various desserts that I'd consider serious relationships with. He stares at the liquid in his glass, frowning. "A man shouldn't have to read about what his child likes on paper." He sounds wistful, a bit forlorn. I wonder if he's mad at my mom. "I'd rather hear your answers than read them. What are your hobbies?"

Does watching *Real Housewives* count? "I dabble in a few things, but nothing has caught my eye yet. Except for baking. I'm an excellent baker." My buttercream and cream cheese frosting is to die for.

"Your cousins Akiko and Noriko raise silkworms," he says, naming the twins. In the royal biographies, hobbies are listed first for females. "Sachiko enjoys mountain climbing. The Imperial Household Agency had a conniption over that—a princess in cargo pants. Very cutting edge." He smiles over the rim of his glass as if we're sharing a private joke. "Your grades. How are they?"

Subpar at best. But my father is a Crown Prince, so I shine up the truth a little. "Great." So good, I've earned entrance into two community colleges and one state school. I sip the cider to keep from elaborating.

"Do you keep your room clean?" He swirls the liquid in his glass.

My room might give you suffocating-in-garbage stress dreams. "I'm pretty tidy, I guess." All of his questions have driven me to a single conclusion: I am remarkably unremarkable.

His chest puffs with pride. "You're like me. When I was a boy, I was very organized." He considers me for a moment. I realize I'm hungry to know about him, too. Questions burn. What else was he like as a boy? Did he get into trouble? *Please have gotten into trouble.* But before I can ask, he says almost begrudgingly, "And your mother? How is she?"

I roll the champagne glass between my hands. "She's good. Still single." My eyes flash to him. No reaction. Guess my plan for a twist on the classic *Parent Trap* won't work. I'll admit it. I had a tiny sliver of a thought to reunite my parents, make them fall madly in love again, and then get them married. A girl can dream.

"Does she still have a mug collection?"

"Yeah," I say warmly. "Her favorite is one that says 'Bigfoot doesn't believe in you either'."

"How about the one that says 'I'm quite frond of plants'?"

"No. I broke it when I was seven." I remember in vivid detail. Mom made me hot chocolate. The outside scalded my hands and I dropped it. She wept and then called herself silly.

"I gave her that one." His posture relaxes. "She laughed like a hyena."

I pause, suddenly understanding her reaction. The mug tied her to another life. To my father.

"She's a teacher?"

"Yep. Mom is super self-deprecating about it. You know the quote, 'those who can't do, teach'?"

"I'm not familiar," he says. "But I understand."

"Her students love her, and the faculty are gaga about her. She's accomplished so much great stuff," I gush.

"And she made you."

My father waits for me to catch on. Comprehension is slow, but when it dawns, warmth spreads from my toes to my ears. He tips his glass to mine. I'll cheers to that.

"She always wanted to teach." His voice has a soft edge to it, a flicker of appreciation and respect. His expression turns wistful. "Are you . . . did you have a happy childhood?"

I answer automatically. "Yes. The best." I launch into my favorite childhood stories, like the time I dressed as a pirate for almost a year in elementary school. Mom was totally on board, blackening my teeth every morning, making dishes with limes so I wouldn't get, you know, scurvy. Those were the days. I tell him about my friends—how Noora has total boss skills, how aggressively sweet Hansani is, how cutthroat Glory can be.

I leave out living in a town with dueling confederate and rainbow flags. And the box of unaddressed Father's Day cards next to my stash of romance novels.

He inhales audibly. "Your life would have been very different if you'd been raised here."

"How so?"

"Well, for starters, you would have been given two very specific names. The first would be an official name that ended in -nomiya. It means *imperial member*." Right. His name.

Makotonomiya. "The second would be a personal name. Scholars would have drafted a list of options. I would have picked one, then sent my choice to the emperor. For approval, of course."

"Of course."

"The emperor would have written your anointed names on washi paper and placed them in a lacquered cypress box with the gold chrysanthemum emblem. The box would have been sent to the palace, then to the hospital and placed on your pillow, right next to your head," he says in a low, warm voice. "After the naming ritual, you would have been bathed in a cedar tub."

"That sounds nice."

He swirls the liquid in his glass. "A floral emblem would have been chosen for you."

My breath makes little clouds. The fireworks are over. Near the pond, fireflies appear, dancing over the water in concentric circles. It's cold. Even so, I'm not ready to go inside yet. "What would you have chosen?" My eyes are as wide as saucers. My heart is open. I want this to work so badly. I want my life to be different. Better. More whole. Superhero epic.

"*I chose the purple iris.*"

The vase in my room—a single iris. He thought about me. He cares. My eyes sting. I bat my lashes against the tears. If he asks about them, I'll say it's the breeze.

"It stands for purity and wisdom."

My emotions swell. Since I'm no good at hiding them, I say, "Mom said she didn't tell you because she knew you wouldn't want to leave Japan. You would be like a tree without sun." *And she didn't want the royal life,* I think. Their impasse led to separation. It was the only solution. I understand, but it's still hard to accept.

He nods. "My duties are to Japan."

I swipe at my nose. "I get it. I've seen all the Spider-Man movies." Thanks to Glory. She's a Marvel freak. "Power, responsibility, and all that."

The wind ruffles his hair. He slugs down the rest of his drink. "I had no intention of living in America permanently. That was never an option."

I nod and gulp. If I don't dwell on it, his words won't hurt as much. He plays with the empty glass in his hands, thumbs skirting the rim.

"But if I had known I had a daughter, I would have found a solution." He studies me, waiting until my eyes raise to meet his. "I would have swum across oceans. I would have scaled mountains. I would have crossed deserts. I would have found a way."

The twist of pain in my stomach eases. Hope floats in my chest. That's something. That's more than a start.

That's a *beginning*.

8

A small gathering, they said. A celebration dinner in your honor. Just family. No biggie. But also, did we mention the meet-the-press section beforehand? How about the handbell ringers? What about a brief concert by the imperial house orchestra? No? Sorry, our bad.

The quiet evening has started with a not-so-quiet bang. In other words, a balls-to the-wall welcome reception. It's a shock to my system after the quiet walk with my father. A reporter from the imperial press club stares at me. His press badge reads Shigesada Inada, Japan Gazette. So far, his questions are little bits of fluff wrapped in cotton. "What is your favorite color?" None of the press carry notepads or recording devices. It's odd. Also, they're all men.

Red for the blood of my enemies, I think. Truth: I'm a little punch drunk. The transpacific flight is nipping at my heels. "Blue," I answer serenely.

Mr. Fuchigami stands close to me. Correction: he *hovers.* He's more nervous than Tamagotchi in a room full of vacuum cleaners. When I answer in a way he approves, a pleasant sound emanates from his throat. So far, I've accrued five happy noises. The reporter bows and thanks me gratuitously before leaving. Across the way, my father is being interviewed, too. Akio is also present, hanging around the edge of the room like a Gothic painting.

"Are we nearly done?" I turn to Mr. Fuchigami once we're alone. "I'm so tired. I can smell colors. Or maybe it's the cocaine." At his bug-eyed stare, I say, "Joke! I'm joking." I'm the only one laughing. Back in Mount Shasta, that would have killed. Noora once laughed so hard at one of my jokes that milk came out of her nose. True story.

"The dinner bell should ring soon," he assures me. "The family usually enjoys drinks after in the parlor, but you don't need to stay for that."

I eye a cloisonné case with a fish scale background in the corner. It's elegant and tall and fits in way better than me. We're in a reception hall with celery-colored carpet bordered by a lacquered parquet floor, its walls the same color as the lightwood. Elegant and airy, it's a part of Tōgū Palace, but separated by a series of sliding shoji screens. The press, handbell ringers, and orchestra aren't allowed past this point.

My room is a three-minute walk away. If I think too much about bed, I'll fall asleep. A change of subject is in order. "The press was so kind."

Mr. Fuchigami appears surprised. "Of course they were. They are members of the Imperial Press Club, handpicked by the Imperial Household Agency."

A flush of embarrassment heats my cheeks. I've been plunked down in the center of a maze, and the keys to finding my way out lie in a vortex of royal protocols, traditions and rules I haven't got the first clue about. I swallow down the giant ball of stress. I'll figure out what to do later. Procrastination has served me well in the past. My mission: survive the night. It feels as ominous as it sounds.

The dinner bell rings. The group splits, and the gaggle of reporters and handbell ringers disappear through a door.

"This way." Mr. Fuchigami leads me to the formal dining room. The long table is dressed up in starched linens and gleaming silvers. A white-gloved attendant pulls out a chair for me. My heart sinks when I see where I am seated. "Not by my father?" I gaze at Mr. Fuchigami.

A single shake of his head. "No. Seating has been carefully considered. We've placed you next to your extended family. This way, you'll have optimal and equal time with each member." He pauses, considers his next words carefully. "As the daughter of the Crown Prince, it is paramount you show attention to each. There should be no favorites. Now . . ." He opens his hands. "Please, go ahead."

The tables have gone quiet. Everyone stands behind their chairs, and all eyes are on me. It's clear my family is waiting for something. My father smiles. Close to him sits twin girls, no doubt Akiko and Noriko, the charms in the imperial bracelet. I see why. They're strikingly beautiful, with oval faces and lips the color of ballet slippers. So alike and perfect it's a bit creepy, as if they sprung fully formed from one of the silk tapestries.

Their father is my father's brother and second in line to inherit the throne. He's down at the end of the table, too. His wife is next to him, and though she's dressed immaculately, her face is tight, pale, and withdrawn.

"I'm sorry?" I whisper to Mr. Fuchigami. I'm so confused. "What's going on?"

"They are awaiting your introduction." Mr. Fuchigami says it like that explains everything. When I don't launch right in, he goes on. "Say a little about yourself." With that, he bows and leaves. *Leaves.*

I stare down at my toes. The flooring is carpet and patterned with circles. I'm standing in the middle of one. I've been put on the spot, literally and figuratively. "Oh, um. Hi." I glance up. My body feels like it's on fire. I do a little finger wave, then remember I haven't seen anyone wave since arriving. I jerk my arm back down. "Konnichiwa. I'm Izumi. But you all probably already know that. I live in Mount Shasta, California, but I suppose I also live here now, I think." I tug on my ear and actively search for a balcony to swan dive off of. "What else? I have a dog named Tamagotchi." The twins narrow their eyes in unison and whisper behind their hands.

Nobody ever says anything good behind their hands.

I feel myself starting to unravel. "He's a really good dog. Kind of. One time I tried to swaddle him and put him in a field of flowers, like a newborn photo shoot. He nearly bit my face off. Though I guess that's not great . . ." I trail off. Nearest to me are two boys and one girl around my age. They smile like they're forcing themselves to. *End it. End it now.* "Anyway. Izumi. Mount Shasta. Nice to meet you." I bow. It doesn't feel right at all. I fall down into my chair, trying to make myself as small as possible.

There is a pause. Everyone continues to stand until my father takes his seat. Then conversation resumes. I'm just dying in a puddle of my own embarrassment. The only consolation is that Akio is not present. No doubt he's somewhere on the property, lurking.

"Well, you did your best," the boy next to me says. He's around my age. "Yoshi." He holds out a hand for me to shake. I discreetly wipe my hand on my dress before I do, pleased with the familiar gesture. "Second cousin, official name Yoshihito, seventh in line to be emperor. Son of Asako and Yasuhito."

He nods at his parents. They sit diagonally from us—a small, affable-appearing man beside a woman with a diamond necklace that must have cost a king's ransom. Their smiles are warm, if a bit apprehensive. Understood. I'm not the only one trying to get a handle on the whole Crown-Prince's-illegitimate-child situation.

"Please, you must call us Auntie and Uncle," Asako invites, inclining her head. Yasuhito repeats his wife's sentiment with a friendly bow of his head. I appreciate a man who supports the woman in his life.

"Now, I know what you're thinking." Yoshi snaps his napkin and lays it across his lap. A lock of hair falls into his eye. All in all, he looks like a J-pop star who fell through a trapdoor into royalty. "You would be correct. In the past, distant cousins have married. But these days, it would be frowned upon." He sticks out his lower lip.

"Bummer," I say, flatly. I copy his move with the napkin. Another white-gloved attendant holding a silver pitcher fills my water goblet.

He drops the pout and exchanges it for a grin. "Oh. You'll do fine. I like you."

I like him, too, in a purely platonic, non–kissing cousins kind of way. I don't think I need to make that clear. He reminds me a little of Noora. They both have the same take-a-bite-out-of-life approach, something I aspire to have.

"You're embarrassing her." The girl across from me chastises Yoshi. She has a small oval face and her dark hair is pinned half-up. A glittery diamond on her left hand flashes as she takes a sip of water. "Don't listen to my brother. I'm Sachiko." She introduces herself, then the man sitting next to her. "My fiancé, Ryu."

"Nice to meet you," he says, nodding.

"Don't worry, Sa-chan," Yoshi says. He turns to me. "I've decided to take you under my leg."

It takes me a full five seconds to decode his message. "I'm pretty sure you mean *wing*."

"*Wing?*"

I suck in a breath, happy to explain. Finally, something I know. "The phrase is 'take you under my wing.'"

His face screws up. "Why would I say that? I don't have wings."

"The term isn't about humans, my God," the guy next to me huffs. He looks very similar to Yoshi. Must be his brother. But his hair is shorter, his back is straighter, and he seems wound tight. He straightens the silverware and refolds his napkin into a symmetrical triangle. "It's from observing birds sheltering their chicks under their wings. Obviously."

"My brother." Yoshi confirms my suspicions. "Spent four years in Scotland studying ornithology and linguistics. If you ever have trouble sleeping, ask him about his thesis on the captive rearing of the black grouse."

Sachiko laughs. Their brother is less than pleased. Their antagonism is familiar, comfortable—makes me feel as if I've slipped on an old sweatshirt. Still, he bows a grumpy head. "Masahito," he says.

"Are you finding your rooms acceptable?" Uncle Yasuhito asks. His mouth twitches under his mustache.

"More than acceptable," I say. An attendant offers me a hot towel with tongs. A glance at Yoshi shows he's unraveled his and is wiping his hands. He throws it into a silver bowl another attendant holds behind him. I pluck the towel from her.

Auntie Asako says, "The palace has recently been renovated."

"Oh yeah, it's like a Nate Berkus dream." I turn, placing my used towel in the silver bowl. I whisper a thank-you, but the attendant doesn't recognize it. His stare is locked on a spot on the wall.

Uncle Yasuhito's forehead wrinkles. I've confused the poor man. "Nate Berkus?"

My smile is bright. "He's a famous designer in the States. Oprah's best friend."

Light shines in Auntie Asako's eyes. "Ah yes, he is like Shoji Matsuri. He designs cat homes." She nudges her husband. "Remember, he designed something for me. Would you like me to give you his contact information?" Her voice drops to a whisper. "He's very discreet."

Not totally sure what she means, but some things are better left unknown. "No, thank you. I'm more of a dog person."

Yoshi draws my attention. "She's got an original Warhol cat in that home." His eyes roll. "The irony."

The dust of conversation settles. A bowl of almost clear soup is set in front of me. Pearled vegetables float around a gold leaf topped with . . . caviar? My fingers twitch over my place setting and the multiple utensils. Forks, knives, and spoons taunt me. *Hello, Zoom Zoom. You don't know how to use any of us, do you?* I am a fish out of water—or rather, a girl out of Mount Shasta. My nerves simmer and my stomach flips. Family members observe my hesitation and I shift, feeling too much like an ant under a magnifying glass.

Under the table, a knee careens into mine. Yoshi very deliberately holds up the spoon beside all the knives. "Leg," he mouths.

I grin and mentally promise Yoshi my firstborn. Why am I not eating already? *Get in my belly.* I dip the spoon in, and across the table, Sachiko winks at me. I make eye contact with my father. His wary gaze asks, *Everything okay?* I answer with a nod, my princess version of a thumbs-up. All good. The room seems to take a breath.

And so it goes.

It's as if I'm being served calculus equations, but my second cousins are taking on the mantle of patient, conspiratorial teachers. With every new dish, they demonstrate what each utensil is and how to use them. Dinner passes in a blur of haute French cuisine—foams, gels, and powders. Between second and third courses, conversation dwells on the emperor and empress, who are visiting the Okinawa prefecture.

"You don't see them often?" I ask my second cousins.

Masahito inspects his crystal glass and wipes away a smudge with his napkin. "Their Imperial Majesties' first duty is to serve the people."

"Yes, they are mother and father to all of Japan." Yoshi says, then drops his voice to a whisper. "The emperor is not a god, but he is not a man either. We may live on the ground, but he still lives above the clouds."

Dessert is served—fruit in the shape of an iris. It's special, just for me. Another welcome. I bask in it. But this moment is fleeting, I realize with a start. Only by the grace of my cousins did I succeed.

After dinner, drinks are offered in the parlor. That's my cue; the sandman beckons. Sweet sleep is only moments away. We rise from the table, and I bid my father goodnight. Aunties, uncles, and cousins watch me leave. I can't help but feel the weight of their gazes on my back, the pull of their misgivings. They're asking the same question I'm asking myself: Will I measure up to the imperial height?

THE TOKYO TATTLER

Japan weighs in on
new imperial family member

March 23, 2021

Her Imperial Highness Princess Izumi (pictured) arrived at Narita International Airport yesterday afternoon sporting casual dress, leggings and a sweatshirt. Imperial blogger Junko Inogashira was present. "The clothing certainly wasn't within protocol. What's worse is that the princess didn't address or wave to the crowds. Many waited for hours and were completely slighted when she left immediately. I heard from an airport employee the princess was rude to her assigned imperial guard when they stopped to use a restroom, too."

Is the princess letting her new title go to her head? Janitor Chie Inaro doesn't think so. He met the princess during the abovementioned restroom break. In an exclusive interview with *The Tokyo Tattler,* Inaro had only glowing things to say about the princess. "Beautiful, beautiful girl—the epitome of grace. She used my handkerchief to wipe her hands," he gloated, showing off the white square cloth, now encased in glass. "I'd like to keep it. But my son wants to auction it off, says we'll make a fortune." A fortune indeed. At press time, the handkerchief's current bid was ¥2,000,000. Inaro plans to put the money toward his retirement.

Since arriving at the airport, the princess has been locked up tight on imperial grounds. The Imperial Household Agency has declined to comment on how she's faring. We can't help but wonder why this princess is being hidden away . . .

9

Seventy-two hours in Japan, and I am no closer to reaching the imperial height. In fact, my growth is distinctly stunted.

From my seat, I stare up at Mariko. Mariko stares down at me, her honey-colored eyes cool and assessing. "Focus, Izumi-sama." Her voice implies I am doing anything but. Her look also implies I am the human equivalent of a Band-Aid found in someone's salad. Others are also present: Mr. Fuchigami smiles benignly, and a butler, eerily efficient and polite, stands ramrod straight. Rain splatters against the windows.

In front of me is a place setting. I take a deep breath, feeling my waistband stretch on my exhale. This morning, Mariko wrestled me into a matching twinset and pleated skirt.

I glance at the table. It's a selection of crystal glasses, gleaming silverware, and porcelain plates inlaid with a gold chrysanthemum. My hand drifts over the second fork on the left. Mr. Fuchigami sucks in air through his teeth. He's dressed in a staid suit, silver-streaked hair neatly parted and styled.

My hand changes direction. Mariko frowns.

If we were in *Downton Abbey*, Mariko would be Mary—churlish, a little cold, and serious to a fault. She is the driving force behind my three-hour etiquette lessons each evening. We practice bowing and different ways to say thank you. There are dress and glove fittings. Based on her frosty attitude,

I have drawn the conclusion she does not like me. Quick fact: as a member of the royal family, I have no right to vote, carry cash, or have social media accounts.

Mariko speaks. "We won't be able to accompany you to the wedding."

Prime Minister Adachi will be wed in just over a week. I'm attending as my first official duty.

"Yes," Mr. Fuchigami agrees. The two are in total cahoots. "You'll be seated with your father. You are expected to know this."

"You won't be able to look to other family members for support," Mariko adds. She must have spied me on the first night at the family dinner when Yoshi took me under his "leg." Despite my royal blood, nothing is inherited. I need a pick-me-up. I reach for the plate of senbei crackers in the middle of the table. They're made of rice and still warm, fresh off the grill. "No more crackers." The plate is whipped from the table. My mouth hangs open as Mariko holds it hostage. "Now, which is the fish fork?" She nods at the table.

Again, I stare at the place setting. At the extra small, small, medium and large forks. I start by eliminating the possibilities. The extra small utensil is an oyster fork. The next size up is the salad fork. That leaves medium or large. My odds are fifty-fifty. Not bad. But in a blinding moment of clarity, the answer comes to me. "This one." I hold it up proudly.

Mariko arches her brows. "Are you sure?"

"I'm sure?" I say it like a question.

"You're right." She doesn't seem happy about it, but she does place the plate of senbei back on the table.

Mr. Fuchigami clears his throat, stepping forward.

"Perhaps we should practice your Japanese. Ogenki desu ka?" He launches right in.

Mariko crosses her arms, clearly ready to enjoy the show. The butler begins to clear the place settings.

Table etiquette to a second language. I shake off the whiplash. In addition to a crash course in culture and table manners, I have to learn Japanese, starting with the hiragana and katakana alphabets and memorizing common phrases, such as: "Genki desu." *I'm fine.* A perfect response to his question, *How do you do?* Truly, it's been a blur of conjugating verbs and perfecting the palatal *d*. Japanese is hierarchical to boot. There are different levels of formality, all depending on the speaker and their relationship to the person.

Mr. Fuchigami nods approvingly. "Ojōzu desu." He nods to the table; along with the senbei, there is a dried fruit platter and selection of nuts. "Nanika meshiagarimasu ka?"

I cock my head, thinking hard. "Ano . . ." That's a space filler in Japanese, the equivalent of saying *um*. A genius word. I use it a lot.

Mr. Fuchigami takes pity on me. "Nani ka meshiagarimasu ka? Would you like something to eat?"

I perk up. "Hai. Ringo ga Asako desu. Oppai tabetai!" Translation: *I like apples. I want to eat a lot of them.* Only . . . Mr. Fuchigami's face turns the color of a tomato, and he can't meet my eyes. Mariko chokes. The butler drops a crystal glass. It doesn't break, but it clinks against a place setting, taking a chip out of the priceless china. "What?" I ask, alarmed. Mr. Fuchigami can't even look at me.

Mariko rubs her eyebrow. "You've mispronounced the word *a lot.*"

"*A lot?* It's oppai, isn't it?" I say it a few more times to get the hang of it. "Oppai, oppai, oppai."

Mariko's eyes go wide. "Stop. Saying. It."

"Your Highness," Mr. Fuchigami says slowly, carefully, quietly. "The correct pronunciation is ippai. The word you said refers to . . ." He can't say it. His eyes flicker to Mariko.

Mariko can't say it either, but her hand drifts up, fluttering around her breasts.

"Oh." My eyes grow wide. I've just sung "boobs, boobs, boobs" to the royal chamberlain and my lady-in-waiting. "Oh!" A knot twists in my belly. "Sorry," I murmur. The butler is gone.

Mr. Fuchigami checks his watch. "I need . . . I have a meeting." I glance at the antique clock on the wall. Zodiac animals mark the time instead of numbers. We were scheduled for another hour, right up until lunch with my father.

"Sorry," I call out again as Mr. Fuchigami hastily bows and leaves. Eye contact is too much to ask.

"We're done," Mariko says abruptly, then trots after him.

Alone, I push away from the table. I wander from the dining room through the living room, catching my reflection in a black and gilt mirror. I still look pretty good—my makeup hasn't budged, and every hair is still in place. But isn't that how it always is? Pretty on the outside, slowly crumbling on the inside?

My steps take me to the entryway. After slipping on shoes, I'm out the door and sitting on the concrete step. I hug my legs. My vibe is glum, totally insecure. The air is cool and it's drizzling, but I stay dry, protected by the porch overhang. Movement catches my eye—Akio. He's as handsome as ever.

The wind lightly tousles his damp hair. He's wearing some sort of dark coat. All in all, he's fit to be on the cover of *Vogue*. Whatever. So annoying.

He eyes me, brows lowering into a definitive glower. Yesterday, I overslept, and a tour of the wild duck preserves and a fishing party had to be rescheduled. Later on, a clock was delivered to my room . . . by Akio's request. I cross my arms and return his frown. His deepens in response. I'm pretty sure he's commanding dark forces to gather upon me. Likewise, buddy. Likewise.

I shift away from him and covertly dig my phone from my bra. I succumb to my pathological need to share my humiliation and text Noora.

> Me
>
> Today I mispronounced a word and accidentally told my chamberlain I want to eat boobs.

I wait for her response, turning the phone over in my hands and wondering what the AGG has been up to. I wish I could stalk them on social media, but their accounts are private, and Mr. Fuchigami made me delete all mine. Royal protocol. There's also a ban on consuming media on imperial property. No tabloids. No newspapers. No television.

Finally, Noora's name lights up my phone.

> Noora
>
> Bah. Could happen to anyone

I'm not sure I can do this

Strongly disagree

Remember that time Glory said you couldn't eat a whole pie from Black Bear and I bet you could and you actually did?

Your point is . . . ?

My point is: I believe in you.

Riiight, because being a princess is the same as eating pie.

It's not. But you're still fantastic. Men weep at your feet. Women want to be you. Birds fall from the sky stunned by your glory.

That help?

Me
A little.

Noora
Good.

Noora buoys me. She's never steered me wrong. Okay, there was that one time she convinced me to shave my eyebrows and draw them on. My phone buzzes.

Noora
Also still waiting on that bodyguard picture

Glory
Ditto

Hansani
Yes please.

She's added the girls to the text thread. Ever so discreetly, I check Akio out over my shoulder. He's staring off into the distance, hands clasped in front of him. I hold my phone, snap, then send. His head swivels. "Nani o shite imasu ka? Did you just take my photograph?"

I rise, brushing off my skirt. "No. Of course not." My voice is heavy with a dose of as-if-I'd-ever.

The screen lights up. I glance at it.

OMG. Make out with him already.

I'd go down with that ship.

I bet he smells amazing but
kind of rare, too, like his cologne
is made with panther tears.
#sexpanthercologne

I mute all. Akio grunts. Such a poet this man is.

He shifts away. Not so fast. Remembering the clock sitting on my nightstand, my blood heats. I sidle up next to him. He's making a show of canvassing the estate, like he can't see me.

"Akio?"

"Your Highness." So stiff. So formal.

"I've been wondering. How does one become an imperial guard?"

He scowls, as if this is the worst time he's ever had. One can only hope. "I prefer *close-protection officer*. I believe Mr. Fuchigami supplied you with my qualifications."

"He did, but it was mostly police credentials." I toe the cement with my sensible navy heeled shoe. "Is there like some imperial—sorry, close-protection officer school you have to attend?" I widen my eyes and put a hand over my mouth. "Have you ever killed someone? And if so, did you like it? I bet you have, and I bet you did." It's always the strong and silent types who are hiding something. "Tell me, do you have a locked room where no one's allowed?"

"Don't be ridiculous." His hands are folded in front of him. His back is perfectly straight. "It's a basement. Better temperature control down there. You know, for the bodies."

My eyes narrow to slits. "It's scary because I can't tell if you're joking or not."

He breathes a deep, impatient sigh.

"I think we should establish the chain of command. Am I, like, your boss?" Please say yes. Please say yes.

The muscle in his jaw twitches. He may have cracked a tooth. If so, I know an excellent royal dentist. Mr. Fuchigami squeezed in a physical and a full dental exam yesterday. I'm still wearing the Band-Aid from the blood test. Crime shows hold true. DNA doesn't lie. I am the Prince's daughter. "Your security and safety are paramount," he says. "They come first."

"Meaning . . ."

Now I have all his attention. "Technically, I am the boss of you."

Oh, he is smug.

I purse my lips. I don't care for that at all. "Has anyone ever told you charm isn't your strong suit?"

His patience has run out. "Charm doesn't keep royalty alive."

Touché. "I think we got off on the wrong foot." *I was late. You had a clock sent to my room. Let's just call the whole thing off.* "What's your favorite movie?"

"Why do you want to know that?" His gaze is sharp, suspicious. The rain starts again. Fat drops hit the pavement.

"I just think we should get to know each other better. You tell me something about you, and I reciprocate. You know, it's how you make friends. It's *bonding*." *Then, once I find out all your secrets and vulnerabilities, I will use them to destroy you.* Just kidding. Kind of.

His lips twitch. He scans the estate again. Silence stretches on until he finally says, aggrieved, "I am fond of *Die Hard*."

I blink twice. "*Die Hard?* Like Bruce Willis, 'Yippee-ki-yay, mothereffer'?" I would have taken him more for an *American Psycho* fan. You know, suits, business cards, a predilection for order, and hiding bodies in closets.

He sighs. "My parents worked a lot. It was on television when I was young." My stomach twists with sympathy. He nods. "Are we finished, Your Highness?"

Akio gestures to the entrance. Chatter comes through his earpiece, and lines form around his mouth. "Everything okay?"

"There is some commotion at the gate," he huffs.

"Commotion?"

"Reporters hoping to get a glimpse of you." The chatter in his earpiece increases. "Are you ready to go inside? I'm needed at the gate."

I shrug. Seems unnecessary since I can't even see the gate from the palace, but I say, "Sure." It is easy to acquiesce when it's your only option. Plus, apparently, he's the boss.

He touches two fingers to the back of my elbow, steering me indoors. There's a little spark. So what if he looks like The Rock and Daniel Dae Kim had a baby and raised it in the Japanese wilderness? I'm sure this attraction is only one-sided. I've had too many unrequited crushes to waste my time on another. I decide to focus all my energy on hating him. Good thing he makes it easy.

"Hey," I say to Akio. "I had a thought."

"A dangerous pastime," he murmurs.

I choose to ignore his comment. "Don't feed the bears" is a saying in Mount Shasta. "Do I have a code name? I'm pretty sure I get a code name. I'd like to choose it."

His fingers fall from my elbow. A pity. "Yes," he says. "As a matter fact, you do have a code name."

"I knew it!" My twirl is the glee-filled kind. "What is it? Sidewinder or Lightning or maybe Pegasus?"

"We were calling you Butterfly."

Huh. "That's nice, I guess." A little soft, but okay.

"Then, the tabloids gave you the moniker The Lost Butterfly, so we had to change it."

I perk up.

"I suggested it," he baits.

"What did you suggest?" I look up at Akio with stars in my eyes. The possibilities are endless—*Sunshine, Moonflower, Cherry Blossom.* My thoughts are a runaway train. Maybe he likes me. Maybe he's not as mean as he seems. Maybe I've terribly misjudged him and this is just a rocky start to a friendship that turns to love that will last the ages. Our affair will inspire folksy campfire ballads.

It's the first time I see Akio smile. It's part evil, part satisfied, as if he's just won a bet with himself. "Radish."

10

I have lunch with my father, just the two of us at the palace. My earlier conversation with Akio lingers around me like a miasma, but all in all, the atmosphere is good. Casual. The place settings are informal, ohashi the only utensil. I lighten up and relax a bit. A special treat has been prepared—ayu, a troutlike fish caught in the Nagara River from the Gifu area. It is served whole over a bed of rice, once a currency and now a sacred grain.

"Very fresh," the chef informs us with a proud smile. "Caught this morning."

"It's considered a delicacy," my father says as the chef leaves. I haven't managed a taste yet. I'm watching my father, observing how he'll eat the fish.

He brings the bowl to his face, then uses the ohashi to grasp the tiny sweetfish and take a bite, starting with the head. I blink. Oh, okay. That's how it's done. I pick up my ohashi and copy his moves.

My teeth sink into the fish. I wait for my gag reflex to kick in, but it doesn't. The skin is crunchy and salty, but gives way to a softer, sweet inside, tasting like watermelon. My saliva glands kick into overdrive. Just like that, I'm all in. If ayu is on the menu, I'll have two.

We dig in.

My father explains how the fish are caught, painting a

picture with his words. The canvas is shaded in purple and blues, the bruises of nightfall. A single firework rises over the river. It signals the start of the evening fishing. In that moment, the towers of Gifu Castle are caught in relief. The fishermen wear grass skirts, indigo tunics, and pointed caps. In specially made bamboo baskets, they carry leashed cormorants, dark feathered birds with hooked beaks. They ease into the water in long wooden boats, torch blazing at the bow. The birds dive under the water and catch and keep the fish in a special pouch in their throat. A snare prevents the bird from swallowing the fish.

My father says, "The relationship between cormorant and man is very important. To the keepers, the birds are family. In the wild, cormorants live seven to eight years, but with the fishermen, it can be much longer. The record is thirty years."

My bowl is empty. My stomach is full. My soul longs for it to be night and to be on the shores of the Nagara River. I wipe my mouth with my napkin. "I'd like to see it sometime."

"The high season is in the summer. I'll ask Mr. Fuchigami to schedule it . . ." He trails off. We both realize it at the same time. I won't be here. In two weeks, I'll be gone.

After lunch, we walk. The sun is shining and heats my head. Black hair is the worst. The gravel beneath my feet is still wet and little puddles dot the lawn. Japan is mercurial. I mean, pick a temperature.

My father says, "Your lady-in-waiting is working out? Your lessons are going well?" He's discarded his suit jacket and tie and his sleeves are rolled up. He's more relaxed outdoors. I remember he loves the mountains, hiking, and such. This is his happy place.

"Yes," I say. Mariko is working out. The real question is: Am *I* working out? I think it over, licking a smudge of Nutella from my thumb—the last bit of my newest obsession. After lunch yesterday, the chef served dorayaki—Nutella between two castella pancakes. Boom. Mind blown. I ate it and ascended to a higher plane. Since then, the chef has kept me in steady supply, and I love him so much for it.

"Is this how you were educated? I mean . . . did you have tutors who came to the palace, and have etiquette lessons like they ones I've been getting?"

"No. I attended Gakushūin. My classmates—all five of them—were handpicked." I wonder what that must have been like, knowing everyone your age had been selected to be around you. He waits a beat, then says, "I looked over your schedule. Mr. Fuchigami is keeping you quite busy. I hope it's not too rigorous."

The light disappears under the arching trees, giving us shade. My burning head screams in relief. "I'm very thankful for the opportunity to learn." Sometimes when I speak with my father, I don't sound like myself. It's not the same tone I'd use with my mom. If I were with her, we'd be knee-deep in potty humor. Or at least, I would be. I know she secretly loves it, though. She's a closet deviant. You kind of have to be, living next door to Jones.

The path widens and the gravel stretches into a circle. We've come to a clearing. A building winks in the sun, glass on all sides. "I assume you share your mother's appreciation for plants. I thought you might like to see the greenhouse." I do. I do. I do! At my smile, he opens his hand. "After you."

Don't need to ask me twice. The door is heavy and opens with a creak. Mom has greenhouses on campus, but they're all plastic poles and sheeting. This one is beautiful, a piece of artwork and fit for . . . well, fit for a prince, I guess. Fans lazily turn, circulating hot air. I feel two pink splotches form on my cheeks. There are three rows of long, wooden tables.

It smells like the earth after the rain, like my mom when she comes home from work with soil under her fingernails. I miss her. We've texted and talked on the phone, but it's not the same. You get used to seeing certain people every day.

I walk in-between two rows, taking in the tiny pots holding plants with broad leaves. Their crooked stems droop with delicate red, white, and pink flowers. "Orchids," I say, swallowing. "Mom's favorite."

My father lingers at the door. He raises a brow. "Are they?"

I study him. Is this some wild coincidence, or does he grow these for my mother? The look on his face says he doesn't want to talk about it. "Tell me more about your school," I say, but you bet the moment I get the chance I'll be texting my mother. Something along the lines of: FYI, my father, your former Crown Prince lover, keeps a greenhouse full of orchids. Aren't those your favorite flower? Just thought you might like to know.

He takes the out and dives in to talking about his studies. The air in the greenhouse fills with all the unsaid things; he can't tell me about his time with my mother, and I can't tell him how I really feel. How I'm not sure I'm equipped to be a princess. Not sure if I belong. The tough stuff will have to wait for another time.

Eventually, the heat in the greenhouse gets to me. We settle into a couple Adirondack chairs on the edge of the lawn.

Cool wind slaps against my cheeks, and it's refreshing. Mom would really love this. It's totally her vibe. I'd like to say so out loud, but I hold back. She's the giant pink elephant in this intricate garden—my mother, his former lover. Does he feel it, too? I don't like not being able to talk about her, treating her as blasphemy. I don't care if this makes me a total dork, but truth: I love my mom. She's one of my favorite people.

"You seem quiet," he says.

"I was thinking about Mom—" I cut myself off before I can go on.

My father sits back, sighs. "Yes."

"You don't . . . I mean, it's okay if you don't want to talk about her." *But let's talk about her.* About how much you loved her, and how much you still do. Let's talk about how wonderful and happy she is, but a little sad sometimes, too. Let's talk about how you both get the same look in your eye when the other is brought up.

He stares at the greenhouse and thinks for a while. "The truth is, I loved college, America, *and* your mother. That period in my life is painful to recall. From the beginning of our affair, I knew it couldn't last. Everything was like a beautiful dream. But like all dreams, it had to come to an end. And that's how I treat it now, as a bit of a fantasy."

I clasp my hands together to keep them from fidgeting. I can hear it in his voice. He can't even entertain the possibility of a relationship with my mom. *The dream is over.* But then what does that make me? "I'm here, though." Tangible proof he and my mother existed.

He smiles at me. "You are. And it is a gift. It's hard to

reconcile the two events, you here now and me back then. I hope that makes sense."

"It does." In a weird way.

He pats the arm of his chair. "Be patient with me?"

"If you promise to do the same for me," I say back lightly. We're in a place where we're both ready to reach now.

"Of course," he promises. He focuses back on the greenhouse. "So what's on the docket for tomorrow?"

"Uh, I think Mr. Fuchigami said something about sericulture?" My royal profile is a little slim. A hobby is in order. Mr. Fuchigami pitched ichthyology with a concentration in carp. A nonstarter. I piped in with how much I enjoyed baking— too common. Tomorrow, we try sericulture. Truth: I'm not one hundred percent sure what sericulture is. Next, I'm going to suggest falconry. The imperial household employs a falconer and everyone knows all epic quests start with birds of prey.

"Good luck, though I don't think you need it. Mr. Fuchigami reports you did splendid with the mock banquet setting this morning. All eyes will be on you at the wedding instead of the bride." He smiles with pride again. He's practically beaming with it. I have no desire to dim the lights.

"Yeah," I agree, smiling right back. Then we sit together, him and me, near the greenhouse that may or may not have been built for my mother.

11

Sericulture should come with multiple warnings.

Warning one: the event involves facing off with ultra-perfect twin princesses to whom you can't help comparing yourself.

Warning two: there will be photographs. The occasion will be documented and released to the press (in other words: don't eff it up).

Warning three: worms. Worms. WORMS. Nobody mentioned sericulture was the production of silk through rearing of silkworms.

I stand in front of a table. Akiko and Noriko are across from me, their gazes hawklike. It is truly an art form to look down your nose at someone the same height as you. Between us is a piece of parchment paper filled with leaves and the writhing bodies of about a thousand silkworms. Surrounding us are imperial minders: ladies-in-waiting (mine and the twins'), chamberlains, photographers, and a guard or two. Akio included. We've taken to giving each other the silent treatment, communicating exclusively through third parties.

A flash erupts. Picture number four.

Japan is surly this morning. A storm swept through outside Tokyo last night. Howling winds and rain threatened to whip the cherry buds from their branches and kept me tossing and turning. Now, the air in the open room hangs heavy like a frown. Also it smells sour, like wet tatami matting.

Noriko—or is it Akiko?—whispers to her twin. They both possess the same high cheekbones, winning smiles, and even teeth. Blunt bangs frame their perfect faces.

Their lips twitch with laughter. My God, even their laugh is pretty, reminiscent of the sound of temple bells. "Cousin," one says, voice low enough so only I can hear. Another camera flashes. I fix my face into an easy smile. Mariko is watching—with concern? Mild annoyance? Hard to tell. But I see her, and it feels as if she sees through me.

"We were just commenting how lovely your dress is," the other one purrs.

I look down. Smooth the light pink fabric over my stomach. Feel the pinch of the elbow sleeves. "Oh. Thanks—"

"Yes," the other twin agrees, all snide and snotty. "It makes you appear so slim."

I dig my fingernails into my palms. I want to punch their noses. How hard is it to get blood out of linen? A million curse words fill my mouth.

The royal silkworm breeder and his assistants enter the room. They're clad head-to-toe in khaki like exotic zookeepers, carrying baskets filled to the brim with mulberry leaves.

One of the imperial photographers whispers something to Mr. Fuchigami. The chamberlain smiles. "An excellent idea. We will take a photo of the three princesses together."

Akiko and Noriko step around the table in unison, and it makes me jump. I shall now forevermore call them the Shining Twins.

A bold silkworm has left the safety of the mulberry and

parchment cradle. It inches its way toward my pinkie nail. The little chalk-colored fella is slightly hairy and fat—its rotund body reminds me of how my stomach feels every Thanksgiving. Forget the AGG and the Black Bear Diner, these suckers are really living their best lives, crunching on mulberry while being gently warmed under lights.

Another flash. The Shining Twins pose demurely for the camera, but the picture has caught my face downturned. "Your Highness," Mr. Fuchigami says. I tip my chin up. The Shining Twins move in closer.

"I admired you at the family dinner," one says.

"I wish I could eat like you," the other says.

Whoa. Shots fired. Still, I smile sweetly for the camera. *Flash.* I turn slightly left. This twin has a little mole beneath her eye, a beauty mark. "I bet I could make you." I say it loud enough for both to hear.

Finally, one says behind me. "Oh, Aki-chan, our cousin is funny."

I focus back on the silkworms. The one making a run for it has disappeared.

"You must have learned that from your father," says Akiko.

I did not learn that from my father. Could not have learned that from my father. We just met. The Shining Twins are reminding me I am the Crown Prince's mess. They're here to clean me up. My eye twitches. What is their deal? Is it the limelight? They can't stand sharing it? Am I stepping on their silk-covered toes? Either way, I am now positive this day is going to end up with a girl in jail. It's me. That girl is me.

Baskets of mulberry leaves are held out. The cameras go wild. This is the moment they've been waiting for—we'll place the branches on top of the silkworms, feed them, and take part in an ancient ritual six thousand years old. This picture will state I am but the spoke in a wheel on a car of a train where everything is working perfectly. It's wonderful and slightly terrifying to be part of something bigger than yourself. This institution, this title will outlast me. My knees buckle. I feel small, not up to the task.

Something tickles my arm. I glance down. It's the Thanksgiving silkworm. His back arches and he thrusts upward like he's a bloodhound, sniffing for the scent of mulberry. He can't find it, so he resumes a steady course up my arm. Rationally, I know he can't hurt me. Emotionally, I feel as if it's a full-out declaration of war. I want him off me. *Now.*

I shake my arm. Thanksgiving refuses to budge. Damn those sticky legs adapted over decades to climb trees. Right now, I hate evolution more than anything.

The twins are placing mulberry branches on the silkworms, easy as you please. They're way too calm. It makes me suspicious, but there's no time to dissect if they may be responsible (they totally are). Thanksgiving is digging under my sleeve. Oh my God. If he makes it into my dress, I'll die. *Die.*

I get a flashback to summer camp, sixth grade. A bee crawled under my sweatshirt. Panicked, I'd stripped the garment off, only I hadn't been wearing an undershirt or a bra. I ended up flashing the entire lunchroom of Camp Sweeney. Now, I am at the precipice of a similar situation.

I raise my hand, ready to flick the rare Koishimaru silkworm. As far as I'm concerned, it's him or me. I don't care if the cocoon you weave is used to restore priceless ancient artifacts or if you're considered a national treasure. Sayonara, silkworm.

A body wedges itself between me and Akiko. A hand sweeps over my arm, capturing the silkworm. I look up. It's Mariko to the rescue. Lips pinched, she opens her hand and dumps the silkworm back onto the mulberry leaves. Thanksgiving has disappeared into the masses. Mariko melts into the background again.

Mr. Fuchigami waves his hands and says something in Japanese. The imperial photographers put their cameras down. They exit the cocoonery. I'm a thousand percent sure I've messed up. Mr. Fuchigami confirms this when he says, "Don't worry, Your Highness. If we didn't get a good shot, we'll edit the photographs." I've ruined the carefully constructed photo opportunity.

The Shining Twins are smug. Now I understand the power dynamic between us. I am at the bottom. Time creeps on. I feel the blood drain from my face, pool at my toes, then out of my body. Here they come. Tears, hot and sticky gather in my eyes. As if it couldn't get any worse, I cry right in front of the Shining Twins.

That afternoon I lounge in the living room and watch Mariko like a cat as she sorts through a pile of gloves. A text comes through. At the alert, Mariko fixes me with a shrewd look. She has a thing about my phone and my pathological attachment to it. My eyes are still a bit puffy. I wept some of the car ride back to the palace. Mariko and Mr. Fuchigami kept up a steady conversation in Japanese. Wow. Talk about uncomfortable. Now, Mariko is giving me a wide berth. I shrink down so I'm in full recline, legs dangling over edge of the couch.

> **Unknown number**
> **Are you ready to step out of the celestial limelight?**

> **Me**
> **Who is this?**

> **Unknown number**
> **You don't know your favorite second cousin?**

> **Unknown number**
> **I am devastated. Insulted. Deeply wounded.**

Despite my gloomy mood, I smile. *Yoshi.*

> **Me**
> **How did you get this number?**

> **Yoshi**
> **Google is your friend.**

> **Me**
> **Srsly?**

Yoshi

No. I asked for it. Nobody
questioned why. Amazing what
people will give you when you're
royalty.

Yoshi

But a warning: you really can find
anything on the Internet these days.
The right YouTube video and I could
give myself a vasectomy.

Me

Would you really do that?

Yoshi

Course not. Deprive the world of my
superior sperm? Unlikely.

Yoshi

You didn't answer my question.

Me

What was your question exactly?

Yoshi

Are you ready to step out of the
celestial limelight?

Me

Dunno what that means.

Yoshi

Tokyo, darling. I'm talking about a
night on the town.

My gaze shoots to Mariko. She disappeared and brought
back more gloves. Good Lord.

Me

Can't. I've got a glove fitting.

Yoshi

That's a real thing? Never mind. Not
talking about right now. Nothing
good happens until after 9 p.m.,
after all.

Me

I don't think it's a good idea.

Yoshi

I disagree. This is probably the best
idea I've ever had.

I look out the window and consider his words. Trees sway
in the breeze. It promises to be a nice evening weather-wise,

but escape is impossible. The landscape is dotted with at least a dozen imperial guards, Akio included, and an equal number of cameras. But I am stuck and restless and still a little sad.

I purse my lips. All events outside of the palace have to be sanctioned. Though no one has said it outright, it's understood that I am not allowed to leave alone. Princesses belong in heavily guarded towers.

> Me
>
> **Say I wanted to. How would I get past all the security?**

> Yoshi
>
> **You just leave it up to me. Come. Let us break rules and hearts. Have a wake-up-with-a-tiger kind of night.**

> Yoshi
>
> **You in or out?**

I recall how the ride from the airport to Tokyo was like peering through a keyhole. Yoshi is offering me a way to unlock the door and open it wide. Isn't this what I wanted, the city spread at my feet? Noora and I would do this together. If she were here, we wouldn't hesitate to sneak off into the night with the promise of adventure just around the corner, so it's totally on-brand for me. In the name of all best friend relationships everywhere, I am practically obligated to say yes. Plus, I need a friendly face. I tap out my response, my chest light with anticipation.

Me
I'm in.

12

The sun sets. Eight thirty rolls around. I tell Mariko I am tired, making a big deal of yawning and stretching my arms. An actress I am not, but she buys it. It's easier to sneak out than I thought; Yoshi gives me detailed directions on what not to wear: no cardigans, nothing with a block heel. I'm dressed down in jeans and a T-shirt that reads Riots, Not Diets—Izzy clothes. It's nice to wear them again.

He also gives me detailed directions to get through the estate. The path leads to a short stone wall. I hoist myself over, and that's it. I'm off imperial grounds and on a sidewalk next to a highway.

It's night. Cars zoom by. A hundred feet away, an imperial guard patrols. My heart stops in my chest as he notes my presence, then quickly starts again when he dismisses me. I am no one to him, just one of the many pedestrians out and about. Why would he be suspicious, anyway? I guess people just trust princesses will stay put. Big mistake. I walk the opposite way, keeping my stride casual, and my head down. I pause when I get to the 40 sign with a red circle around it where Yoshi said to meet.

In no time, a car stops in front of me. It's a clunker. The engine rattles and smoke pours from the window as it opens. Yoshi sticks his head out from the front passenger seat. "Get in," he says, smile broadening. He's wearing sunglasses, a multicolored silk jacket with a holographic tiger, and his hair is whipped into peaks. It's mesmerizing. "I like your outfit," I say, climbing into the backseat.

"Please," Yoshi says. "This is me at a three."

A skinny man in a velvet jacket is in the driver's seat, a cigarette clamped between his teeth. Jazz plays on the radio. The car jerks and enters traffic.

"This is Taka," Yoshi says. In the mirror, the man lifts his chin to me. "He's an Uber driver by day, ceramicist by night." My cousin leans over the seat, cups his hand over his mouth, and pulls a face. "Don't ask to see any of his art. Awful." All this he says loud enough for Taka to hear.

Taka grunts and points a finger at his own shiny head. "I'm not bald. This is by choice. Okay?" Male egos. So touchy.

Yoshi cackles. "You are a weird motherfucker, Taka."

Taka smiles. His front two teeth are gold. It works on him.

"Um, how long have you two been friends?" I ask, checking my seat belt. I thought Noora's driving was bad. The city zips by: The Ritz Carlton and hostess clubs, kimono shops and boutiques selling leather handbags.

Neon lights reflect in Yoshi's sunglasses. "We met last night." At the face I make, he says, "Don't worry, you're in the best of hands. Plus, we're already out. Once the kimono has been opened, it cannot be shut."

Right. I should probably tell someone my whereabouts, just in case. The AGG has a strict no judgment policy. I tap out a text to the group.

Me

Out with my cousin in a strange
Uber. If I die please make sure
my headstone reads: Killed by a
bear (or something equally epic).

They answer with a thumbs-up. All taken care of. Now
can I relax and enjoy. The night is clear, the city is bright,
and in no time, we're pulling to a stop outside of a restaurant.
Taka parallel parks in a spot nearly too small for his car, but
he somehow squeezes in. Yoshi opens my door and offers me
his hand. I take it and he spins me in a pirouette. Taka lights
up another cigarette.

I'm still a touch dizzy as I follow the two men to a restaurant across the street. The front isn't much to look at—a brick
facade, two lights illuminating a plain white sign with kanji,
red lanterns hanging under the eaves, and menus display the
pricing. A large window showcases the kitchen. A man in
a crossover indigo jacket and a hachimaki around his head
sweats over steaming pots and a flaming grill.

Yoshi reaches the set of double doors first. We enter. The
red lanterns continue inside and cast the room in a warm,
crimson haze. Hip-hop plays low, voices meld into one another, and bottles clink. It's packed, and the patrons take
note of us. Our royal presence radiates outward, ripples,
then stills. They recognize us. I swallow and start to back
away, but Yoshi blocks me. "Izakayas are the most demo-
cratic places you'll find in Tokyo." As if to prove his point,
the crowd resumes their chatter, their drinking, their noisy
eating. They don't care.

We slide into seats at the bar, me between Yoshi and Taka. Farther down is a group of salarymen. To our left is a squad of girls with bright pink hair. Their skirts are plaid, and they all wear the same shirt—white with a man's face on it. He's delicate, kind of elfish, with a sharp chin and the same bright pink hair as the girls.

I grab a menu. It's in Japanese. I plan to point, say hai, and hope for the best. Yoshi plucks it from my hands. "You don't need that." He throws it to the side, then orders for us, starting with liquid courage. An indigo bottle is placed in front of us. "First rule of sake." Yoshi picks up the flask and one of the matching ceramic cups. "Never pour for yourself." He pours a shot for Taka and me. I reciprocate, pouring one for Yoshi.

We hold the cups close to our faces and sniff. Sweet notes rise up and we toast. "Kanpai!" Then we sip. The rice wine goes down cold but warms my belly. A few more sips and my limbs are warm, too. Scallops and yellowtail sashimi are served. We sip more sake. By the time the yakitori arrives, our bottle is empty and my cheeks are hot.

The group of salarymen have grown rowdy, their ties loosened. Yoshi winks at the pink-haired girls and they collapse into a fit of giggles. My God, to have such power over the opposite sex.

Gyoza is next. The fried pork dumplings dipped in chili oil burn my mouth but soak up some of the sake, and I sober a little, just in time for the group of salarymen to send us a round of shōchū, starchier than the sake but delicious all the same. We toast to them, to the bar, to the night, to Tokyo. My stomach is near bursting when the chef places agedashi—fried tofu—in front of us. Finally, Taka orders fermented squid guts. I don't try it, but I laugh as he slurps them up.

Yoshi pays our check. "What do we do now?" I ask. I'm not ready for the night to end. I feel light. *Free.* My cheeks hurt from laughing. The possibilities are endless. Taka suggests making our way to a local school. A mountain cultist who follows a blend of Buddhism and Shinto will be walking on hot coals. I'm interested.

Yoshi slams back the rest of his drink and Taka rubs his stomach. "No. I've got a better idea." My cousin flashes me a smile that is in no way reassuring.

We follow Yoshi, stumbling next door to a karaoke bar. The group of salarymen join us, along with the pink-haired girls who Yoshi throws an arm around.

One of the salarymen walks next to me. His collar is open. He's young and cute, with a flop of dark hair that falls into his eyes. He wants to practice English. "Sūpā," he says, pointing across the street.

"Supermarket," I reply.

"Soopuhrmahket," he says back slowly. "Ohime," he says, pointing at the front of my chest.

"Izumi," I say.

He shakes his head. "No. Ohime."

"Princess," Taka says from behind me.

"Princess," the salaryman says.

The forbidding from earlier creeps back in, but Yoshi seems to think everything is okay. No one has tried to pull out a camera and snap a photo. I go along with it, allow the alcohol to dull my inhibitions, my misgivings.

The karaoke bar is rowdier than the izakaya. The walls

are glass and it's like we've landed in some futuristic vampire movie. We go up a flight of narrow stairs to the private booths and drop into vinyl seats. Drinks arrive—sake with muddled kiwi, martinis with chocolate shavings, and bottles of beer.

Yoshi tells me how he lived off imperial grounds for a while. What a time it was. Then he asks me my favorite color, my sign, where I get my hair cut, my blood type. "B positive," I say, which is also my life motto. The pink-haired girls are singing. The song is by Hideto Matsumoto, the man from their T-shirts. A rocker turned rebel icon who committed suicide at thirty-three—he is a cult legacy, Yoshi explained. Fifty thousand people attended his funeral.

"We're not compatible at all. I'm type A." He pouts. "And you don't speak any Japanese at all?" he asks, picking at his beer label.

I swallow, tasting chocolate from the martini. "Not really. I'm learning now." Old insecurities tickle the back of my neck. It's an odd sensation to blend into this bar but still be an outsider. I recognize myself in their faces—in their dark eyes, hair, skin color—but not in their mannerisms, their customs. I thought Japan would be different. I thought I'd slip into the country like an old coat. While some things are familiar, there are things I'll never understand. Tonight, I've stepped out the door and into Tokyo, but it's not my home.

I give Yoshi a brief rundown of my family history. How I was lost before I was born. He stares into the neck of his beer bottle. "Heavy stuff. I get it." His eyes rise to mine. "I think you and I are more alike than not. I can't imagine trading my family, but I can perfectly picture trading circumstances. I've never felt at home being a prince."

Same, I think. I nod, because there's nothing more to say. Yoshi understands what it's like to be a part of something but not fully belong to it. I can't help but wonder if that will be my fate here, too. Am I chasing a ghost? Am I doomed to wander?

Taka takes the microphone. He starts singing something slow and a little melancholy, like a lullaby. The salarymen shrug out of their suit jackets and slow dance with the Hideto super fans. Confetti falls from the ceiling.

"I miss my apartment in the city," Yoshi says.

I smile softly at him. I know this feeling well, of wanting something different, a place to call your own. "I would've liked to see it."

He shrugs. "It wasn't much, but it was mine. I came and went as I pleased. No chamberlains hanging about, looking over my shoulder, shuffling me from event to event. What about you?"

"What about me?"

Yoshi says, "I miss my shitty apartment. What do you miss?"

Alcohol always makes you more honest. "Mount Shasta," I blurt and realize it's true. I miss my house, my friends, my mom and my stinky dog—the comfort of the familiar. You don't really know what you have until it's gone. I describe it all to Yoshi—the quiet life of a small town, how everything moves slowly.

"So go home," Yoshi says, picking at his beer bottle label. "Sounds like a nice enough place."

"It's not that easy." My throat feels dry, so I take a drink. "I don't know. Don't listen to me." I frown into my lap. I'm killing the mood.

Yoshi laughs. "We're a sad pair, aren't we?"

"Super sad." I stare glumly at the table littered with empty glasses.

"Don't worry. I've been here before," he says. "I know exactly what we should do to make this better."

"What should we do?" I echo.

"Sing." Yoshi pats my back. "We sing." Then he takes up a post at the karaoke machine and motions for me to join him. We scroll through the options. I perk up when I find something I recognize, something I know by heart. If anyone is wondering if I can rap the entire lyrics to Warren G's "Regulators," the answer is yes.

Yes I can.

More confetti falls from the ceiling and sticks in my hair. Yoshi and I drown our sorrows, our earlier conversation dissolving into the night. I've rapped and tried my best at a Hideto Matsumoto ballad. Time is a nebulous thing. There are no clocks in the karaoke bar. Taka slow dances with one of the pink-haired girls. Yoshi is dozing off. The salarymen are singing a Bruce Springsteen ballad, and they've dedicated their session to me. I don't know why. I tried to explain he was from New Jersey, but they insisted. Who am I to argue? I stand and wobble.

"Bathroom," I say to Yoshi when he pops an eye open.

"It's downstairs to the left." He rouses. "Want me to come with you?"

I shake my head and walk off. I use the wall for support. Wow, I am drunk. Slowly, I make my way to the bathroom.

My vision is blurry. Miracles of all miracles, I find the bathroom. A one-stall affair with little light and chrome stalls. Back in the hall, I can't remember which way I came from. Left or right? My odds are fifty-fifty. I head left, slipping through a black door.

The thump of music snuffs out. Instantly, I know I've made a mistake. The door slams shut, inches from me catching it. I'm outside. The alley is narrow, with a couple dumpsters and crates stacked against one wall. My stomach recoils at the smell. Now I know where all the fish waste goes. I try the door. Of course, it's locked. All right, I'll just have to walk around then, make my way back to the front of the karaoke bar. No problem. It's all good. Only—there's chain link fence all around me. There's a gate wide enough for the dumpsters to fit through, but it's padlocked. I look up to the sky for an answer. Chain link up there, too. I'm in some sort of dumpster cage. Super. I'm trapped.

My phone is in my back pocket and I take it out and try Yoshi. No answer. I give it a minute or two. Then try again. And again. And again. "C'mon, answer." I shift from foot to foot. Goose bumps have broken out on my arms. A piece of confetti falls from my hair and onto the pavement. He still doesn't pick up.

The door swings open. No way could he be that fast.

I'm right. It's not him. It's the young salaryman I practiced English with. He must be lost, too. The karaoke bar should do something about that, like placing a guard at the door or a tank full of sharks or a leashed bear to indicate danger lies this way.

The salaryman sways back and forth. He burps and

undoes his zipper. I turn my cheek as he teeters to one of the dumpsters and relieves himself. He finishes with a shake and stumbles backward, almost into me. I make a little noise and he whips around.

"Sain," he says.

I stick up my hands. "I don't know what that means."

He draws closer. "Sain." He laughs. It echoes off the building. I am all too aware I am trapped with a stranger who is bigger and stronger than me. A warning light blinks in my head. *Danger. Danger. Danger.* My breath quickens. He's crowding me now. I can smell the beer on his breath, see food between his teeth.

"Whoa." I back up more. My body hits a dumpster. I've cornered myself. "You're kind of violating my safe space here, buddy." My arms go up. He leans in. I whimper, close my eyes, and brace myself.

I hear the door click. There's a whir of movement, the sound of shuffling feet. The warmth from the salaryman's body is gone. I pop open an eye, then another. I clutch my chest.

It's Akio. He's dressed in a plain gray hoodie, jeans, and tennis shoes. He is positively wrathful, holding the salaryman by the neck against the brick wall. It's one thing to read about Akio's qualifications on paper and quite another seeing them come to life.

My skin tingles. Right, so I shouldn't find this attractive. Wrong time.

Akio bites out something in Japanese. I don't understand a word he's saying, but all in all, it's threatening.

The salaryman's face is turning splotchy, red and purple

with a hint of blue. His hands flail at his sides. "Sain," he chokes out. The salaryman raises a hand, opens it. A piece of paper and pen fall out. I don't have to be fluent to understand—he wanted my signature. An autograph, that's all. But someone really should have a conversation with him about boundaries.

Akio's mouth is a tight white line. He lets go, and the salaryman slumps to the ground, holding his neck. My bodyguard crouches and speaks lowly to him, and the salaryman fishes his wallet from his pants. Akio opens it, removes the identification, and takes a photograph of the ID, then flicks it back to the salaryman.

Akio stands. Our eyes meet. "I don't think he'll be a problem. But I know his name and address."

I'm still in shock. "What are you doing here? How'd you find me?" I say, eyes wide—but there's no time for him to answer. The dumpsters still smell like rotten fish and I've definitely eaten and drank way over my stomach's limit. Really, I have no choice in the matter. The landlord has nailed an eviction sign to my stomach. Rent is overdue. Everybody out. I lurch forward. Just like that, I throw up.

13

I'm in an imperial vehicle, complete with chauffeur and tinted windows. In the backseat, I wait for Akio, who's popped into a convenience store. We're on a quiet street. A crumpled newspaper lies on the sidewalk. It has my face on it. I open the car door, reach out, and swipe it up at the same time Akio reappears, black plastic bag in hand.

I scoot back in the car and he follows me in.

"I told you to stay in the car." Then he knocks on the partition, signaling the driver to go. The car starts and we pull away.

My mouth is dry and I might have dragon breath, but still I speak. "Does that usually work for you? Telling people what do and expecting them to blindly obey?"

"Yes," he states unequivocally.

"That's ridiculous," I huff, shivering. The heat is on, but I can't seem to get warm.

Akio snorts, then moves, slipping off his sweatshirt. The white T-shirt he wears underneath bunches up and I catch a glimpse of his abdomen, watching his muscles flex and pull. Our eyes connect. He pulls down his shirt. I flush. "Here." He hands me his sweatshirt.

"I'm fine." I stick up my chin, cross my arms.

"Fine. I'll use it to clean the vomit from my pants." I wince. There are little speckles of barf on his jeans. What did I eat that was orange?

When he puts it that way, it seems like a waste of a perfectly good piece of clothing. No need to punish the sweatshirt and reduce its existence to a barf rag. I'm sure it would much prefer me. I slip on the hoodie, and it smells nice. Not like cologne but clean, like detergent. It contrasts the scent of my hair, which has picked up and carried the fried snail odor from the izakaya. So much yuck.

The black bag crinkles and Akio draws out a bottle of clear liquid with a blue label. "Drink."

It's cool in my hands and the label reads . . . "Pocari Sweat?"

"It's a sports drink. Contains electrolytes."

I unscrew the lid, sniff and take a sip. It's good, with a grapefruit aftertaste. I didn't realize how thirsty I was. In no time, I've drained half the bottle. Akio pulls out a triangle-shaped package wrapped in plastic. Inside is sticky rice wrapped around ginger. "You should eat something, too."

One look at the food and my stomach rolls—it's not ready yet, maybe never. "No thanks."

Akio shrugs and puts it back in the bag. We sit in silence. I drink the rest of the Pocari Sweat and watch the neon lights of the city catch Akio's face and soften it.

"How did you find me?" I ask.

"You were never lost. At least not to me," says Akio. Cryptic much? I rub my eyes. The night has caught up to me. I am sober, tired, and in no mood for riddles. He goes on. "I put a tracker on you."

My mouth hangs open. I bolt upright. "You put a *tracker* on me?"

He nods casually. My outrage grows even more.

"Where?" I ask, voice climbing in volume.

His eyes glitter. "Your phone."

I drop my phone like a hot potato. Then I pick it up and thrust it at him. "Remove it."

He casts the ceiling a pained glance. "It's standard protocol."

"Remove it. Right now." I shake my hand in front of him.

Taking the phone, he snaps the case off. He fishes a little tool of some sort from his pocket and uses it to jimmy the phone open. He extracts a small metal disk from the guts of my phone, snaps the case back on, and holds it out to me. He arches a brow.

I yank it from his fingers. "Not okay. Line crossed," I say, my words sharp. "Any more trackers?"

"None I'm aware of."

My phone buzzes. Yoshi is texting.

Yoshi

Where'd you go?

Yoshi

Please tell me you're okay.

Yoshi

I knew I should've gone to the restroom with you.

Yoshi

My God, did you fall into the toilet?

I tap out a response along the lines of *It's all good and I'll see you tomorrow*, then finish with thanking him for an awesome night. No need to get into the story of dumpster cage and my imperial rescue. I'd rather not relive the humiliation again just yet.

I stare at Akio for a moment. Anger still burning bright and hot, I say, "You know, maybe a tracker wasn't enough for me. Might I suggest a shock collar?" Horrible, horrible inventions. "Might make things easier. That way you can just press a button and zap me whenever you think I'm doing something wrong."

He grinds his teeth.

"Well?" I ask.

"You're actually waiting for an answer. I thought that was a rhetorical question." We glare at each other. Oh man, if my eyes could shoot laser beams. Then he runs an aggravated hand over his head. "I'm sorry."

I blink and wait for the earth to swallow me whole, for strange shadows to streak across the sky signaling the end times. Did Akio just apologize? It takes a moment to register. He did.

I smooth my jeans and look out the window at the park we're passing. A couple kisses under a cherry blossom tree, their bodies lit from behind by a street lamp. Blooms flutter around them like paper snow. The buds have just opened and already they're dying. Mono no aware—it's a Japanese phrase expressing a love for impermanence, the ephemeral nature of all things. "Sneaking out, using a bathroom, and a wrong turn hardly seems like the end of the world," I say to Akio.

"You're right." His voice is even, calm. "Again, I'm sorry. I'm not angry with you. I'm mad at myself. You could've been hurt and it would've been my fault."

"Forget it," is all I say.

When I was five, I decided I didn't need training wheels anymore on my bike. So without my mom's consent or help, I removed them. I rode for five sublime seconds sans helmet, then took an epic fall. I needed two stitches to the back of my head. The blood was copious and glorious, and so was my mom's fear. Her only defense against such helplessness was to become righteous with anger.

We don't talk for a while. I get tired of staring out the window but don't want to look at Akio. The tabloid article brushes my thigh. My face is on the front—a picture of me the first day at the airport. Burning curiosity gets the better of me. "What is this?" I thrust it at Akio. He has no choice but to take it.

Surprised, he studies it for a moment. "It's a picture of you at the airport when you first arrived."

Akio must have had some training on how to deflect. The art of dodging. "Very helpful. What does it say?"

"I don't think I should tell you."

That bad, huh? Now I have to know. "You said you were sorry. If you want to make it up to me, tell me what the article says."

"You'll forgive me if I read you this?"

I nod.

Akio rubs a hand across his face. "It's a newspaper called *The Tokyo Tattler*. It's not considered reputable."

"Noted."

"For the record, I am against this."

"Also noted. Now read."

His sigh is beleaguered. "It reports on the clothing you wore at the airport. An imperial blogger was interviewed. She was of the opinion you should have dressed up more." That hurts. "In addition, she remarks on your behavior, saying you were rude to your imperial guard during the restroom break and refused to acknowledge the crowd once outside. She paints you as snobbish and challenging." Okay. That hurts more. A lot more. "However, a janitor seemed to like you. He's selling the handkerchief you used. The money will help fund his retirement. It finishes by wondering why you haven't been seen in public and suggests you're being kept hidden away."

I expel a breath. It's worse than I thought. Actually, I didn't even think that much about how I'd be portrayed in the tabloids. There's the media ban, and I've been so focused on my father. . . . I'm dumbstruck. "Japan hates me?" I squeak out.

"Like I said, not reputable." Akio folds up the article into a perfect square and sets it on the seat beside him. "People are always rooting for those above them to fall."

"I didn't ask for this. Any of it."

"I understand." Do I detect a slight softening of Akio's sharp features? "But we cannot change the circumstances of our birth, can we?"

I suppose not. Plus I wouldn't trade it or go back in time. So far it's been worth it just to get to know my father, but wishes come at a price. This one comes in the form of public scrutiny. I rest my head against the back of the seat. "You know, I'm very good at a lot of things. Spelling, for example. In fact, back in the States, I was a hangman champion." At his silence, I explain the game.

"You were best at a game that teaches children if they don't spell correctly, they may be put to death?" I open my eyes and peer at him. His lips quirk up just a fraction of an inch. Akio is making a joke.

I smile back. "You're right. We, as a society, probably don't discuss that enough."

His laugh is low and husky. Could we be getting along right now? Wonders never cease. I guess a heart does beat inside that cold, super fine chest. "Isn't there any magical imperial wand we can wave and make them say nice things about me?" I ask. "Or better yet, maybe I should have an interview and set the record straight."

"Sometimes, silence is your greatest weapon." He shifts. "Famous Japanese proverb."

"Really?"

He laughs again. "No. I just made it up."

I cross my arms. "Don't you think sarcasm is beneath you?"

"I don't know. Probably." He stares directly at me. "What I do know is these tabloids are beneath you. They don't deserve your time and attention."

I touch my chest. "Why, Akio, I think that's the nicest thing you've ever said to me." He says nothing. I break eye contact. We're in a tunnel now, shiny tiles on all sides. Not much to look at, but I suddenly find it fascinating. "I'm not sure."

"Not sure about what?"

My smile is rueful. "Not sure if the tabloids are beneath me or not." Most times, I feel so small.

Akio leans forward and captures my gaze again. He splays his legs, rests his elbows on top of his knees. "They are. Trust me."

I make a dismissive gesture, but inside me, the rising tide of resentment against Akio eases. The tunnel stretches on. I cast my eyes skyward, tapping my fingers on the seat. Do I dare ask for more? Last time I tried to befriend Akio, he called me a radish.

"I am sorry." His voice is quiet. "You know, a superior once suggested I am not the easiest person to get along with."

I perk up and look at him. "You don't say."

A ghost of a smile. "I have a tendency to be stuck in my ways."

The tunnel ends. I recognize the crumbling rock walls around the imperial palace. We're almost home. I pick at my thumbnail. "I'm sorry I threw up on you." If he can try to do better, so can I. I'll start by setting my clock thirty minutes ahead. And I'll stop comparing him to vampires and serial killers in my head.

"I've seen worse," he says.

"In the police force?"

He dips his head, but doesn't say anything else. I won't press him on it. Maybe someday he'll want to tell me. "It doesn't seem fair. You've seen me at my lowest. I'm afraid the only way we can tip the scales back to even is if I know something embarrassing about you."

He thinks for a moment, regards me through half-lidded eyes. "Not sure I should trust you."

"If you can't trust an imperial princess who constantly runs late and sneaks out, who can you trust?"

"Good point," he states matter-of-factly. "How about this: when I was little, my school mates called me Kobuta." At my blank expression, he says, "It means piglet. I had very chubby cheeks."

My fingers curl into the cool leather seat. "Wow. I'm definitely going to need to see a picture."

He shrugs. "I loved cookies. I'm not ashamed."

The car rolls to a stop. The palace gate creaks open. "My mom calls me Zoom Zoom." It seems only fair I share my nickname as well.

He half grins. "It suits you."

I bounce a little in my seat. The car starts forward again. We only have a couple minutes left together. Can I trust him? Should I trust him? "I'm not sure I'm cut out to be a princess."

"I see," he says. "You're in excellent company then. I'm not sure I'm meant to be an imperial guard." He's serious. There's a sort of fragility in his confession. I'm not sure, but I might be the first person he's ever told this to.

The car stops and we jerk away from each other. I don't know why, but it feels as if we've been caught. The chauffeur opens the door. I step out and cold air assails me. I feel suddenly alone, lost again. I turn, hanging on to the open door. "Thanks for saving me."

The Adam's apple in Akio's throat works. He inclines his head in the deferential way I've seen others do with my father. "It's my job." I get out of the car and start to move toward the door. I hear Akio before I head inside. "But . . . you're welcome."

14

I find myself with a day off. Rare. Unprecedented. Inconceivable. Mr. Fuchigami says I may go anywhere in Tokyo. And I know exactly where I want to spend the day: the Imperial Dog Kennels. Honestly, it's needed. It's *really* needed. Even though Akio told me *The Tokyo Tattler* was beneath me, it's been hard to get the article off my mind, hard not to overthink everything I might do wrong. Tomorrow kicks off a series of events. I'll accompany my father to assorted public outings. Cameras and press will be present, a soft launch of sorts before the prime minister's wedding. My nerves are frayed. What will the press say about me? I smiled too much? I didn't smile enough? A royal puppy pile is definitely in order.

Now we're en route. It's a fine day, the sun bright, not a cloud in the sky. Cherry blossoms have finally bloomed and weigh heavy on branches. Mariko sits beside me, the stink of I'd-much-rather-be-anywhere-else radiating from her body. There is also a lint roller noticeably tucked into her purse and a pack of tissues because dogs make her "sneeze." Akio is across from us. He is distracted, a bit off today. More grumpy than usual. Every couple of minutes, his phone buzzes, and he swipes to ignore, but he doesn't turn it off. Have I mentioned his scowl? It is noteworthy.

I wonder if maybe it's his girlfriend. He's never mentioned one. I imagine the woman Akio might date, his female equivalent. I know the type. I've seen her in comic books and action movies before. Beautiful. Deadly. Plays war games for fun. His phone buzzes again.

"Is something wrong?" I ask finally.

He shakes his head once. "Nothing, Your Highness." His grip on the phone tightens.

Mariko speaks to him in Japanese. I frown at her. I don't like it when she does this, and she does it often, on purpose, to cut me out of the conversation. Worse is when I can tell she's speaking about me, because I hear my name interspliced between angry-sounding words. This time my name doesn't tumble from her lips, but I do understand one word: okāsan. Mother.

Akio's response is clipped, terse.

Mariko's mouth dips in concern.

Now I *have* to know what is going on. I nudge my lady-in-waiting. She whips her elbow away from me and holds it, rubbing it like I've hurt her. "What's going on?" I ask lowly.

"Everything is fine," says Mariko. Clearly, it is not.

I direct my stare at Akio. "Is something wrong with your mother?"

His posture is rigid. "It's really nothing, Your Highness. My mother needs medication and my father can't leave her right now to go to the pharmacy. He is asking I pick it up. I have informed him I cannot leave work."

"Oh." I slump back in my seat, thinking. It's obvious what needs to be done. "Where's the pharmacy?"

"Pardon?" Akio says.

"The pharmacy. What is the address?" I overenunciate.

He bristles, shaking his head.

"Name and address, please," I insist.

He says it quietly, but I hear. Before I can forget it, I roll down the partition separating the seat from the chauffeur. "There's been a change of plans," I say loudly. "We're going to . . ." I give him the pharmacy address. "Then we're going to . . ." I turn to Akio. "What's your home address?"

"I don't think—"

Mariko chimes in, "He lives in Kichijōji, near the temple." At Akio's WTF look, Mariko says, "If that's where the princess wants to go, that's where we'll go."

Akio chews on the situation, and after several moments, he spits out, "Ten minutes at the pharmacy and ten minutes at my parents' house. Then we'll go to the imperial kennels."

I shrug. "Whatever you say." I remember our conversation on the porch back at the palace. *Technically, I am the boss of you.* "You're the boss, after all."

Soon enough, we're outside the pharmacy. Akio makes me promise twice I won't budge an inch before darting out.

"This is a kind thing you're doing," Mariko says, a bit begrudgingly. "Our parents know one another. My mother worked as a lady-in-waiting while his father was an imperial guard. What's happening to his mother . . ." She trails off. "It's so unfair."

I swallow. It's the first kind word Mariko has ever said to me, and it's making me emotional. "That's nice of you to say."

Mariko harrumphs, remembering she doesn't like me. "Yeah, well. Anything to avoid the kennels, I guess."

The car door swings open and Akio is back inside the car, plastic bag in hand.

Half an hour later, we're pulling up alongside a curb to a little house situated between two concrete towers. Beyond the gate, a tall man with sparse gray hair peeks through the curtains. Akio's father. They share the same flat-lined mouth and hooded eyes. Good to know broody eyebrows run in the family.

The screen on Akio's phone lights up. "My father sees the imperial vehicle and knows you're inside. He offers his hospitality. Don't worry. I'll make excuses." Akio starts to climb from the car. I follow after waiting a beat for Mariko, who shakes her head. Fine, she can stay in the vehicle.

Akio doesn't notice me. I'll be damned. He really does believe when he gives an order that it's blindly obeyed. He goes through the gate and I catch it. His steps echo on the mossy flagstones, and mine do, too. He whips around. "You're not in the car."

"Yes, Akio, I would love to meet your parents and see your childhood home. Thank you so much for asking." I smile at his face, blinking back.

"My mother is ill."

"I gathered as much. Is she contagious? Is there a concern for my health and safety? Or hers?"

His head shakes. "No. But—"

"Then please . . ." I stick out a hand, my grin stretching. "Lead the way."

He sighs through his nose very loudly before resuming course. His father greets us at the door, bowing low, then hops off to brew tea after making me comfortable in the living room. Once I'm settled, Akio disappears down the hall, white bag in hand.

Of course, I don't stay where I'm put. The room is simply furnished—a navy couch and wooden chair with clean lines. Shelves of books line a wall and are crammed with various texts, the brightly colored spines adding splashes of color.

There are framed photos pinned up in the hall, and I walk over to them. It's a timeline of Akio's life. Akio as a newborn, toddler, preschooler, and it's true: his cheeks are those of a squirrel hiding nuts. What counteracts the adorableness is Akio's tiny frown. So he's been that way since birth. Next, I come to a large photograph of his elementary school entrance ceremony. His mom wears a kimono, his dad a suit, and Akio sports a brand new randoseru, a hard-sided backpack. I keep going, and note he's an only child. Ha! I knew it. We can smell our own. It's probably why we butt heads so much. We're used to getting our own way. I'm probably better at sharing, though. Noora would totally corroborate. The last photo is recent, one of him looking dashing in an imperial guard uniform. His parents stand by his side, beaming with pride.

At the end of the hall, there are two doors. Both are cracked open. In one, I see Akio's back. He's folded his big body into a chair and sits next to a bed. Holding his mother's hand, he speaks softly to her. He turns and I dart into the other room.

There is a futon, television, and desk. Posters are tacked up. Model planes litter every available surface. I touch the nose of one, sending the propeller whirring.

"This used to be my room." I startle at Akio's voice.

"Used to be?" A fine layer of dust coats the shelves.

"I live on the imperial grounds. Staff housing."

I nod vacantly. Though I'm surprised. Seems I haven't put

enough thought into getting to know my imperial guard. No time like the present, I guess. "Model planes, huh?" He's silent. Okay, another topic then. "Is your mother all right?"

"She's fine." He steps into the room. The door is still partially shut. It's so quiet in the house. It feels like we're alone. Like we're the only two people in the universe. "She has early onset dementia." With one finger, he stops the propeller from spinning. "My father retired from the imperial guard for her. Now he spends his days as a nursemaid, filling the holes in her memory."

"I'm sorry."

Another shrug, like it means nothing. Nothing at all. But I imagine it's a terrible weight to carry. "She has good days and bad days. Sometimes she wanders. He doesn't like to leave her alone." He pauses. "Thank you for this."

It's my turn to shrug. "Of course. I'm a big fan of moms in general." Well, all women, really, because we're awesome. The corner of his mouth tugs up. It's nice to see him smile again. It means something to me, making him happy. I look at my shoes. "You know, I thought, maybe it was your girlfriend calling you."

He sounds amused when he answers. "Did you?"

I risk a glance up. Yep, definitely amused. "It's not that it matters to me, per se. But I guess I should know if you have other commitments that might distract from your job." I purse my lips. Scan the room. Act casual.

"A girlfriend wouldn't distract me. I wouldn't let it," he explains. Probably true. "But for the record, I don't have a girlfriend."

My lips twitch, but I contain the grin.

"What about you? Do you have someone at home?" His voice is light, casual. "Someone that might distract from your imperial duties? I guess I should know that as well, just in case, for security purposes."

Fair is fair. "No. I had a boyfriend, but we broke up a year ago. He took way too many mirror selfies." For the record, one is too many.

He makes a strange expression. "I've never taken a mirror selfie."

"Good to know."

I've made a full lap around the room. I'm back in front of Akio now. On the wall behind him are photo collages of Akio at different ages with friends and teachers.

"I've never even taken a selfie," he says.

"Even better." Although my phone is full of them. Mostly Noora and me hamming it up, pretending to pinch Mount Shasta between our pointer finger and thumb. I study a green plane with a silver body and yellow stripes on the wings.

"That's a Mitsubishi A6M Zero, flown during the war. The majority were converted to kamikaze aircraft toward the end."

I am familiar with the term. Kamikaze. Divine wind. My mind fills with images of planes twisting from the sky like angry hornets from a nest, then exploding on impact, pilots still inside them. "Would you do that?"

He blinks. "Die for my country? Yes, I would." It must be a requirement of being an imperial guard. The thought of Akio taking a bullet for me is too much. My throat is dry. I don't want to talk about it anymore. "Mariko said your parents worked with hers."

"Most of the imperial positions are legacies, handed down over time."

"Like the monarchy," I say.

"Yes."

Another thing we have in common. We were born to play certain roles. Our destinies were predetermined.

We're standing close now. For a long time, he stares at me. I wonder if he feels it, too, this wall of electricity. I start to get self-conscious. "Is there something on my face?" I wipe my cheek, searching out crumbs or a smear of blush gone wrong. What am I saying? Mariko would never allow that to happen.

A headshake. "No."

"What's the look for, then?" We've drifted even closer, chests almost touching. I stroke the inside of my palms with my thumbs. Our breaths have synced.

"I'm just trying to figure you out."

Is that all? "Good luck. Better men than you have tried." Not true. For a princess I've kissed a fair number of frogs. My voice lowers. "Let me know when you've got an idea."

"I thought you were a bit silly at first." Wow. Give it to me straight. "But I was wrong. . . . I think you're very serious about the things you care about. I think you lead with your heart."

We gaze at each other.

A throat clears at the door. Much like the night in the car, we spring away. The wall of electricity fizzles out. Akio's father speaks in Japanese.

"Tea is ready," says Akio roughly.

Tea is served in the living room, brilliant green ocha in a blue china glazed bowl. As we sip, I steal looks at Akio, blush, and turn away. His last words repeat in my head.

I think you lead with your heart.

THE TOKYO TATTLER

Spotted: The Lost Butterfly and Crown Prince Father around the town

April 2, 2021

While Their Imperial Majesties Emperor and Empress Takehito are out of the country on an official visit to Vietnam, their son His Imperial Highness Crown Prince Toshihito has stepped out on the town in a flurry of unofficial public events with his daughter, Her Imperial Highness Princess Izumi.

On Monday, the two attended the 42nd Asia-Pacific Festival and Charity Bazaar in Tokyo. While walking and viewing, the princess went ahead of her father to greet His Excellency Ambassador Sam Sorm at the Royal Embassy of Cambodia handicraft booth—a literal misstep. Guess no one informed the princess that she should have waited for her father, the Crown Prince, to say hello to his Excellency first. It's most likely the princess was merely honoring one of her own American traditions. Ladies first, isn't that what Westerners often say?

On Wednesday, the two attended a gallery opening. Princess Izumi struck up a conversation with attendee and controversial artist Yoko Foujita, who has been a critical opponent of the imperial family. Imperial Household handlers were quick to curtail the conversation, but *The Tokyo Tattler* managed to get an exclusive picture of the two chatting (see inset).

Finally, on Thursday, the father-daughter duo was spotted at the opening season baseball game. They were seen in the imperial box, wearing matching hats and sharing a cup of kakigōri (see inset, picture of HIH Princess Izumi *pointing* at the players). Later, the two greeted the opposing teams, and the princess seemed to favor one of the players too long.

Prime Minister Adachi's wedding is up next—the entire imperial family will be attending officially, with the exception of the emperor and empress. One person not on the guest list? The prime minister's sister, Sadako Adachi. The two have been embroiled in a nasty feud since Sadako penned a scathing tell-all accusing the prime minister of infidelity and having ties to the yakuza. It's rumored the prime minister fired a staffer for mentioning his sister in his presence. Too bad reporters won't be allowed inside the überposh wedding and reception. Like the rest of Tokyo, we'll only be able to watch from the sidelines. But what a view it promises to be...

15

"There." Mariko carefully pushes a final pearl pin into my hair, then steps back to assess me. My lady-in-waiting blocks the full-length mirror. Her chin dips in approval. "You're ready."

She shifts, and I see myself. Well, she's certainly worked her fairy godmother magic. My nails have been buffed, shined and painted a nude color. No more kinky pink for me. My bangs have been trimmed into a blunt edge that skims my brows. My hair twists into a low bun and is adorned with freshwater pearls. My floor-length gown is silk jade and shimmers in the light.

Mariko places a matching clutch in my hands. It's light. "Lipstick and some cover-up, in case you get shiny. Oh, and I put your phone in there. But please keep it on silent." I arch an I-can't-believe-it brow at her. Most days she's hiding my phone, playing keep-away with it until after I finish the day's task.

She trails me to the front door and rattles off more instructions. "Make sure to walk behind your father when entering a room. Only speak to people you've met or know. I wish we'd had time to go through photographs of everyone attending and sort out their political affiliations, but just don't show any favoritism. And don't point." The last few days, Mariko was quick to note when I made mistakes—at the charity bazaar, art gallery opening, and baseball game. My sins are many.

I keep walking, a nervous knot forming between my brows. It might help if my father was here, but he has back-to-back events this evening. We're meeting at the wedding. Akio will be my escort. Speaking of . . .

He stands in the middle of the living room in black tie and his hands at his sides. Some of my anxiety melts away. *Whoa.* Akio in formal wear. Slow clap.

"Do you need anything else?" Mariko asks.

"No. Thank you so much, though." I keep my gaze trained on Akio.

"Just remember to sit up straight. If you need a moment, excuse yourself to the restroom . . ." She trails off.

Akio smiles at me. I smile dumbly at him. "I'll let you know when we're on our way home," he says, keeping his eyes on me.

After a moment, Mariko says, "Of course. I'll have the room ready for when she returns."

Akio dips his head, and she excuses herself. Two lamps offer the only light, making the room feel cozy. "The car should be here soon. I'll call and see where they are," he says.

"No," I blurt, stopping him. "Another minute, please." I am suddenly nervous again. The prime minister's wedding is a red-carpet event. Outside will be the press. Inside will be my family and the upper echelon of Japanese society. I'll be carefully cataloged. I study the hem of my dress. Is it too long? Will I trip on it? It's all too real.

I take a deep breath, try to detach. I think about Mount Shasta, hoping it will anchor me. But then I remember what I'm missing this weekend. "It's senior prom tomorrow night." A few days ago, the girls sent me pics of trying on dresses. It's an eighties theme.

"Is it?"

I'm surprised he's not forcing us out the door. I'm in no hurry. Neither is he, apparently.

I'm jittery, unable to filter my thoughts. "You know what I'm going to miss about not going?" Aside from the warm punch, bad lighting, and that awkward moment where you run into your ex-boyfriend and the girl he cheated on you with? "I'm going to miss the dancing. Will you dance with me?" I'm a bit sheepish. But feeling brave, kind of, and beautiful, at least.

He shuffles his feet, rubs his chin. "I'm not sure."

"Please. Just one dance." A little more time in this room where it's safe and warm and there aren't any prying eyes. "For the prom I'm missing. That's all." Truth: I'd probably slow dance with Noora. We've done this before. Then Hansani and Glory would cut in. Because it is understood: we are each other's one true loves.

"We don't have any music."

"Oh, I can fix that." I take out my phone, scroll through the options, hit play, and turn the volume all the way up. Setting the clutch and phone on coffee table, I fold my hands in front of myself. It's Akio's move. I won't make him dance with me if he truly doesn't want to.

But then, he's in front of me, placing his hands on my hips. There's a slight tremble right before he tightens his grip. I place my hands on his shoulders. We rock back and forth stiffly. It's very middle school. "I've never heard this music before," he murmurs.

"Not many people have. It's the Mount Shasta Gay Men's Chorus."

"Doesn't sound like a whole choir."

I scrunch my nose. "It's actually just two people, Glen and his partner, Adrian. They're both lumberjacks and believe Bette Midler is a national treasure. They'll fight anyone who says otherwise." Their entire album is covers of her greatest hits. Right now, we're listening to "The Rose."

"It's nice. I like their voices, especially the deeper one."

"Yeah, that's Adrian. He pretty much carries the ensemble." Akio reminds me a bit of Glen, a rough-around-the-edges type.

We go quiet. Listen to the music. Scoot closer. Somehow, my head finds itself on his chest, and his hands find themselves interlocked on the small of my back. I lick my lips, enjoying this soft glow of happiness. "Have you figured anything else about me yet?"

He makes a noise in the back of his throat. "Well. Let's see . . . you have this habit of talking with your hands. Your fingers are very demonstrative. You also hum when you eat, it's like you can't control how happy food makes you. I like that you take joy in such simple things."

I want to tell him I've figured him out, too. He's stoic, but not cold—far from it. He loves deeply. I saw the way he bent toward his mother, the tender way he touched her brow, how he offered her a glass of water.

"Akio?" The song starts again. I put it on a loop. Clever me. "Since we're getting along so well, there *is* something I've been meaning to speak with you about." We do a half-turn. I wait a beat. "It's my code name, Radish."

"You don't like it?"

"No. I don't. I kind of hate it, actually." Especially since the root is known for irritating the digestive tract.

"A radish is a very formidable vegetable," he says, then adds quietly, "They're my favorite, in fact."

I'm glad he can't see my smile. "Is that true?"

"Didn't used to be. But I find they've grown on me. Often overlooked, the radish is hearty and packed with vitamin C." My pulse races, gallops away. His heart hammers, too. I can feel it. "But we can change it if you wish."

"No. I guess it's okay." I look up. Rest my chin on his chest. Curl my fingers into the starch of his shirt. "When we met, I thought you didn't like me."

We stop dancing. Our toes, our chests touch. His gaze is soft, a little wary. "I probably like you too much."

I'm frozen. His eyes are half-lidded and hazy. I could kiss him. I *should* kiss him. I rise to stand on my tippy-toes. His head bends. So close.

But then, he pulls away. Shakes his head, clears his throat. "We should go. I don't want to make you late."

I swallow. "Right. Of course." What just happened? My head is spinning. "Thanks for the dance."

"Of course," he says.

I smile a bit, unsure. "I'm much less nervous now."

"You shouldn't be nervous. Anyone would be lucky to speak to you." His stance is rigid, but his words are soft.

My smile grows genuine. He moves and opens the door. I slip through, just a princess off to the ball.

16

Outside the New Otani Hotel is a parade of shiny luxury vehicles. Men dressed in coattails and women draped in furs alight from Jaguars, Bentleys, and Maybachs. Approximately 250 of the who's who of Japanese society has been invited. Royal watchers have turned out in droves. Behind a barricade, they wave tiny Hinomaru flags and snap pictures of the guests.

The Imperial Rolls-Royce glides along the curb and stops. Akio steps out from the front seat, his earpiece and frown back in place. The door opens, and he extends a hand to me. I place my gloved fingers in his and let him pull me from the car. It feels like I'm in an old-world drama. It's all so very *Great Gatsby*.

Cameras rise. *Click. Flash. Snap.*

"I don't like how crowded it is out here," says Akio. Imperial guards surround me. We blaze a path. No more photos for me. I am a tiny piece of silk caught in a gust of wind. We slip through glass double doors. More flashes. The doors swing shut. The crowd dims, redirecting their focus on the Tesla pulling up with a well-known movie actress inside. Outside the ballroom, a harpist plucks the wrong string, eyes wide and frightened at Akio's I-eat-tiny-villagers approach.

We cross the threshold, passing a table piled high with ornate envelopes. At Japanese weddings, cash is king. The prime minister and his bride will be doling out the gifts, and each seat will have a beautiful, handmade paper bag stuffed full of little spoils underneath it.

An arm hooks through mine, stealing me from Akio's side. "Ugh, finally, you're here," Yoshi grouses. "This evening has been dreadful so far. Uncle Tadashi cornered me and wouldn't stop waxing on about his prize cock." My brows go to my hairline. "All he talks about are his chickens and roosters." Yoshi peers at Akio in a why-are-you-still-here? sort of way. "Stand down, man. My God, it's a party. Try to look happy."

Akio says nothing, just bows and dissolves into the crowd. Glasses clink. Women laugh. A man in tails plays a Bösendorfer piano. Yoshi's parents, Auntie Asako and Uncle Yasuhito, approach us.

"Can you believe it?" Auntie Asako says, fingering the diamonds around her neck. "A prime minister descended from the Tokugawa clan marrying a narikin? I never thought I'd see the day."

Uncle Yasuhito grunts in agreement. They chatter about the bride and how, in addition to being new money, she's so much younger than the prime minister. Across the room, a woman gives Yoshi the stink eye. She's severe-looking but beautiful, wearing a sleek black gown. "Who's that?" I whisper, nudging Yoshi.

He plucks two glasses of champagne from a passing tray and hands one to me. "*That* is Reina, my imperial guard."

Uncle Yasuhito hears and says, "Yoshi hired her himself."

"Insisted on a woman, because I'm a feminist like that." Yoshi puffs out his chest. He's wearing black tie like everyone else, but there's a hint of sparkle in his lapels. "She wears the most beguiling pantsuits and does handicrafts in her spare time, mostly scrapbooking. She knows ten different ways to kill a man with a piece of paper. She scares me, and I like it." He mock-shivers.

"Yoshi is half in love with her," Auntie Asako says indulgently.

He sends Reina a dazzling smile and she scowls.

Across the room, Auntie Asako nods at a woman. The woman nods back, then resumes her conversation with a much older man in full military regalia. A father and daughter? They share the same thin lined mouths and heavy brows. "The Fukadas," Uncle Yasuhito says at my questioning look. "He's a general with the Ground Self-Defense Force. His daughter is the son he always wanted."

"They look as if they hunt people for sport," I say, the champagne warming my belly and cheeks.

The three laugh and it feels good, like I'm on the inside.

Opposite the father-daughter-people-sport-hunters is a group of girls, the Shining Twins at the center. They meet my gaze head-on, whisper something to their friends, then laugh. No doubt it's at my expense.

Yoshi sucks in a breath. "Yikes. You've caught the attention of the Gakushūin clique. Careful now, slowly divert your eyes. The moon is full tonight, which means their powers are at an all-time high."

I do as he says. Gakushūin. I remember the name from my father and Mr. Fuchigami. It's where Mariko goes. "Gakushūin?" I ask more loudly than I mean to.

Auntie Asako touches the bracelet on her wrist, a confection of diamonds and sapphires that complements her dress.

"It's the most exclusive school in Japan, maybe in the world."

Uncle Yasuhito nods. "All the young royals and scions of prominent families attend. Yoshi was first in his class when he graduated."

"You would have most likely gone there." Auntie Asako looks me up and down. "Where did you attend school? I've heard California has some wonderful private institutions."

"Mount Shasta High School, by way of Mount Shasta Middle School."

Her smile falls. "Public education?"

"Yes," I say unequivocally.

She shudders. "Well, if anyone asks, say you were educated abroad."

"Careful, mother. Your elitism is showing," Yoshi huffs.

"What?" Auntie Asako touches her chest. She turns to her husband as Yoshi pulls me away. "What did I say?"

"On behalf of my family, I apologize," Yoshi says.

"It's fine." Really, it is. I'm not ashamed of the schools I went to.

"It's not fine. Don't try to hide your feelings. Clearly, you're devastated." Yoshi gives me a lopsided grin. I return it. I'm so glad he's here with me.

He steers me deeper into the crowd. We skirt around a lumbering yokozuna, a grand champion sumo wrestler. Yoshi smiles at guests, then gives me the lowdown on each one, filling my ear with who's who: The President of the Bank of Tokyo. A rice vinegar manufacturer. Two brothers who own one of the largest and oldest whiskey distilleries, and they've come all the way from Hokkaido, the Wild West of Japan.

There are members of the Kuge and Kizoku families—Japan's

former nobility, counts and countesses abolished after World War II. They lost their titles, but not their snobbish, social standings. They resent my grandfather, father, my uncle, and now my cousin Sachiko for having relationships with commoners—and by extension, me, too. Yoshi doesn't say so, but I can read between the lines. It's understood. Even though I'm full Japanese, I'm too American, not enough blue in my veins.

There are also captains of industry, like a famous tech manufacturer whose company starts with the letter *S* and a car titan whose family name starts with the letter *T.* Topping it all off are the Kasumigaseki, Tokyo's bureaucratic beehive.

We come to the tables, circular with white linen cloths and low flower arrangements—lilies and pine branches to symbolize the crests of the two joining families. Seating is assigned. People shuffle around, examining place cards. Yoshi and I part ways. He'll be with the extended imperial family at another table. Rather than family, the most prominent members of society are given the honor of sitting with the bride and groom. It's hierarchical—meaning, the Crown Prince, his daughter, my uncle, and his love spawns (aka the Shining Twins) sit with the PM and his bride. My aunt, the twins' mother, should be here, but she's absent. I'll try to remember to ask Mariko if she's ill.

I drop down into a black lacquered chair and try not to burn to ashes under my twin cousins' withering stares. Things I wish I could say to them: Don't you think this is a little cliché, being mean to the outsider? Relational aggression is a terrible plague among young women. When did torturing others become a rite of passage?

The prime minister enters, my father next to him. The

bride follows behind. In a white silk gown overlaid with pearls, the prime minister's new wife is the definition of a unicorn bathed in other unicorns and glitter. Her diamond tiara glints in the candlelight as she takes a seat.

My father greets me. "You look lovely."

"Thank you. You look lovely—um, I mean, nice, too." I preen under his attention. We smile at each other. The room waits for my father to sit before doing so.

Speeches are given. My father toasts to the bride and groom. Everything's in Japanese and I don't understand most of it. When he's finished, the Shining Twins whisper to each other just loud enough for me to hear.

"He forgot to mention Adachi's sister," Akiko says.

Noriko clucks her tongue. "He should've said something about her not being here. How unfortunate it is she could not join us."

My father has made a mistake. I wonder how that could happen, but it makes me feel better. We're all fallible, I guess.

Dinner service begins. It is an elegant choreographed dance by servers in white gloves and coattails. More speeches are given. My father chats with the prime minister. I chat with the bride. She's a former diplomat, but now she plans to stay home full-time and support her husband. We slurp a clear soup with dumplings and eat savory custard with eel and mushroom, grilled baby ayu, and bowls of sticky white rice with red beans. Mariko told me clearing one's plate is polite. That I can do.

My father wipes his mouth with a crisp, white napkin. "Izumi-chan," he says. "You seem very happy this evening."

"I am," I say back. A slow dance. A wedding. A girl in a

ball gown. What could be wrong?

"Japan is agreeing with you."

"It is." A waiter clears our plates. My stomach is near bursting. "I don't want this to end."

"Your Highness." The prime minister draws my attention. He's older, his black hair streaked with gray. His first wife died of heart disease. "Thank you so much for attending this evening. My wife and I are honored by your presence."

Technically, I didn't have much of a choice. But I am glad to be here. "It's a beautiful event. Thank you for having me." I remember Akiko and Noriko's comments earlier. "It's such a shame your sister couldn't attend." My smile is bright, expectant. Ready to receive the PM's warm reception, maybe he'll answer with a fun anecdote about his sister. Maybe my father will thank me for coming to his rescue. Maybe I have a future in diplomacy. "I bet you wish she could be here."

My father nearly chokes on a bite of rice. The conversation around me flatlines. I look around, clueless. There is a suspicious quirk to Akiko's and Noriko's mouths, like the sharp edges of knives. The prime minister hangs his head, curls his fist around his napkin. Then he starts to speak in Japanese— softly at first, then louder as he gains momentum. His wife hurries to soothe him.

I don't understand. "What—"

"*Izumi.*" My father's voice is harsh, full of censure. He's never used this tone with me. "The prime minister and his sister aren't on good terms." He drops his voice, and says under his breath, "She accused him of horrible things. We don't . . . we don't speak of her. *Ever.*"

My father enters the fray and tries to placate the prime

minister, who continues to rant and wave a hand at me. Now I know what the word *catastrophe* looks like. The room is folding in on itself. Guests avert their eyes. The prime minister goes on and on. My twin cousins laugh into their napkins. There's absolutely nothing I can do to stop it. Finally, the prime minister grows quiet, but his body still hums with anger.

"I'm so sorry, Prime Minister Adachi," I say. He's furious in his silence. All I can see is the top of the prime minister's head. He's ignoring me now. I've been ostracized. I touch my father's arm, but he won't look at me. It's true the blows you least expect hurt the most. Something breaks inside of me. "My sincerest—" I push back from the table. "E-excuse me." I stumble over my words, over my dress. Humiliation unfurls in my chest, slices it open, and burns a path up my throat. I remember Mariko's advice. "Bathroom," I manage to get out.

"Gaijin," Akiko spits out as I pass.

Just in case I didn't hear it the first time, Noriko repeats it. "Gaijin."

My cousins set me up.

Head down, I escape.

17

My flee is legendary. I am Cinderella running from the ball, but I won't be leaving behind a glass slipper, and I won't be waiting for a prince to rescue me.

My eyes glisten from trying not to cry. I refuse to give the Shining Twins the satisfaction. I'll break down in the car, my room, the bathroom—somewhere with a little more dignity.

Akio shadows me. I don't miss the way he positions his body, shielding me from the people as we exit. I wish I could tell him thank you, but I might crack and break open, all my insides spilling out. I've embarrassed my father. Myself. Japan.

The walk from the ballroom to the car is a blur. Mercifully, the Imperial Rolls-Royce is waiting. As soon as I'm in, we're off.

Akio holds a handkerchief out to me. "What happened?" he asks.

I dab underneath my eyes. I don't want to say it out loud— how big of a fuckup I am. My God, I thought . . . I thought I had it all figured it out. Stupid. I am so stupid. "What does gaijin mean?"

"Who called you that?" he barks out.

"It doesn't matter." Again, I don't want him to know how much my family hates me. It's all so embarrassing. "What does it mean?"

He unbuttons his suit jacket. His lips twist. "It means

foreigner. And not in a good way."

"I see." My jaw locks.

"You will tell me who said this to you and I will take care of it."

I'm touched by his defense. "What will you do? Beat up the other imperial princesses because they were mean to me? You're sweet. But I prefer to fight my own battles." Though I don't know what kind of armor I have left. The Shining Twins managed to find my thinnest skin and tear right through it with their beige nails. "Besides, they're not wrong . . ."

It's true. I *am* a foreigner. If I'd lived in Japan before last week, I would have known about the prime minister's sister. I would have known to wear a nicer outfit to the airport. I would have known to walk behind my father at the stupid craft bazaar. I would have known which artists oppose the imperial family. I would have known attending a baseball game and greeting players was an act of diplomacy, and that pointing was rude.

He harrumphs, which I didn't know a human could actually do until now. Reaching over, I grab his hand. "It's really okay." It's not, though. There is still a painful ache inside me. The disappointment in my father's eyes, the way he spoke to me—the memory makes my stomach twist. There may be no crying in baseball, but there are definitely tears in princessing.

Akio's fingers tighten on mine, then his hand slips away. He sighs, rubbing his eyes. "This is poor timing." Dark eyes pin me in place. "You make me wish for all the things I shouldn't."

"I do?" I sniffle, feeling a little better. I lean forward, hoping he'll take my hand again. Maybe he'll cup my cheek and tell me everything will be all right.

"Your Highness," he says, over-serious.

"Akio." I match his tone, half joking. But then it registers—his body language isn't mirroring mine. I feel the first piercing sting of rejection. I sit back. Now we're both stiff. At odds.

"A hundred years ago, imperial physicians wouldn't even touch the emperor or empress without gloves." His hands ball into fists. "When a prince or princess rode through cities, villagers would avert their eyes. They were not worthy to look upon the children of gods and goddesses."

I have a scary, icky, deep foreboding about where he's going with this. "It's a bit archaic, don't you think? That doesn't happen now."

His face is guarded. "You're right, it doesn't. But the idea still exists. It's taboo."

"What are you saying?" My voice is small.

"I think you know what I'm saying."

"I think I'm going to need you to say it." When Forest cheated on me, I made him tell me all the lurid details, though I already knew most of them. I wanted to read between the lines, see if I could glean what faults of mine drove him away. Don't we always blame ourselves?

"Our dance . . . it was a mistake." Ah, I totally see it now. It's in the set of his shoulders, in the tenseness of his jaw. Regret. My vision blurs. "I got carried away. It was my fault. I crossed a line." So noble of him to take the blame. "It won't—it can't happen again."

My fingers curl into my palms. I'd like to get out of the car now. What I wouldn't give to be magically transported to my room. Tears start to fall, but I ignore them. All of Mariko's work on my face, ruined. I focus out the window at the dark starless night, praying for time to move faster.

"Please don't be upset," he says quietly.

Izumi will be upset. Izumi will be extremely upset, thank you very much. I can't seem to get anything right—I'm a black belt in humiliation.

"Say something," Akio says when we arrive at the gate.

Say something? What is there to say? The winding drive up to the palace takes an eon. I use my gloves to mop up my face. Too bad they can't clean up the mess I've made.

As soon as the palace is in view, I dart toward the car door. The vehicle stops just as I pop the handle and dive out, but Akio chases me.

"I'm sorry," he says.

I twirl around. "No." I try for a lighthearted tone, even go for a little laugh. I don't quite nail either. "It's totally my mistake. I misread the signals. Stupid, right?"

"Izumi—"

Wind ruffles my dress. "It's *Your Highness,* isn't it?" Akio blinks, taken aback, but I'd rather have his anger than his pity. I soften my tone. "Wouldn't want any lines to be blurred."

His takes a big breath. "Will you require anything else this evening?"

My chin trembles. "No. Thank you."

"Goodnight, then. If it's okay with you, I'll wait here and make sure you get safely inside." It's totally unnecessary. Still, I manage a sharp nod.

Ten wobbly steps and I slip through the door. I listen for

the sound of the car driving away, but I don't hear it. He's still out there. A knot twists and tightens in my belly, and I sink to the floor.

God. I'm such a fool.

18

I'm shaken awake by tiny yet strong hands. What fresh hell is this? My gummy eyelids slide open.

"Izumi-sama," Mariko says. "You must get up now."

Bleary-eyed, I sit up. Damn, I feel like roadkill. Nothing like crying yourself to sleep. "Wha—"

"The Crown Prince is waiting for you." Mariko is in much distress. She buzzes about the room, arms full of clothes and slippers. I throw my legs over the bed.

She dresses me in under fifteen minutes. I am of little help. My arms and legs are wooden and stiff like a doll. "Did you even wash your face?" Mariko *tsks*, wiping my cheeks with a cold washcloth. Though she's being gentle, it slaps me awake. A little makeup, a brush raked through my hair, and I am pushed through the door.

The hallway seems brighter than usual, but it could be my crying hangover. Tears are really a bitch. Mr. Fuchigami and a whole gaggle of chamberlains are gathered outside my father's office. Butlers and valets are also hanging around, loading monogrammed luggage into a waiting imperial vehicle.

"Good morning," I say warily.

Mr. Fuchigami is solemn. "Your Highness. The Crown Prince is in his office."

I swallow and nod. My heartbeat pounds behind my ears as I knock on the door and slip inside.

My father exhales seeing me. "Izumi. Please come in. Sit down." I shuffle forward and collapse into a chair with a dainty *thud*. My father sits behind his desk. He's in a suit and tie, pristine, though he appears a little tired. Guess we both had a rough night. My head is pounding and I'm pretty sure my face is still puffy. I didn't have the heart to look in the mirror.

"Feels like I've been sent to the principal's office." I clasp my hands in front of me. "If this is about the prime minister's wedding—"

"We need to talk—"

We speak at the same time. Pause. Stare at each other.

"You first," says my father, opening his hands.

My fingernails dig into my palms. I try to look at my father, but my chin doesn't seem inclined to go in that direction. Instead, it points down at my lap. "The prime minister's wedding . . . I'm sorry." My cheeks heat thinking of the moment—of the Shining Twins' smiles, of how I embarrassed my father, of Akio's stinging rejection.

My father says nothing. I force my chin up and wish I hadn't. His mouth is a flat line. He drums his fingers against his lacquered desk. "We were fortunate media wasn't allowed at the event. I cannot imagine the consequences in the papers. Pictures of you running from the wedding would be all over on the cover. The speculation . . . or if they actually found out you insulted the prime minister." He shakes his head. "It would have been awful."

"I'm sorry," I say again. Is there a word for *lower than low*? "It's just that Akiko and Noriko said you didn't mention the prime minister's sister in your speech, and so I thought, maybe I should mention it. . . . I was only trying to help," I finish weakly.

He shakes his head. "The feud has been public and very ugly. I'm sure you misheard."

"But . . ." I say, flabbergasted.

He leans back, and that's the end of the discussion. "It doesn't matter how it happened. As members of the imperial family, we're expected to be beyond reproach."

"I get it," I say evenly, though I kind of don't. I apologized and tried to explain myself. Did I ever stand a chance in this new world? You don't know what you don't know, and you'll be blamed for it. He scrubs a hand over his face, seemingly at a loss for words.

Heads bob outside the window; valets are loading luggage. I peer out the glass. "Is someone going somewhere?"

He straightens up. "Yes." He's still a bit off. *We're* a bit off. "I'm leaving."

"You're leaving?" Oh. Wow. Just give me a moment to scoop my heart up off the floor. "When? Where are you going?"

"I was supposed to depart early this morning, but I delayed so I could speak with you. It's an unscheduled trip. The emperor, my father, isn't feeling well." At my concerned look, he waves a hand. "Nothing serious. He's fatigued, I believe. Too much traveling. I've been asked to fill in for him."

I shake my head, stupefied. "How . . . how long will you be gone?"

He sighs. "Sixteen days."

This math is easy. My flight home is in a couple days. I open my hands. "I guess this is goodbye, then." I start to stand.

"Izumi. Wait. Stop."

I sink back into my seat and lift my chin high.

"I'm doing this all wrong." He grasps a heavy silver pen and fidgets with it. "I don't want this to be goodbye." He clears his throat. I sit perfectly still. "I wonder if maybe we should extend our time together." His eyes level with mine. "I'd like you to stay."

I suck in a breath. I'm not being kicked to the curb? This is unexpected . . . and not such an easy decision on my end. The girls and I had big plans for the spring, packing in breakfasts at Black Bear Diner and polar bear swims in Castle Lake before we leave for college and go our separate directions— Glory to the University of Oregon, Hansani to UC Berkeley, and Noora all the way to Columbia. I'd planned to stay local at College of the Siskiyous, near my mom. Months are all we have left after a lifetime together.

I frown. "I can't miss graduation. You could come, I guess," I blurt out. Don't know how mom would feel about that. Maybe it'll be a surprise. Everyone loves surprises, right?

He dips his chin. "I'd need to check my schedule."

"Of course," I'm quick to say. "If you have time." It sounds snippy.

"I'll speak to my secretary." He pauses, taps his pen. "You haven't answered my question. Will you stay?"

"I don't know." I hesitate, still reeling from the last twenty-four hours. It's been a roller coaster. Do I stay on the ride, not knowing how it ends? Right now, I'm just trying to catch my breath.

He regards me carefully. "Izumi-chan, may I ask why you came to Japan?"

I lace my fingers together and stare at the samurai sword behind his desk. The blade is polished to a high sheen. I can see part of my reflection, the gentle upturn of my eyes. A dragon curls around the hilt. Originally, I thought coming here was to get to know my father. But it's bigger than that. "I came to figure out who I am, where I come from." *Find somewhere I belong.*

"History is important," he says. He thinks for a moment, coming to a conclusion. "Stay. Mr. Fuchigami suggested Kyoto, and I think it's an excellent idea. You'll see the countryside and continue your lessons. When I return, we'll attend the emperor's birthday together. It's a national holiday and there is a big to-do. You'd meet your grandparents."

I twiddle my thumbs, feeling the pull of his promises, but I'm still upset. I can't shake Mr. Fuchigami and my father making plans for me behind my back. I suddenly understand Yoshi's desire for distance from the imperial family. It's hard not to feel like a pawn on a chessboard. Chamberlains moving you about. All these men deciding what is best for you. "I should talk with Mom." I wait a beat. Really contemplate it—Kyoto, a part of the country I haven't seen. I know my search isn't over. This opportunity is too big to let go of just because I'm pissed. You know, don't cut off your nose to spite your face, that whole thing.

"Okay," he says slowly. Clearly, he was anticipating more excitement. He doesn't have a lot of experience with teenagers, I guess. All I can say is: welcome to the jungle, buddy.

"Is that all?" I stand.

"That's all." He stands, too. "I'll be leaving for the airport in . . ." he checks his watch. "An hour."

"I'll let you know what I decide."

We face off.

"All right," he says.

"All right then," I parrot, then leave, spine straight and unforgiving.

In my room, a breakfast service has been laid out next to the floor-to-ceiling windows. I pluck up my phone and settle at the antique table. I dial my mom and peek under the silver dome—Wagyu tenderloin served with scrambled eggs, black truffle and chives. All delicious, but I can't find my appetite.

Mom answers on the first ring. "Zoom Zoom!" Her voice is happy.

"Mom," I say.

"Oh no. What's wrong?"

Just by my tone, she can tell something's up. Man, I miss her. "My father asked me to stay in Japan, and he wants me to go to Kyoto," I expel in one breath. Outside the window, a crane swoops and lands in the water. I definitely don't scan the lawn to check for Akio. "Mom? You there?"

"I'm here." She sounds uneasy. "Just needed a moment. Your father wants you to stay?"

"Yes." My stomach churns.

"I see. Well . . . what do you want?"

"I want to stay, I think?" Should I tell her about the wedding? My father? Our discord? It's on the tip of my tongue, the whole messy story. But then, I picture her reaction, the worry on her face. How hard it would be for her to know I'm hurting while I'm an ocean away.

"I'd feel more confident if you didn't pose that as a question."

With my finger, I trace the edge of the crane's neck through the glass. *Why'd you come to Japan?* my father asked. "I want to stay. I know it means missing more classes, but I haven't had enough time here." I stop. Pause. Collect myself. I can hear her breaths through the line. I wish I could see her. Map the expression on her face.

She sniffles.

"Oh my God. Are you crying? If you want me to come home, I will. Why are you crying? Is it because of school? Do you think I'll miss graduation? I promise I'll be home for that. Don't cry. Please don't cry."

"Oh, it's not about any of that." There's some shuffling, a discreet blowing of the nose. "I don't really care about classes or graduation, though I'd love to see you in your cap and gown. I just want you to be happy." She sighs. "I guess I'm finding it hard to share you. I'm not equipped to let you go. This mothering thing is hard, know what I mean?"

I do not, but I can imagine. "Yeah."

Another sniffle. "I'm being silly. Go to Kyoto."

"You sure?"

"I'm sure. You have my full blessing."

I exhale a sigh of relief. "Thanks."

"No problem." Her voice is lighter now. "Also, I want to encourage your independence, but maybe touch base more often?"

"Got it. Will do." Suddenly, I'm hungry. I pick up the heavy silver fork, nibble on an egg, and look at the crane—it lifts a leg, takes one slow, long step, then launches out of the water.

"You know, how much children push their parents away directly correlates to how secure they feel in the relationship."

"So I've done a good job then?"

"Absolutely. The very best." I lick my fork, feeling calmer, surer. My course is set. I know where I'm headed, at least for now. I settle back and watch as the crane circles once, then disappears into the tree line.

Messages

9:17 AM

Me

On my way to Kyoto. Might not
be back stateside for a while.

Noora

Jealous. I just ate an entire pizza in
my underwear.

Glory

Whoa.

Hansani

A lot to take in here.

Me

I miss you guys.

Noora

Ditto. Japan has stolen my best
friend. Totally heinous anus.

Glory

That's not a saying.

Noora

Well, I'm making it one and I'd love
your support.

Me

Anyway . . . you all mad?

Hansani

Of course not.

Glory

Nope. Some horses are meant to
run free.

Noora

Just don't be a stranger, okay?

Me

Got it. One more thing?

Noora

Yes.

Me

If you all were trees, know what
kind you'd all be?

Glory

If this is a pun . . .

Me

. . . tree-mendous.

Noora

I'd totally go out on a limb for you.

Glory

Please stop.

Hansani

What happened with hot
bodyguard?

Me

Ugh. Don't ask. Made a fool
of myself. Now it's beyond
awkward. That's what I get for
trying to branch out.

Noora

Don't worry I'm here. I won't leaf
you alone.

Glory

You two actually need help.

I smile at my phone, lean back in the plush velvet seat, and listen to the *click-clack* of the train as it speeds toward Kyoto. We're in a private carriage—me, Mariko, Mr. Fuchigami, and a security team headed by Akio. As for the imperial guard, he's made himself scarce. Naturally, I don't jump every time a door between the cars opens or shrink in my seat hoping to avoid him. That would be pathetic. I'm not a total sad sack. Just kidding. I am. I really am.

My phone buzzes in my hand. It's my father texting: *Departure okay?* I tap out a three-letter response: *Yep.* Instead of informing him myself I'd be going to Kyoto, I had Mr. Fuchigami do so. Now we communicate purely by text. Just call me Petty LaBelle. He may have posed Kyoto as an opportunity to learn, but it's hard not to feel as if I'm being hidden away. You know, the whole thing where imperial families ferret unwanted members to the countryside and abandon them?

I put my phone away and stare out the window at Japan's countryside, watching the scenery zip by at 320 kilometers per hour. Mount Fuji has come and gone, as have laundry on metal merry-go-racks, houses plastered with party signs, weathered baseball diamonds, an ostrich farm, and now, miles of rice paddy fields tended by people wearing conical hats and straw coats. Japan is dressed in her best this morning, sunny and breezy, with few clouds in the sky as accessories. It's the first official day of spring. Cherry blossoms have disappeared in twists of wind or trampled into the ground. Takenoko, bamboo season, will begin soon.

Mr. Fuchigami sits across from me. He nods to the window. "See how the villages huddle together?" I do notice. They're clustered, surrounded by rice paddies or farmland. "Not many people live in higher altitudes. The mountains are the domain of the gods," he says. Shinto is the state religion. My grandfather, the emperor, is the head of it—the symbol of the State and the highest authority. "Even today, it's considered taboo to live so high."

At the word *taboo*, I remember my last conversation with Akio. I stand abruptly. "Excuse me." I skirt away, heading for the door.

In the bathroom, I wash my hands and contemplate splashing water on my face to see if it will cool the lingering burn of embarrassment, but Mariko spent half an hour on my makeup this morning. I wait a few minutes, letting my body sway with the train's movement. There's something soothing about the rocking. Alas, I can't stay here forever.

I hit the button for the door and it slides open. My head is down. I'm not looking where I'm going and I run right into a solid body. Eff my life. It's Akio. Sadly, my imperial guard is just as handsome as ever, but a little broodier. Even better.

"Your Highness." His voice is dry. So formal. "I didn't see you."

I can't quite look at him. I don't want to. The eyes are the windows to the soul, after all. "Right. I'll make sure to alert you of all my future movements." It's a bit snippy. A lot snippy. But the best defense is a good offense. And that's all I know about sports.

His unsure gaze searches my face. "If you would like another imperial guard, I would understand. A replacement can be here—"

"I don't think that's necessary." I lift a shoulder, doing my best to convey through body language that what happened between us means nothing at all. "No reason we can't still work together. I've forgotten about it already." Lie. Big lie. I haven't forgotten. I cannot forget. *I still have your sweatshirt. I still can feel your hands on my waist, the way your fingers dug into my hips.* "It was a mistake. A misunderstanding."

His lips press together. "Right."

The connecting car door slides open. "Izumi-sama, lunch is about to be served." It's Mariko.

"Sumimasen." Akio bows. "I've a security briefing to lead."

I try to smile, but I'm pretty sure I fail. Akio stares at me for one agonizing moment, then leaves. Mariko watches him. I give myself a pat on the back for keeping my eyes trained on the window. Small steps.

"Everything okay?" She frowns, searching my face. "You seem a bit off."

"Just peachy," I respond tightly.

She takes a deep breath. "Akio's in a mood today."

"Yeah." I straighten. "Are you hungry? I'm hungry."

I breeze past Mariko. Lunch is placed in front of me. A bento box. Akio stands at the back of the train. No, I will not look at him. But do I feel the weight of his stare, or is it just wishful thinking? My neck heats. I glance back. Oh, he's watching me, face blank. I remind myself this is his job. That's all he's doing. No need to read into it.

A distraction is necessary. I could spend the time on homework. I've arranged to finish up my classes online. But instead, I reach into my bag—some designer purse that looks like a large envelope with handles—and pull out my headphones. I plug them in and listen to hip-hop and "The Rose," the song Akio and I danced to.

The music drowns out the sound of the train, the rustling of Mr. Fuchigami turning his newspaper, the chatter of Mariko on the phone, and most importantly, my thoughts.

I let out a frustrated breath, ball up the piece of parchment paper, and toss it to the side. It's late, the hour nearing midnight. Lights are turned down low. I shiver in the drafty room. Built in the late 1800s, the Sentō Imperial Palace was refurbished, but kept all of its ancient charm and appeal—a tiled roof that swoops into elegant curls, huge wooden exterior doors, floorboards cut from rare keyaki wood, and golden screens separating rooms. If I am to find my Japanese soul anywhere, this would be the place. There are no tabloids here, no high-profile events, no distractions.

My hands are stained with ink, and the blue Nabeshima rug is littered with my sacrifices. I've been practicing kanji at a high table for hours. The house retired long ago. I am alone with all my failures. Picking up another sheet of washi paper, I place it on a cloth and weigh it down with a polished stone.

I dip the brush in ink. Making ink—grinding powders, mixing colors (golds, silvers, azurite), and adding glue—can take hours. Someday, I might be able to do this. But it's a master's skill, and I am a novice. It is the way of kata, the practice of doing something over and over again until it is second nature. Calligraphy is part of the imperial identity. Therefore, it is part of mine now.

I draw the brush downward, creating the first stroke for

the word *mountain, yama*. It ends in a giant splotch. I drop the brush, and ink splatters all over the paper. Another one bites the dust.

"You're overthinking it." It's Mariko. Her pinstriped pajamas are buttoned all the way to the top.

I startle. "I didn't think anyone else was still awake." She hesitates at the door. Inwardly, I sigh. "You hungry?" I gesture to the plate of dorayaki pushed to the corner of the table.

"I could eat." She shuffles forward and joins me at the table. We nibble in silence for a while. Mariko's serious face glows in the lamplight. "May I see?" She edges the piece of paper with the ruined script toward her.

I squirm in my seat. She studies my handiwork and doesn't try to hide her displeasure. I actively wish for the power to light things on fire with my eyes. "I knew it. You are over-thinking. Because of this, you are too heavy-handed. You are forcing the lines rather than letting the lines be the force. Let me show you."

She takes up the brush, dips it, and, on the same piece of paper, executes the first stroke. "Do not think about the character you're making. Only think about the line, the single movement. It's like a dance, ne? If you concentrate too much on the final steps, you will miss the present ones." Another stroke, one more, and she has completed the pictograph. It is beautiful, worthy of hanging on a wall, and I say so.

She shakes her head. "I still have much to learn, but it is passable. It doesn't have to be perfect, however. Kanji is an expression of the soul."

I fiddle with the edge of the paper. "It's overwhelming how much there is to learn."

She nods. "I understand. When I came to Japan, it was quite intimidating."

I inspect her, surprised at this news. "You weren't born here?"

"No. I was born in England. My father is Japanese. My mother is Chinese. We moved here just after I turned five."

"I didn't know that." How could I not know that?

Her brows draw tight. "You never asked."

"I bet you were fluent in Japanese, though."

"I knew some," she says. "But my entire education had been in English. When we arrived, my parents enrolled me in St. Peter's International School in Tokyo. I had to learn everything from scratch. Worse, I was terribly made fun of. Children can be so cruel."

I think of Emily Billings in an almighty rush. All the nice things anyone has ever said to me are dust in comparison to that one moment in time. I gulp. "How did you manage it?"

She stares at the table. "Some things you just get through. I was near proficient by the end of kindergarten."

My mouth quirks upward. "You really do learn everything you need to know in kindergarten."

"And sumo. I used to watch with my nanny and practice the wrestler names." She taps the paper. "*Mountain* was a personal favorite." She sighs. "I blend in most of the time. But in some ways, I will always be a foreigner."

"I insulted the prime minister," I blurt. "Asked him about his sister not attending the wedding. And as I was leaving, my cousins called me gaijin."

She has the good grace to wince. "Ouch."

"Yeah." I hunch over. I stare at the washi paper. *Mountain* was my latest attempt. But before that was *sky, middle,* and *sun.* I focus on the *sun* character—Japan's national emblem. The first emperor, Jimmu, was born swaddled in golden rays. He descended from Amaterasu. How could you ever go wrong with the light at your back?

She makes a noise in the back of her throat. "Those girls. Their mother is around too little and their father gives them too much, as if material things will make up for her absence."

"Please. Don't make me feel bad for them."

"I'm not. They're terrible. Believe me. I'm not surprised they said something like that. They don't attack unless they feel truly threatened." I feel a smidgen better. She juts her chin at the washi paper. "I wouldn't waste any time thinking about them. Focus on kanji instead."

"Is this your idea of tough love?" I give her the side-eye. "Because you should know it's my least favorite kind of love."

Mariko doesn't reply, only raises her eyebrows. At length, I set a new paper in front of me, dip the brush, and tap out the excess ink. I keep my hand light and patient and think only of the here and now. The line I'm making, and not the word. It only takes a second or two, but when I sit back, I grin. It's a little wobbly at the top and too thick at the bottom. A little weak, but with a promise of strength. It definitely could be fine-tuned a bit. But I like it. It is an expression of my soul, after all—my messy, messy soul.

Mariko peruses my effort. "Still needs work, but better."

I examine her, then brighten. "Oh my God! I just figured something out."

She comes to attention. "What? What is it?"

My smile is sly. "You like me."

"What?" She scowls. "I do not—"

"You like me," I say with a firm nod.

"Stop saying that."

"You like me and want to be my friend."

"If anyone hears you, they're going to think you've lost it." Mariko's lips purse. She crosses her arms and huffs out. "I respect that you are trying. It's not easy. You're rising to the challenge. It's . . . admirable, I guess."

"Uh-huh." I give her a knowing look.

Mariko can't even. Her sigh is long and drawn out, aggrieved. "Do you want help practicing your kanji or not?"

"Yes," I say beaming, then sing, "*friend*."

THE TOKYO TATTLER

The Lost Butterfly holidays in Kyoto

April 21, 2021

Despite fatigue cutting short His Imperial Majesty's tour of Southeast Asia, preparations for his eighty-seventh birthday are well underway. All imperial family members will be present. A formal audience has been scheduled where Her Imperial Highness Princess Izumi will officially be introduced to her grandparents for the first time.

Recently, Tokyo Tattler correspondents and locals have spied HIH Princess Izumi out and about in Kyoto. Spottings have mostly occurred in the evenings (inset: Princess Izumi seen visiting a temple and geisha house last week).

While HIH Princess Izumi holidays in Kyoto, her twin cousins have been carrying the imperial workload, attending official duties on behalf of their mother, Her Imperial Highness Princess Midori, who hasn't left imperial grounds in weeks.

And what of her second cousin, HIH Prince Yoshihito? Our palace insider said the two have grown close. In an exclusive scoop, HIH Prince Yoshihito was just seen boarding the imperial train. His destination? Kyoto.

20

Kyoto used to be a city of shopkeepers, Shirasu tells me. The bamboo farm we stand in the middle of has been in his family for five generations. It has supplied bamboo to the imperial family for just as long.

Shirasu is wrinkled and slight, his body like one of the strips of paper fortunes fluttering outside of the temple we visited earlier. My nostrils still burn from the incense. We traveled here by car, an hour on dirt roads blanketed by old-growth forest, mist rolling in at our heels. It's almost prehistoric. When we stepped from the car, I expected a saber-toothed tiger to dart from the underbrush. Shirasu greeted us instead. Still, it's as if we've stepped back in time. His home is simple with a thatched roof. He insists it's all he needs. We've traveled deep into his twenty thousand square meters of bamboo grove. He chats up a storm in broken English.

"My father thought about selling farm years ago. We traveled to Tokyo to make deal with big company." The name, he's forgotten. His back is bent with age. "That day, first bombs dropped on city." He mimics an explosion with his hands. "Everything gone. I hide under desk survive. My father not so lucky." He goes on to explain how his father died of a head injury. How little fires sprouted up everywhere, melting doorknobs and bottles. How he played in the ashes with other children while waiting for transportation back to Kyoto. His mother brought him back to the farm. They never spoke of selling it again. Until he was old enough, she tended the bamboo and sold it. His father's name is inscribed at Yokoamicho Park in Tokyo. I promise to visit someday to pay my respects.

In the past two weeks, I've memorized the most common kanji characters, covered every square cultural inch of Kyoto—teahouses, Kabuki plays, umbrella-making—and attended evening etiquette lessons with Mariko. Please note how I fold my hands in front of myself, how my steps are half the length they used to be, how I smile without showing too many teeth, how I laugh behind my hand and how, instead of pointing, I gesture with an open palm. To top it all off, I've been practicing Japanese with Mariko and Mr. Fuchigami. I can roughly communicate now. I'm not all the way there, but I'm definitely much further down the road. Things have changed fast. *I* have changed. The sour feelings toward my father have eased, too. I am woman enough to admit when I am wrong. Kyoto has been good. I am thankful.

"Some bamboo grow ninety feet in two months!" Shirasu exclaims. I peer up at the imposing stalks. They're thick and planted far apart. How easy it would be to slip through the gaps and get lost. Sunlight glints through, thick and warm like honey. Wind rustles. I am reminded of Shintoism. How gods dwell in hills and trees. I feel that presence here. "Patience is key." Shirasu stops. At his feet is a crack. "Bamboo take time to grow, to spread root. Three year before it surfaces. But after that . . ." He makes the same motion as he did when speaking about the air raids.

He kneels. "Best bamboo underground." He removes a small pick from his pocket. His hands are gnarled knots.

He works the soil until he upends a lily-white bulb. With his thumbnail, he demonstrates its ripeness. "Tender," he says. "Like apple." He hands it off to his son. The boy is a farmhand now, absorbing his father's words like gospel. Someday, he'll take over. The son places the bulb in a basket.

Shirasu bows and invites me to enjoy the property. "Dōzo," he says. *Do as you please.*

I return with a nod. "Dōmo arigatō gozaimasu."

He hopes we'll visit again soon. Perhaps in June, to see the emerald-colored frogs that stick to the stalks and attend Gion Matsuri, a festival where women dress in summer kimono and the shops are decorated with art. There are floats in the evening and music spills onto the streets.

I leave Mariko and Mr. Fuchigami behind and travel deeper into the forest. Here, the bamboo is taller, still spread out, but the leaves are broad and eclipse the sun. Shirasu keeps his plants cut at six feet, but for some reason, in this section they've grown wild. The footsteps behind me are Akio's. He's my shadow. Stopping, I trail my hands over a stalk, trying to feel the god within.

I catch Akio in my peripheral vision. His face is drawn tight, lips white with strain. Little beads of sweat dot his forehead. "Are you all right?" Could he be sick? It's hard to imagine the imperial guard falling ill with a pesky virus.

"Fine." He's stiff.

"If you say so." I keep wandering. The bamboo grows taller still. Leaves sway and dip, skirting our shoulders. Mist clings to my ankles. It's like the earth is exhaling.

"Forest is getting a bit thick, don't you think?" Akio's voice sounds choked.

I study him, realizing what it is—he's claustrophobic. Strong winds sweep through. A leaf tickles the back of Akio's neck. Fear flashes in his eyes. *Thwack.* Holy shit. Akio has grabbed the offending stalk and broken it in two. Damn, he's strong. He's also having a bit of a mantrum, still hacking away at the bamboo.

"Whoa." I step to him. "Easy. The bad piece of bamboo is gone." I touch his shoulder. He stills. "That's it. The sun's getting real low, buddy."

He glares at me over his shoulder, then his gaze drops to my hand. I jerk it away as if I've been burned. There's still a spark between us.

The bamboo falls from his hands. "Did you just quote *The Avengers* to me?"

"Yes." I'm not ashamed.

He wipes his hands, mutters to himself. "If I was an Avenger, I wouldn't be the Hulk."

My eyebrows meet my hairline. "You wouldn't?"

He scoffs. "No. Obviously, I'd be Tony Stark. Iron Man."

I laugh. He does not. I take a breath. "You're serious?"

Blank stare. "Well, I'm certainly not the Hulk or Hawkeye."

"Yeah, Hawkeye is the worst." I mean, he's got a cool love story. But a bow and arrow? C'mon. "What about Dr. Strange?" I'm sorry as soon as I ask it.

Akio snorts. "A white guy who uses ancient Chinese mysticism?"

"It is a touch problematic," I say. "There could be more Asian representation." Or just some. One, really. One Asian superhero. It doesn't seem too much to ask.

We laugh together. I stare at my feet. Rock back on my heels. "So, small spaces, huh?"

He shakes his head. "My family visited a bamboo forest like this when I was younger. Not a farm. More like a tourist destination. I got lost for a few hours. Couldn't find my way out." His arm lifts, fingers brushing my hair. I resist leaning into his touch. "Leaf," he says, holding up a little piece of green and letting it flutter to the ground.

Right. On that note. "We should probably go." I don't wait for him to answer. I start walking. Akio keeps pace. I don't want to leave things like this, strained and confused.

I stop abruptly. We nearly collide. I jump back, not wanting to touch him again.

"Akio—"

"Your Highness—"

We speak at the same time. He extends a hand to me. "Please."

Now that I have the floor, I'm not sure what to say. I swallow. I wish I could read him better. I wish I could touch him even more. "I'm sorry for how I acted on the train." I press on. "And in the car ride about calling me *princess*."

"I understand." He nods as if it's nothing.

"I just don't want you to think that I think of you that way. I don't believe I'm above you." I pause. "I didn't mean it."

"You should mean it." He's so earnest.

I sniff. I'm such a crier. "I've also been thinking you were right."

"About?"

"Me and you. I know it can't happen. It was just a foolish mistake." I breathe deep. Let the tears dry for a moment.

"Plus, if I dated you, people might think I'm shallow because you're too good-looking." I stick up my nose. It's all about my public image these days.

His laugh is dry. "People would think I've betrayed my monarchy and that I am a shameless opportunist."

Touché. "Definitely don't want that."

"So that's it." Our gazes meet a moment, then dart away. "That's it."

Why does it feel as if I'm losing something all over again? "We can still be friends though, right?" I've missed talking to him.

He shifts slightly. Moves a little bit closer. The tension eases, like a spring coil slowly releasing. He sticks out a hand for me to shake. "Friends," he says definitively.

My palm slides against his. Our fingers clasp. One shake. Then, we hold on a moment too long. Slowly, we disengage. It might be the last time we touch. I want to remember the feel of his rough palm, the warmth there.

We amble together through the forest. "You remember the way?" asks Akio. Oh, he's still a little scared. How cute.

"Absolutely," I say reassuringly.

His brow knits with nerves. "Can we agree to forget about my little freak-out? The embarrassment is worse than the actual incident."

I mime zipping my lips. Then, I unzip them. "I won't tell anyone, but you should know, I do find the whole *vulnerable imperial guard* thing very endearing. Makes you human."

"Yeah?" His mouth quirks into a begrudging smile.

"Oh, yeah it's my favorite. Close second is *grumpy, nonverbal imperial guard*."

He laughs. The tension eases from his body. Mission accomplished. I made him feel better. Totally what friends do.

I lead him through the forest. We catch up, and I ask about his mother.

"She's doing as well as can be expected," he says. "I call as often as I can, but I haven't been able to visit—" He cuts himself off, but I get it, the distance between them. It's something I created. I wish I could make it up to him. I could ask for a replacement and relieve Akio of his duties here. But I don't want to lose him. Selfish, I know. Against my better judgment, I start to suggest something. "If you want . . ." I'm really going to offer it. "If you would like to go home, I'd be okay with it."

He looks at me sharply. "Is that what you want?"

"No," I say way too quickly. "I would understand, though. I'd be sorry to see you go. I've grown used to having you around."

"I don't want to leave." He exhales gustily. "I've grown accustomed to you as well."

I lick my lips. "It's settled, then. You'll stay."

"I'll stay."

The way he says it, like a vow. I die a little inside.

Mr. Fuchigami and Mariko come into view, cutting our conversation short. On the ride back to the palace, Akio sits up front. I ride in the back with Mr. Fuchigami and Mariko.

"Mariko, do you have a pen and paper?"

She's curious, but doesn't ask questions. She digs around and produces a pad and pencil from her purse. Part of her job is to be prepared. She's got all sorts of marvelous things in her handbag: needle and thread, mints, tampons, even cash. The imperial family doesn't carry any money. Everything is paid for by the Imperial Household Agency. But I do have an emergency credit card from my mom. Just in case.

I scribble something on the paper and fold it in half. "Mr. Fuchigami." I hand him the paper.

He unfolds it and reads, caterpillar eyebrows inching up his forehead. "This isn't something that's normally done." I can't read his tone. It's either you've-got-some-goddamn-nerve or I-unwillingly-respect-this-act-of-kindness. Could be either.

"Onegai shimasu," I say. *Please.* My lashes lower. My heart is caught up somewhere near my tonsils. *Do this one thing for me. For Akio. For his family.*

He stuffs the note in his breast pocket. "I'll see what I can do."

"Arigatō." I bow my head to him.

21

Mariko goes off on an etiquette tangent for most of the ride back to the palace. It's all about how Shirasu failed to execute a full forty-five degree bow when saying goodbye. Her rant is rounding ninety minutes. Must be some sort of record. Truly. We're on imperial property now, gates shutting firmly behind us. The grounds are elaborate and well kept, gardens manicured with potted bonsai trees, all in keeping with the swept-back-in-time theme of old Kyoto.

"I'm pretty sure he has a bad back," I say helpfully. Honestly, I'm only half-listening as I text my mom and the AGG. Mom has sent her daily check-in. *How are you?* I respond with a *Great* and a scenic picture of the bamboo forest. Noora is on some sort of campaign to normalize men wearing short-shorts. I give her two thumbs-up.

"Even so," Mariko says, and I can hear the frown in her voice. "Don't you think he should have—"

I look up and cry out. Cars line the driveway, their trunks propped open. Staff in white gloves unpack monogrammed luggage. There is Yoshi, right in the middle of it all, dashing and resplendent in the sunlight.

"What's he doing here?" Mariko says bewildered. "He's not on the schedule." She's flipping through documents on her phone. Royal itineraries are shared—meaning, every morning, an email is sent from the Imperial Household Agency detailing every family member's movements.

I unbuckle my seat belt and scramble from the car. Mr. Fuchigami hisses through his teeth. I throw a *sorry* over my shoulder as I exit the vehicle. I run to Yoshi and stop short. He grins and opens his arms. I throw myself at him and he catches me in a fierce, smothering hug. "What a very enthusiastic American response," he says holding me close, then adds warmly, "Public affection isn't a thing in Japan, though I'm glad to see you haven't lost your spirit." He squeezes me before letting go.

I squint up at him. His jacket and matching crossover tie have gold threads and . . . do I detect glitter in his hair?

"What are you doing here?" I ask, watching Mariko and Mr. Fuchigami climb from the car. "You didn't tell me you were coming."

We've texted, of course. I told him all about the PM and the Shining Twins. He commiserated, telling me Noriko peed herself in kindergarten because she was too embarrassed to ask to go to the bathroom and that Akiko wouldn't stop eating glue. There was a whole meeting about it—chamberlains, teachers, and a variety of behavioral experts were called to weigh in.

"I've come to visit, of course. Hardly seems fair you're having all the fun in the countryside." His gaze focuses downward. He groans, pinches his nose between his thumb and forefinger. "Please tell me you aren't wearing nude pantyhose. The situation is much more dire than I thought. Seems I've arrived just in time." He smiles at my laugh. Goodness, it's good to see him.

"Your Highness." Mr. Fuchigami moseys over to us, buttoning his suit jacket. "We weren't expecting you."

Mariko frowns. She heard his comment about the panty-hose, no doubt. Each morning, my lady-in-waiting painstakingly chooses my outfit.

Yoshi winks at the chamberlain. "That's the fun of it. It's a surprise. I'm delightful that way."

"Your chamberlain, Mr. Wakabayashi. Has he accompanied you?" Mr. Fuchigami asks, unflappable.

Yoshi waves a hand. "He's inside somewhere . . ." He trails off, eyes cutting down the line of cars. Reina and Akio stand inches from each other, discussing something. "Your body-guard is standing very close to mine. What do you suppose they're talking about?"

"They're probably discussing security." My smile is so wide it hurts.

"No," he says, offhandedly. "Reina is probably vision boarding my funeral. She's angry with me. All because I spoke with her through the door while she was using the toilet. I don't know why she doesn't like that. I feel like it makes us closer, you know?"

"No," I say simply. "I don't know." Even though I kind of do. The AGG have no shame when it comes to the bathroom. Some of our best friend moments were born there.

He shrugs it off and his smile broadens, mischief dancing in his eyes. "Let's do dinner tonight. Somewhere lavish and ridiculously expensive where they'll throw rose petals at our feet." He takes his phone out, scrolls through it. "Have you ever dined kaiseki?"

"Don't know what that is."

"It's a must, then. You'll need something a touch dress-ier." He peers at me. "The chef I'm thinking of doesn't mess around. Takes himself very seriously."

Mariko chimes in. "Perhaps a silk kimono would do?"

Yoshi turns his attention to her, a devilish look on his face. "A kimono would do nicely. You know, I don't think we've formerly met. Cousin, why have you never introduced me to your lovely lady-in-waiting?" He bows to her.

Mariko actually blushes. It's so easy to fall under Yoshi's charms. "I'll need a good hour to get her ready," she says in a pleasant tone she's never used with me.

Yoshi flourishes another bow, looking at her as if she invented cake. "Of course, I'm your servant in all things. You know, if my heart wasn't otherwise engaged to a certain woman that hides weapons all over her body . . ."

Oh good God, enough. "Yoshi," I say, trying to communicate with my eyes.

"Right. Yeah." He turns to me. "I forgot myself there for a moment. Good thing Reina isn't the jealous type. Though I wish she was." He stares at her longingly for a moment, then goes back to his phone. "I'll make reservations for us." He glances up, then shouts to a staff member unloading a perforated duffel as he dashes off. "Careful with that, there's a live animal in there."

We dine in Gion—the geisha district, Kyoto's heart and spiritual center. There are rickety teahouses, master sword makers, and women dressed in kimonos. The restaurant is by invitation only and seats seven, but the chef prefers to keep the guest count under five. His name is Komura, and like the bamboo farmer Shirasu and his son, his two daughters assist him. The sisters light candles in bronze holders and place them around the room. The restaurant is a converted home, the walls a deep ebony stained from years of smoke from the open hearth—it's called kurobikari, black luster. It's a hidden gem nestled between a pachinko parlor and an antiques shop.

The table we kneel at is made of thick wood, its surface weathered, worn, and polished, honed by years of hands and plates and cups of tea.

Yoshi smiles, a gleam in his eyes. "Tell me everything. Do you love Kyoto? Hate it?" He wears a satin suit and matching tie. His hair is slicked back. Very debonair. All that's missing is the white ferret around his shoulders. Famous designer Tomo Moriyama will be debuting live animals as part of his Fall Collection during Tokyo Fashion Week, and Yoshi has one of the first "samples." The chef wouldn't let him bring it in. Luckily, Yoshi came equipped with some sort of harness leash for the creature. One of the bodyguards is walking it right now.

I take a deep breath. Hard to do since my waist is cinched so tight. Mariko certainly worked her fairy godmother magic. My kimono is teal silk stitched with silver threads to mimic rippling water and embroidered with multi-colored lily pads. Hair pulled back in a low bun with a chrysanthemum pin complements the outfit. "Kyoto is a dream," I say quietly. While the restaurant's atmosphere is relaxed—soft lighting, pillows to recline on, low voices, a single silk tapestry on the wall—it is also a cultural minefield, full of places where I might misstep. This whole thing could blow up in my face. I check my posture, the way I hold my ohashi, and remind myself how to bow to thank them at the end of the meal—gochisōsama deshita. My smile is genuine. "Even better now that you're here," I say.

Together we sip the aperitif, a sweet wine. Then the sisters bring the second starter—hassun, bite-sized appetizers arranged like tiny jewels on the plate. We cease movement and conversation while the plates are laid down. Once the sisters leave, Yoshi says, "Oishisō."

"Oishisō," I repeat. *Looks delicious.*

Our conversation resumes and Yoshi says, "I'd been meaning to visit. An old schoolmate lives here. His name is Jutaro. He's a former aristocrat who moonlights as a wild boar dealer."

Whatever that means. I smile.

Yoshi waits for me to begin. In Japan, the most honored guest eats first. That's me. "Itadakimasu," I say, keeping my back straight as I take a bite of prawn. In kaiseki, the focus is on the food's essence and is reflective of the rhythms of the seasons. The meal is heavily influenced by nature. It's May, so our menu will be inspired by spring and feature bamboo.

Yoshi observes me warmly as he digs in. "Look at you. You've changed."

I set my ohashi aside. "I haven't. I'm still a work in progress."

"Aren't we all?" Yoshi takes a drink of water, eyeing me above the rim. "You have. I look amazing, but you look even better. Change isn't the worst thing. Perhaps you could give me some tips. I'd like to improve my media image. You can teach me."

The sisters clear our plates and bring the second course, bamboo shoots boiled in spring water. I cup the lacquered bowl in my hands. "Media image?" I ask between sips.

My eyes flick to Akio. He stands near the entrance alongside Reina. Discreetly, he pulls his phone from his pocket, checks it, and glowers. Whoa, glad I'm not the messenger. But then, he turns that frown on me. What did I do? I rack my brain. Nothing comes to mind.

Oh, there is one thing. The favor I asked of Mr. Fuchigami. But why would Akio be upset about that?

Yoshi waves a hand and says, "I know you adore me, so this may come as a shock. But I'm a bit of a black sheep."

I pretend to be surprised. "You don't say?"

He pats my hand. "Please don't think poorly of me. It's the press. I've been treated quite unfairly. Youngest children are always so misunderstood. If only people could see inside. I'm very sensitive, you know. It's just that I don't like rules. Or being a prince. I want to be free of my gilded cage. Does that make me an awful walking cliché?"

"I'm afraid it does."

"Right. As for my media image, I'd like to keep the godlike adoration. But I'd like them to also be a little frightened of me, too. Like I'll unleash a host of plagues if I become displeased."

"Ah. You want to be viewed as an immature jerk who throws temper tantrums?"

A ghost of a smile appears on Yoshi's face. "You're right. That's not good, either. Thanks for keeping my head on straight. I need to get something named after me. Maybe a hospital or a library. Something that says: 'a soft, giving heart beats inside this large masculine chest.'"

I laugh. The third and fourth courses are served—sashimi, then pickled clams and roasted Kawachi duck. "Yoshi," I say, feeling the gentle pace of the evening, how the meal unfurls like a fan slowly opening, each rib revealing a new part of the picture.

"Izumi," he says.

"I'm so glad you're here. I'm so glad you're my friend. Thank you."

His eyes are a bit guarded. Maybe the serious stuff doesn't come easy. Last time we had a heart-to-heart, we were knee-deep in alcohol. But now, it's just us. Two sober people at a table in a quiet room. But then, he admits quietly, "I'm glad I'm here, too."

After dinner, we wait outside the restaurant while Yoshi takes a phone call from his friend Jutaro (the former aristo-crat who moonlights as a wild boar dealer). I wander, my legs are stiff from sitting seiza. There's a little fishpond with a tin-kling waterfall.

"I received an interesting message while at dinner."

I startle at Akio's voice. "Did you?"

He walks slowly toward me. "It seems a royal physician paid a visit to my mother."

"You don't say?"

He makes a noise in his throat. "There's more."

"I can't imagine."

His eyes drop to me, long lashes creating half-moons on his cheeks. It's really unfair. Mariko has to curl and lather mine in mascara for the same effect. All the best things are always wasted on boys. "Seems she's to be treated at the im-perial hospital from now on."

"What wonderful news." I smile at him. Mr. Fuchigami came through.

"I owe you a debt," he says, voice low and hypnotic.

I play it off, wave a hand. "Pshh. As I've stated before, I'm a big fan of mothers."

"I feel as if you've given me so much. I don't know how to repay you."

I stare at the sky. I've always been uncomfortable with compliments, though I have a pathological need for them. "There are so many stars out tonight."

"Your Highness," he says softly.

I look at him. "Yes?"

He steps closer. "I'm in your debt."

Silence hangs in the air between us. It's cold but I feel warm, like a rock baking in the sun. The restaurant door opens. Yoshi steps out, his gaze flickering between Akio and me.

Akio steps away. "It's settled then," he says, opening the car door. Then, he smiles. It shimmers in the night. Vibrates off him in waves. Ensnares me, forces me to reciprocate.

I try to keep my heart from racing. "Perfect," I rasp, though I'm not sure what I'm agreeing to. Not sure at all. Doesn't matter, though. It's all good. Better than good. Kind of wonderful.

The peaceful mood from dinner continues in the car. The streets of Kyoto are nearly empty, the ride is smooth, and the company is pleasant. Akio drives, and Reina rides shotgun. I'm in back with Yoshi. The ferret is curled in his lap and he strokes it absently, lost in thought.

About a block away from the palace, the car slows to a stop. Akio and Reina's heads dip toward each other. In low, serious voices, they discuss something.

I perk up, trying to see past them. The street is lit funny, not by the usual yellow street lamps. The glow is softer, more orange and hazy. "What's happening?"

Akio touches his earpiece. "The road is blocked." His head moves and I see the disruption. People have gathered in the street. Each of them cradles a paper lantern in their hands. It's like they're holding little moons.

"What is it?" I ask. Did we miss a festival?

"They're here for you, Your Highness," says Reina. It's the first time she's ever spoken directly to me. Her voice is dry, husky. Soothing. "It seems they gathered an hour ago and have been waiting for you since."

"Why?" I blurt.

Yoshi speaks, his voice is quiet. "Kyoto is welcoming you. The people line the streets to celebrate births, weddings, and newly found daughters of the crown prince." He winks, nudging me. "It's tradition. An honor. Go on. Walk among your people."

I toy with the edge of my kimono. "I don't know . . ." I wait for Akio to argue. Insist the security risk is too high.

"It's okay," Akio says. "Imperial guards are in the crowd. The palace is only a short distance. If you'd like to walk the rest of the way, it's fine."

Well. Not really a choice then. "I guess I'll walk."

Akio is first out of the car. My door is opened in no time. A hush falls over the street. I incline my head, fold my hands in front of myself, and shuffle forward. The crowds part until they fall in parallel lines, their lanterns a steady stream of light. Akio, Reina and Yoshi are steps behind.

A couple of imperial guards appear and take the lead, but I'm alone in the middle. I acknowledge people with smiles and small waves. I see Shirasu. He grins at me. I lose my breath, find it again. I don't want to break this spell. I'm completely besotted. In love with Kyoto, with Japan. We come to the end, to the palace gates as they open.

At the gate, I turn and bow. *Thank you.*

Mr. Fuchigami is there, enjoying the lanterns with the rest of the staff. "Your Highness, did you enjoy your dinner?" he asks.

I nod. Can he see how happy I am? How my eyes shine with joy?

He steps toward me. "You've won the heart of Kyoto." The lantern bearers surround me and all at once, they let go. Glowing orbs drift to the sky in a perfect circle of light.

It's beautiful. Truly beautiful. A golden crown.

22

It's nearing midnight and I can't sleep, too drunk on Japanese fine dining, silk kimonos, bodyguards in my debt, and lanterns in the sky. If ever there was question that a girl could fall in love with a city, the answer is yes.

The palace is sleeping. Mariko turned in hours ago, and Reina finally put Yoshi to bed. I creep through the palace corridors, thinking about Mount Shasta and the girl I was there. How there, everything felt wrong sometimes, and how everything feels like it's coming together here, like things are how they should be.

A light is on in the kitchen. I turn and enter. It's modern with clean lines, but the windows and wooden beams on the ceiling are original architecture. The island lights are on. A single figure sits underneath them. I stop short. "Akio."

He turns from his laptop and shoves himself up from his seat, legs squealing against the marble floor. His suit jacket and tie are off. His shirt sleeves are rolled up. "Izumi . . . I mean, Your Highness." He reaches for his discarded coat.

I stick out a hand. "No, don't. It's okay."

He hesitates, jacket bunched in his fist. I map the veins in his forearm. Watch them taper down to his wrist. After a moment, he sets the jacket down. "You're awake."

I shrug and step into the kitchen. "Couldn't sleep."

"In that case, join me, please." He gestures to the island. "I have snacks."

Ah, the *real* three words every girl longs to hear. I cross the room, nodding at the laptop. "Working?"

He scrubs a hand down his face. "Revising the security detail. I've had to reorganize the schedule a bit with your cousin's arrival."

"Sorry about that." I settle into a chair beside him.

His eyes rake over me from head to toe. I'm wearing his sweatshirt, the gray one he gave me after the karaoke bar. It's only half-zipped, and underneath it is a lacy camisole. I jerk up the zipper. "So, snacks . . ."

Akio turns his head and swallows hard. "Right," he says, pulling a couple of plates toward us. I recognize the confections: goma dango, small rice flour balls filled with anko, sweet red beans, and dorayaki. He did mention a sweet tooth that night in the car.

Of course, I go for the dorayaki first. I emit a little groan on the first bite. "Oh my God, I want to have this dorayaki's babies."

Akio clears his throat and slams his laptop shut. He's not making eye contact. "So, what kept you up?"

I set the dorayaki down and swing my feet, hooking them on the base of the stool. "Oh, um. I was thinking about Mount Shasta. You know, my pre-princess days."

His gaze settles on me. I pretend it's the sugar from the dorayaki making me feel all stirred up. "What is it like, where you're from?"

I finger the dorayaki. "It's a pretty hip tourist spot. People like to camp in the forests during the summer and ski on the mountain in the winter. There's literally one stoplight on Main Street."

"Sounds nice." His mouth is one straight, sincere line.

I straighten a bit. "It is, but . . ."

"Go on," he urges.

My heart twists in my chest. "I dunno. It's like . . . the thing that makes it so wonderful—the same people, the predictability—also makes it kind of awful. Like, there are these boutiques on Main Street, and they sell all sorts of tchotchkes. One in particular had a rack of little rainbow key chains with names on them. Still does to this day." I glance at Akio. I have his full attention. "When I was eight, I wanted one so badly. It didn't take me long to figure out my name wasn't there. There were Carlys and Lindseys and Emilys, but no Izumis. I blamed my mom, railed at her. 'Why couldn't you name me Olivia or Ava?' I hated my name. All this happened in the middle of the store. I can make a scene." I smile wryly.

"What did your mom do?"

I slump down. "She just kind of took it. Eventually I calmed down, and in the car, my mom explained. Her parents died in a terrible car accident the summer before she left for college. She said my name was the only way she could give me a memory of where I was from. I never discussed it with her again. But I did start going by Izzy. I erased part of myself to make it easier for people, but it was also easier for me. Sometimes you just don't want the headache, you know?"

"Honestly, I don't. But I'm sorry." Akio's voice is deep and earnest. I hang my head and gaze at my lap. He places a hand over mine, curling it around my fingertips. "You shouldn't be ashamed, though." He quiets, squeezing my fingers before letting them go. "If I could, I would take your sorrows and bury them deep."

I gape at him. "Do you just sit around and practice perfect things to say?"

He stares back at me, totally calm. "Yes. It's really what all imperial guards do. We have a critique group that meets on Wednesdays. My buddy Ichiro works mostly with haiku," he deadpans.

I smile. How many people get to see this funny side of Akio? His dry sense of humor? I think I am blessed to be one of the few.

"What a gross misuse of time," I say.

"I'll report your concerns to my supervisor."

I find another grin.

"Nice to see you smile again." He rubs the back of his neck. "Are you tired?"

"Not in the least."

He looks over his shoulder, through the giant windows and the dark garden beyond. "My mother used to take me on walks when I couldn't sleep. We'd count the stars. Want to try that?"

I nod and smile, playing with the hoodie's drawstrings. "Couldn't hurt."

We steal away. A gentle breeze skirts the highest branches of the trees. It's cool, but not too cold, dark and quiet with the occasional cricket chirp and the sound of our breaths.

A plane flies overhead, white and red lights blinking. I

crane my neck. "Whenever I see an airplane, I always wonder where it's going, who it's carrying."

Akio gazes up. His profile in silhouette. "That's a commercial plane. Probably a twin-engine regional aircraft headed for Tokyo."

I sigh. "That's considerably less romantic than I thought."

We resume course, traveling deeper into the garden. The palace disappears behind the tree line. "So, planes . . . ?" I think of the model aircraft in his bedroom.

He says, "When I graduated two years ago, I decided to enlist in the Air Self-Defense Force."

My face screws up. "Then how'd you wind up here?"

His steps slow a bit. "There was always an unspoken expectation that I would return one day and follow in my father's footsteps as an imperial guard. My mother grew ill, forcing my father into early retirement. I did my duty."

"That seems unfair."

He huffs out a breath. "It feels unfair. But my parents were older when they had me. You know, the last remnants of a postwar generation, brought up to value sacrifice, discipline, and duty."

"Whoa. Gimu. Peak Japanese." Japanese language is subtly nuanced. There is a myriad of words to describe duty, and among them is the gimu—a lifelong obligation to family or country.

"Yes. Gimu," Akio agrees resignedly. "My father is complicated but a good man. He loves my mother, though he shows it in strange ways. The other day I heard him demand she not die without him. We Kobayashis are anything but autocratic." He scratches his head. "His dreams are ending while mine should be beginning."

A bridge arches overhead. I cross my arms. "I used to think the world belonged to me. But I was wrong. I belong to the world. And sometimes . . . I guess sometimes, our choices have to reflect that."

"Exactly." Akio gives a pained sigh.

We're on the bridge now, our steps echoing on the wide, wooden plank deck. Akio falls behind me and I drift to the edge, to the rail where the end posts are capped with upside-down bell-shaped finials. Below, the water lapses against the pebbled shore. Even in the dark, it's a breathtaking sight. I turn to Akio and can't help but smile. I'm still all keyed-up. He stands in the middle of the bridge, watching me. The hard line of his jaw shifts. "Izumi, come here," he says.

I do as I'm summoned. Once in front of him, I tip my chin up. "Yes."

"You know of gimu. But have you studied ninjō?"

It's hard to think the way he's looking at me. I rack my brain. "Ninjō?"

"Ninjō is human emotion, and often conflicts with gimu. A classic example is a samurai who falls for a shogun's daughter. Bound by duty, he cannot act on his feelings."

"Or an imperial guard who wishes to change careers but cannot out of familial obligation?" I say.

He nods and shuffles closer to me. "I have a proposition for you."

"You do?"

"What would you say if I asked you to be Izumi? I'd be Akio. No titles. No duties." He pauses. The muscles in his throat work. "What if we gave in to our ninjō?"

"I'd say it's practically our duty as Japanese citizens."

He cocks his head. "Just tonight?"

"Just tonight," I whisper.

"All right, then." He holds out a hand for me.

I close my fingers around his. I am breathless. The night seems blissfully endless. He uses our joined hands to pull me closer. I can feel the heat radiating from his chest.

Ever so slowly, he brings his lips to the shell of my ear. "I like you in my sweatshirt."

"Oh?"

His hands come to my hips and slide up.

"That's good, because I plan on keeping it," I croak, my throat in danger of closing. Air. I need air. His fingers trace the outside of the sweatshirt, over my collarbones.

"I can't believe I ever thought you were silly." His thumbs caress my cheeks. "I was such a fool, I couldn't see how wonderful you are."

I finger the buttons on his fine shirt. I need to get something off my chest. "While we're on the subject of past grievances, I think I ought to inform you that when I first arrived I took your headshot out of the dossier and blacked out some of your teeth."

He chuckles but stays close, the warmth of his touch bleeding through the fabric of my clothes. We sway back and forth, dancing to the tune of the tinkling water. "Did you?"

I wince. Hide my face in his chest. "That's not all. I also drew on a pair of penis earrings. They were really charming, actually. Dainty and classy. Not overdone at all."

He nods sagely. "That's good to know. Anything bigger would have been much too gaudy."

My mouth twitches. I look up. "I'm very sorry."

After a blistering moment of silence, he asks, "Anything else?" His eyes glitter, feverish and bright.

I shake my head. "No. I don't think so."

He cups my cheek. "Good. Because I'm going to kiss you now."

Akio is a man of his word. Slowly, softly, sweetly, he presses his lips to the corner of my mouth, then the other corner. He pulls back, smiles, and lets out a breath. My heart swan dives with disappointment. "Is that all—"

He swoops down. I tighten my hold on him, understanding the term *swept away*. Our noses bump. Our mouths connect. I feel his stubble, the flutter of his lashes against my skin. There's a sort of push and pull to it. He exhales, and I inhale.

The noises fade into silence. It's just us. Izumi. Akio. One perfect evening.

23

Yoshi stays a few more days. We pal around the city, taking in the local sites, wandering narrow streets lined by small shops capped with ceramic tile roofs. Two nights in a row, we dine at McDonalds, ordering shrimp burgers, chicken sandwiches, sweet corn, and shaka-chicki—fried chicken in a paper bag with a choice of seasonings. The fun is over after forty hours.

We return to Tokyo together. The train ride is eventful. Midway through, Yoshi's ferret escapes the crate and causes a stir. I don't enjoy watching the imperial guards chase the thing through cars. *Much.*

"I'm going to make a fur coat out of that rodent," Reina threatens, resuming her seat. Sweat dots her forehead, and there are little pieces of white fur all over her black suit. An imperial guard has the ferret by two hands and is wrestling it back into its monogrammed leather carrier.

Yoshi pouts. "I can't believe you'd do such a thing to our love child."

Reina doesn't reply, but her narrow-eyed gaze totally speaks volumes. *I seriously hope you die.*

I rise from the plush velvet purple seat, pluck a can of Pocari Sweat from the bar, and seek out Akio in between the cars.

"Your Highness." He bows. I like how his voice has changed with me. It's lower. Softer. Warmer. He's back in his suit, buttoned up and perfect. But now, I know what that starched collar feels like crushed under my fingertips.

I crack the can open and offer it to him. "Pretty sure Reina has reached her limit with Yoshi." He takes the can from me. Our hands brush and we hold still. One. Two. Three seconds. We break apart.

"Gimu," I say forlornly, bringing us both back to earth. Not here. Not now. Maybe never again.

"Right. Gimu." He clears his throat.

I turn and head back for the carriage. "Izumi." I pause. Don't turn. But I'm all lit up inside remembering our searing kiss. A piece of paper is pressed into my palm. I wrap my fist around it.

Back in the carriage, I find a seat in the corner and curl up, my back to the car. Very carefully, I unwrap it. It's five lines. Thirty-one syllables. A waka, a poem, from Akio.

The earth forgets but
I will always remember
Karaoke bars
Pharmacies and cups of tea
And plates of dorayaki

When we arrive at the station, Yoshi and I are whisked away in separate directions.

I'm headed to the Imperial Palace. The streets are dressed up in red banners and golden chrysanthemums, preparations for the emperor's birthday. There's a definite buzz in the air, all meant to induce happy chemicals, all meant to lead one to believe the world is a marvelous place. Still, my stomach rolls, nervous. Kyoto seemed easy in comparison to Tokyo, especially given that I still haven't really spoken to my father, who has since returned. We've texted, but I've kept my responses to vague, generic answers. I'm not angry anymore, but some things are better said in person. Or maybe I was just avoiding the confrontation. . . . Yeah, that's more likely. Totally on-brand. On the seat next to me is a rolled scroll tied with a red rope, a gift for him.

Mariko notes my mood and keeps quiet. Smart woman. We arrive at the palace, Akio opens the car but I stall, smoothing my navy dress and fiddling with the hem of my skirt. I take long enough that my father comes searching for me. He stands on the porch and waits.

"He'll like your gift," Mariko says.

"Yeah," I say, reminding myself that my world doesn't stop or start with my father's approval.

"So . . . I'm getting out of the car now. Okay?" Mariko says slowly. "Remember, we have a dress fitting for the emperor's birthday. Eleven o'clock sharp." She's out, bowing to my father as she passes him.

I count to five and climb out after her. Scroll in one hand, I half raise my other hand in greeting. "Hi." Akio is behind me. His little poem is stuffed into my dress pocket, a reminder that is here with me, always.

"Izumi. Hi," my father says back. We stare at each other in much the same fashion as our first meeting.

"How was your trip?" I ask, walking toward him. The car door slams shut. I don't have to look to know Akio isn't there anymore. Feet shuffle, luggage is unloaded, and the imperial vehicle departs.

"Good," he says. "How was your trip?"

"Good," I say, squinting against the bright morning sunlight.

"What's that?" He motions to the scroll.

"Oh." My hand tightens a bit around the scroll. "Um. It's actually a present for you."

"You brought me back a gift?" He blinks at me.

"Well, yeah. It's not a big deal. Just something I made." I remember the antique chaise in the family room from the French ambassador. The Patek Philippe watch on his wrist from the emperor. The stall of half a dozen Arabian horses from the Sultan of Brunei.

He rocks back on his heels, expression considerably warming. "I have a present for you, too."

"For me?" I ask.

He hums. "It's in my office. What do you say we go inside?"

A butler opens the door. The smell of the East Palace is familiar—light and fresh, with a touch of citrus. It's nice to be back. My father's office is the same, save for a new addition. I gaze at the orchid sitting on his windowsill. It's wrapped in bamboo and tied with a purple tassel. Its yellow and green leaves are long and narrow, striped like a tiger's tail. The blooms are tiny, white, and fragrant.

"Fūkiran," my father says. "Grown since the Edo Period and collected by feudal lords as gifts to the shogun or emperor." He slides the office doors closed.

"I know." I smile because it's familiar. My mother has a woodblock of it above her nightstand. *Neofinetia falcata*. "It's Mom's favorite."

"Yes." My head shoots up. My father's smile is a bit shy, guarded. "I grow them for her."

I play it cool, scroll in my hand forgotten. "Do you?" I knew it. I *KNEW IT.*

He steps forward and fingers the tassel. "You knew the moment you saw the greenhouse." He shrugs, and his face grows contemplative. "I guess I thought I could keep a part of her. It worked for a while. The memories were enough. But having you here it makes me think it might not be. I don't have to keep that part of myself separate. That's why I had the gardener place an orchid in here. I'd like to be the man I once was and the man I am now. Do you think that's possible? Fuse the two together?"

My throat feels dry. "I think anything is possible."

He nods, frowns at the floor. "I'm glad you're back. I don't like how we left things. About the wedding, my reaction . . . I'm sorry. I was angry—"

"You don't have to explain. I get it." No need to relive the embarrassment, how I risked a tabloid scandal, how I humiliated him. I want him to be proud of me, this person he made. Show him I can do it: be a princess, a part of Japan, and his daughter.

"You do?" Relief floods his features.

I make a noise of agreement. "At first, I thought Kyoto was a punishment."

"What? No—"

"But then, I viewed it as an opportunity. You were right," I add brightly. "It's like the time I swallowed a magnet when I was four and mom took me to the emergency room. I cried and cried because she was mad and I was in trouble. But the doctor taught me all sorts of stuff about north and south poles. I ended up actually learning a lot that day. Kyoto was kind of the same. Does that make sense?"

"Perfect sense." He grins. "I do apologize. To be clear, Kyoto was not a punishment. I love it there. It's one of my favorite places. I genuinely thought you would enjoy it."

I'm suddenly touched. "It's really okay," I say. "Let's just move on."

"I'd like that," he says. As far as I'm concerned, the slate is wiped clean. Everything is fine. And it will stay fine as long as I don't mess up again.

My father opens his hands. "So . . . gifts? Should we exchange them?"

I gulp. Stare down at the scroll. "Sure."

We settle into our respective seats: him behind the desk, me across in an upholstered chair. I cross my legs at the ankles and hand over the scroll. "Like I said, it's nothing big. I've just been practicing my kanji." He handles it like a piece of glass, carefully unfurling it to reveal his name. "You don't have to do anything with it . . ."

"It is lovely." His eyes rise to mine. They're misty and genuine. "It's the best gift I've ever received. I'm going to have it framed and put it on my office wall there"—he motions to the back wall—"so I can see it every day."

I'm not crying. You're crying.

"Thank you," he says. He admires the scroll for a while. Then he retrieves a manila envelope from the corner of the desk. He hands it to me. "For you."

I hold it for a moment. It's thick and weighty. "Should I open it?"

"Please."

I bite my lower lip and slip the contents out. Black-and-white photos flutter from the pages. "Tanaka family history . . ." I read out loud.

"Before you left for Kyoto, I asked why you came to Japan. Do you remember your answer?"

"To find myself," I whisper.

"My side of the family is an open book, literally. The imperial family has been cataloged for generations. But your mother's . . . Well, I had a professor at University of Tokyo dig into her family genealogy."

I scan the pages. There's so much history. Names and dates going back a hundred or so years. It's hard to fathom. I have a kamon, a family crest, on my mother's side, a three-leafed holly. I trace the image with my fingers.

"Your grandmother was a picture bride." My father stands, coming around the desk. He finds a photograph on the floor and hands it to me. It's a woman in kimono standing next to a man in a tweed suit. I see my mother in both of them. "Seems your maternal grandmother chose life in the United States over an arranged marriage in Japan, although picture brides were an arranged marriage of sorts. I suppose she was keen on choosing her own destiny."

"Maybe she wanted adventure." I stare at the photo, then at all the papers, all the photos. All too much to possibly go through right now. I itch to start sifting through it. "This is . . . this is the best gift anyone has ever given me."

"Now you know where you come from."

"Thank you." I'm overwhelmed. Elated. I'm not lost anymore.

The clock chimes. The hour strikes eleven. Mariko or some chamberlain will knock soon. Our time is not our own. My father knows it, too. I rise from my seat. He walks me to the door, but stops before sliding it open.

I think he might hug me. But his arms hang loosely at his sides, hands curled into his palms. Yoshi said affection isn't really a thing in Japan. So I hold back, stand by. "It's good to have you home," my father finally says.

I couldn't agree with him more. My face fixes into a smile. I hug the papers to my chest. "It's good to be home."

After dinner, I find Akio outside. The sun is setting, and everything is cast in burnt oranges and blazing reds. Other guards mill around, and my father is in his office. If he glances out his window, he might see me. Better be quick.

I step carefully to him, note in hand, heart beating against my rib cage like a panicked bird. "Akio," I call out, and he turns.

"I think you dropped this earlier." My hand stretches out and he plucks the folded note from me.

At first, he frowns. But then he smiles, understanding. He inclines his head. My stomach tumbles. "Thank you, Your Highness."

I skip away toward the front door and turn at the last minute, in time to see Akio unfold the note and smile so fully it takes over his entire face.

Now I understand
How lonely the sun must be

The unending job
To rise again and again
Setting fire to all it sees

24

A few days later, I'm on my way to an official appearance at a nearby hospital. We sit in the car, Mariko rattling off instructions and bits of information. "Princesses Akiko and Noriko will be there," she says.

Tokyo whips by. Since it's an official imperial visit, the stoplights have been programmed. No red lights. No breaks for me. I can't seem to catch my breath. It doesn't help to know my cousins will be present. Every story needs a villain. I just wish mine didn't come in double.

"Their mother was supposed to attend. She's an honorary member of the board. But she is . . . indisposed," Mariko says carefully.

No need to say more. Princess Midori has been bludgeoned in the press. Once a famous soap opera actress, she struggles now with her role as princess—the expectations are too much. The Imperial Household Agency calls it an "adjustment disorder."

"Ah, sō desu ka," I say. *Yes, I see.*

Mariko calms a little at my use of Japanese. "Your accent is improving."

"Arigatō," I reply.

It only takes a second or two for her to wind back up again. "You'll cut the ribbon with the twins, then tour the new maternity ward while handing out blankets to the new mothers and babies. Remember to keep your hands still. No picking at your nails." Mariko nibbles on her lip. "I confirmed the color of the ribbon, white. The carpet will be blue. Nothing should clash with your outfit." I'm wearing an orange dress and cream pillbox hat. "Perhaps we should practice waving again?"

This conversation is doing my head in. "Mariko." I frown at her.

Her frown equals mine. "Izumi-sama."

"Relax."

She doesn't exactly do my bidding, but she does settle somewhat, long enough for me to enjoy the rest of the three-minute ride. I focus on Akio in the front. A night ago, I found a folded airplane on my pillow, a note on the wing.

> Staring at the clouds
> I find it impossible
> To walk, to run . . . to stay
> How to remain grounded when
> I am always filled with sky?

I'd replied yesterday, tying my poem to a little piece of cake and handing it off under the guise of the chef wanting Akio's opinion on a new dessert recipe.

> Born a foreigner
> I carry two halves with me
> Loose skins I pull on
> To go places and don't fit
> Like apple pie and mochi

Too soon, my musings are cut short. I'm out of the car, being escorted through the back entrance into the hospital. Dozens of royal handlers surround me—a mass of men in black and navy.

The ribbon cutting goes off without a hitch. Cameras flash. It's the whole shebang—the imperial press club, mainstream press, and hospital publicists. I smile robotically, keeping my distance from the Shining Twins. Noriko whispers out of the side of her mouth, "Cousin, your dress is so bright. Good for you. I could never pull that off." Akiko follows up with, "I love how you can just wear *anything*."

Quickly afterward, we're ushered into the new ward. Already, there are a few patients, though I suspect they've been planted there. The new mothers and babies look way too good—combed hair, cashmere robes, pink-cheeked babies swaddled tightly. Hansani has a little sister. A bonus baby, her parents call it. The months after her delivery, Hansani's mom described herself as feeling like warm garbage. She admitted more than a dozen times to forgetting to put on underwear. Also, she pees when she laughs. I didn't want to know that, but there you go. I cross my legs whenever I see her.

Curtains separate the beds. For each mom, there is a tiny, pinkish creature in what looks like a clear Tupperware bin on a rolling rack. I don't know. I'm sure there's a medical term for the cradles housing the tiny humans. The Shining Twins are ahead of me, distributing bears with overlarge eyes. I'm on blanket duty, handmade and crocheted by the empress and her lady-in-waiting coven. A photographer, Mariko, Mr. Fuchigami, and Akio trail me.

I stop and chat with a woman who looks slightly older than me. She gave birth two days ago and isn't quite up and around. She knows a bit of English. I know a bit of Japanese. We meet somewhere in the middle. She wants to know what it's like to be a princess. I dress it up a little, but keep it politically correct. I speak about my love for Japan. Her baby sleeps soundly nearby. I'm about to gush all over the infant when a shout splits the air.

A baby in the next curtain over wakes and cries. Then, another baby wakes. Soon, they're all keening. Then, a clatter echoes. Gunshot? I don't know. Everyone scrambles. Chaos ensues.

Without thinking, I throw myself over the baby in the Tupperware bin. My nostrils fill with the scent of baby powder. My heart beats like a hammer inside my chest. I squeeze my eyes shut and wait. A body covers me. Hands curl over mine. "Stay down." It's Akio.

Seconds tick by. The silence is loaded. Slowly, I raise my head. One by one, people wake from their stupors. A camera flashes. Not a good time for pictures.

"I said stay down," Akio hisses. His words skirt against my neck. I'm all too aware of how he's pressed against me.

"I think we've established I don't follow directions well," I whisper. Akio's hold tightens and I am contained. I manage to turn my head, though. All at once, I see it. Another imperial guard has someone on the ground, knee in his back, one hand like a pair of cuffs around his wrists. It's one of the new fathers. I recognize him from two curtains ago. His eyes were red-rimmed with lack of sleep. Behind him is an overturned cart of blankets. The Shining Twins make a sound. They're farthest away from the cart, shielded behind two imperial guards.

Mr. Fuchigami holds up his hands and speaks. I don't catch everything, but I do hear the word *jiko*—an accident. The new, sleep-deprived dad must have knocked over the cart.

At this, Akio slowly releases me. He exhales tightly. Another picture is snapped. The room comes back to life. The new mother beside me bursts into tears. Hormones plus near-death experience equals not a great combination. I reach out and squeeze her shoulder. Between the sobs and hiccups, I can't make out a word. She is mixing Japanese and English. Finally, she settles on her first language.

I cast a glance at Akio. He's closest to me. My hands are shaking, but he's steady. "What is she saying?" I ask.

Akio listens for a moment. She's repeating the same thing. "She's thanking you. You went to save her son before yourself." His voice drops and he says quietly to me, "You shouldn't have done that."

"Of course I should've," I volley back.

He stands there and exhales slowly. The tension eases from his body. "You're right," he says voice measured, deliberate, *soft*. There's a glint in his eyes, unguarded and affectionate. "My mistake. I won't forget again. You lead with your heart."

That evening, Mariko knocks on my door, a secretive smile on her face. She's hiding something behind her back. "May I come in?"

I eye her warily. Wish I had x-ray vision. What's behind her back? Another schedule? More gloves to fit? "I'm super tired."

"This will only take a moment. I promise." She drops her voice to a highly persuasive purr.

After a moment, I ease the door open and she ducks in. The door slides closed with a *click*. Mariko walks the perimeter of the room, positioning herself in a way that I can't see what she is holding. "Papers don't come out tomorrow, but there's been quite a bit of chatter online about your hospital visit."

My stomach churns. "Do I need to sit down for this?" My father's disappointment after the wedding comes back to me.

"Maybe."

"Mariko." My voice carries a warning tone.

"Fine," she says and whips a piece of paper from behind her back. She hands it to me. It's a printed news article from *The Tokyo Tattler*. "I sneaked it in."

There's a picture of me cutting the ribbon, then another of me thrown over the newborn bassinet, Akio against my back. Still can't tell if it's good or bad. Based on Mariko's enthusiasm, it's probably okay. "This will take me a bit to translate."

Mariko makes an exasperated sound. "I'll read it to you." She plucks the paper from my hands. "Her Imperial Highness Princess Izumi attended the Tokyo Metropolitan Children's Medical Center's new maternity ward today. It hallmarked the princess's first event since returning from holiday in Kyoto." She goes on, breathless. "Joined by Their

Imperial Highnesses Princesses Akiko and Noriko, the new princess cut the ribbon on behalf of the imperial family. She sported a lovely orange A-line dress." Mariko grins at me, proud of her outfit choice. She focuses back on the article. "A bit of excitement happened during the tour of the maternity ward. While handing out teddy bears and blankets, a new sleep-deprived father tripped over a cart and sent it clattering. 'I thought it was gunfire! It was very scary,' Sadako Oyami, our own *Tokyo Tattler* reporter on the scene, said. 'Everyone ducked for cover,' she explains. Everyone except for the HIH Princess Izumi, who threw herself over a newborn baby, protecting him." Mariko waits a beat. Beams at me.

I do need to sit now. I stumble back until I find the edge of the bed and slump down.

She clears her throat, continuing. "Careless of her own life, the princess sought to protect the precious new life first. This is in contrast to her cousins, Princesses Akiko and Noriko, who shoved their imperial guards in front of them." Mariko stops and takes one overexcited breath. Her cheeks are flushed. She is dreamy-eyed. This is what gets her excited. Good to know. "They compare you to the empress after the 1923 earthquake!" The empress rolled up her sleeves and laid bricks for a new school. She refused to leave until the town was fed, the children safe. There is a famous picture of her hugging a mother who lost her son, both of their cheeks coated in dust. "They end with calling you our very own royal."

Words fail me. Mariko seems to know I need a private moment. She places the article in my lap, then glides out the door. When she's gone, I pick it up. I rub my thumb over the last sentence of the article. It's not the royal part that warms me. No, it's the other two words. *Very own*, it says. *Very own*. Yes. That's me. A true daughter of Japan.

25

Once upon a time, shoguns ruled Japan. A rigid hierarchical society was established, lasting for two and a half centuries. Tokugawa, the last shogun, fell in 1868, when two powerful clans (whose names I don't remember) joined forces and seized control. They placed the emperor back in power and threw open the borders. It was the end of feudalism. The class system was abolished. Modern Japan emerged. The country transformed into a world power.

I'm standing in the new imperial palace built on top of Edo Castle, the former seat of the Tokugawa shogunate. In fact, the buildings have been burned and rebuilt a few times. Under my feet, there have been births, deaths, and coronations. Wars have been waged, lost, and won. All of it happened inside this whirlpool design of a citadel.

"Maybe one by the windows?" the imperial photographer asks me, voice echoing. The room we're in is usually reserved for state dinners, but today it is vast and empty.

I adjust the hemline of my Hanae Mori gown—cherry blossom pink with a floral motif and chiffon sleeves—and step to the bank of floor-to-ceiling windows, into the sunlight. I stare out the window while the photographer captures my profile. Crowds are already gathering outside. They've come to celebrate the emperor's birthday, a national holiday. Businesses are closed. The palace grounds are open to the public.

Snap. Flash. "Thank you, Your Highness. I'll confer with Mr. Fuchigami, but I believe I have everything I need."

I incline my head to the photographer. One of these pictures will become my royal photograph. Whenever I see it, I will always remember how it was taken a few minutes before I met my grandparents. I've officially arrived. My father is with the emperor and empress already. Now, I wait in the antechamber for him to fetch me. The photographer leaves. Akio enters.

He checks his watch. "A few more minutes." Before I meet my grandparents, he means.

I worry my lip. "I didn't think I'd be this nervous. Do I look okay?" I ask. "Nothing embarrassing like toilet paper on my shoe or food in my teeth?" I flash him my pearly whites. Please don't let there be anything in my teeth.

His eyes rake over me, head to toe. "You look . . ." Beautiful? Lovely? "Fine."

I laugh. He never fails to surprise me. "Wow. I can't believe I ever thought you lacked charm. I'll take fine, though. I just want to fit in."

The corner of his mouth tips up. "Maybe you're not meant to fit in. Maybe you're meant to stand out." My heart beats heavy and fast. He bows. "You're beautiful, Your Highness." He looks down, hesitates. "I probably shouldn't have said that."

"No, probably not," I say. "But just to clarify, beautiful like a unicorn bathed in glitter?"

"No." My face falls at his emphatic response. "I'd never say something like that."

"No, of course not."

He closes the distance between us. We're a foot apart. Akio's voice is low, husky, and filled with sweet longing as he says, "If I could speak freely, I might say you remind me of Kannon, the goddess of mercy, with dark hair that absorbs the light. A face so lovely it blinded men . . . and yet, so far from a mere mortal's reach." With a single finger, he traces my hairline, leaving sparks in its wake.

"Well that's better, I guess."

He withdraws. His smile is wry. "I guess."

My breath hitches. I'm struggling to form the words to tell him that when we're together, it's as if we're standing at the bow of a ship, like I can feel the spray of the tide and the wind in my hair. "Akio, I—"

"We need to talk," he says at the same time.

His words slash through my haze. "Sounds serious." My lighthearted tone is not convincing. Suddenly, it's as if I've swallowed a nest of bees. My insides hum with apprehension.

Akio's brows dart in. "No, it's not like that. It is serious, but it's good. At least I think it's good."

"Please," I say. "You can tell me anything."

The doors open. It's Mr. Fuchigami. "Your Highness."

The timing is poor, but inevitable.

"I'll find you sometime during the luncheon," I say lowly.

Akio nods, imperial guard mask back firmly in place. I've left my gloves on a window ledge. I retrieve them and head toward Mr. Fuchigami. Akio has moved to the door as well. As I pass him, he lifts a single finger and it brushes along my wrist. It gives me courage. My steps are more surefooted. It's amazing how life-sustaining a single touch can be.

*

My father waits in the hall. He smiles gently, and we begin walking down the red carpet, me following just a step behind. The hallway is lined with evenly spaced bamboo lanterns and I count them as we move.

When we reach a set of doors, he stops. "Don't be intimidated. Just remember, they watch soap operas and sumo wrestling in the evenings," he whispers with a wink. "We'll talk for a while. Then, I'll accompany my parents to the balcony. You may watch in the wings, if you'd like. I did so as a little boy." Only imperials that have come of age can stand on the balcony and greet Japan. It's tradition.

I relax a smidgen. Smile. Talk about a brave face. My father nods to two white-gloved attendants. Doors slide open, folding in like neat origami. I understand now. These pocket doors are part of the Japanese way. We are all just a bigger part of the whole.

He'll enter first. Imperial protocol. I'll follow behind. This, I do alone, without Mariko, Mr. Fuchigami, or Akio at my back. I square my shoulders. Take a few easy breaths. Remind myself pressure is okay. It's how diamonds are made.

The Audience Room is vast. Various representatives are present, including the Grand Chamberlain, Mr. Fuchigami's boss's boss. There is a stillness, a silence like that of a temple. But it's not cold. The room is made entirely of cypress. The walls are papered in fabric with bamboo patterns. It's warm, inviting. In the center, the empress and emperor sit in upholstered silk chairs, a table and tea set between them. Simple. Domestic.

I approach and go into some sort of trance where I bow and deliver the correct honorifics. When finished, I stand vision downcast and wait. From the corner of my eye, I see my father. He's standing, too. Nothing seems to move for a while. Not even time.

"Please," the empress speaks. Her voice is warm and dry. "Sit."

Chairs are produced. My father and I sink into them. I place my gloves in my lap, fold my hands on top of them, and keep my gaze trained there. An attendant pours tea, setting the cup and saucer on the table in front of me. My hands are shaky as I pick them up.

"Izumi-chan," the empress says.

Her use of the affectionate honorific surprises me. My eyes dart up then back down, embarrassed. But in that one moment, I am able to fully see her. Her character shows through her features: An oval face with a small nose and kind eyes. Wrinkled skin the color of parchment paper. Hair glowing gray, parted down the middle and pulled back into a neat twist. She is wearing a kimono of brown silk with gold and silver bars. She is full of grace. "Your father speaks very highly of you."

Another glance up. This time, my gaze bounces between the empress and emperor. There's an unimpeachable aura about the two. My grandfather is small, approaching his ninth decade. A pair of round spectacles is perched on his nose, and dark circles hang below his eyes—he hasn't fully recovered from his fatigue. His suit is slightly ill fitting. It's as if he's shrinking in time. His court name is Takehito. The -hito at the end signals the highest level of virtue. "Sono yō na shōsan ni atai shimasen," I say, deflecting the compliment.

"Mr. Fuchigami reports your studies are going well," the empress says, eyes gleaming. With a dainty, speckled hand, she picks up the teacup and takes a slow sip.

"I still have much to learn," I reply serenely.

The empress presses her lips together. "Yes," she says, placing the teacup down with a distinct click. "You haven't chosen a hobby."

"I haven't, but I do enjoy botany." Whew. Way to think on your feet, Izumi.

She tilts her head. "That would be acceptable. Your father has a fondness for orchids." Could she know my father's affinity for orchids is in direct correlation with his affinity for my mother? "Much too finicky for me. I prefer azaleas. When I was a little girl, I used to drink the nectar from the flowers."

I brighten a little. "I did that, too." Mom had azalea plants all over our property. She taught me how to pull the blossom from the stem and slurp from the tip of the flower like her mother had shown her. I always thought it was something unique to us, to our family. But maybe it was more. A connection to Japan, an invisible tether. "Is there a variety you prefer? I quite enjoy the omurasaki."

I've caught her attention. "It is a lovely bloom," she says. "Your mother is a botanist?"

"She teaches biology at the collegiate level and botany is a passion of hers, yes."

She eyes me shrewdly.

The emperor taps his fingers against the armrest of his chair. "It would be better if your parents were married."

My insides turn to dust.

"Please don't," my father says to *his* father.

My grandfather waves his hand like the emperor he is. "Fifteen hundred years of monarchy and we've never had a child born out of wedlock."

"That's not true." My father is flushed. "Or are you forgetting the former concubine quarters, now horse stalls?"

The emperor raises his bushy eyebrows. "You should marry her mother. Have more children. A boy."

In Japan, only males may inherit the throne. It goes against my grain. I've had heated discussions with Mr. Fuchigami about this. Japan had female empresses up until the eighteenth century. Then in the nineteenth century, the Meiji Constitution blocked female heirs.

My father says, "It might be time the laws are changed."

My heart stalls. Most women born into the imperial family marry commoners, like my cousin Sachiko. She's engaged to the heir of a rice empire. When they wed, Sachiko will officially leave the imperial family. She'll lose her title. It seems I'll follow the same path someday, *way* into the future. But my father is suggesting that I might become empress. Whoa, that's a can of worms I'm not ready to open now.

"Izumi-chan," the empress says, "What are your thoughts on this?"

Think about what you would normally say, then do the opposite was Mariko's last bit of parting advice to me. But I owe it to myself and to all women to say something about gender biases. Actually, I have quite a few thoughts. I am my mother's daughter, after all.

Carefully, I set my teacup down to consider the most diplomatic response. "The Imperial Household Law stipulates that only men whose fathers are emperors may inherit the throne. However, some scholars may argue that such law violates the principle that men and women be treated equally as set forth in Article 14 of the constitution."

"You've studied the constitution?" The emperor eyes me keenly.

"Yes," I say evenly. Thank you, Mariko and Mr. Fuchigami. "Historically, there has been precedence for females to reign." I list off the eight empresses, speaking in my own self-interest. Might as well. Men have been doing it for years. "We might even argue the goddess Amaterasu was the first to rule," I say lightly.

My father smiles behind his hand.

The empress takes a sip of tea. "I am inclined to agree with you."

"What of tradition?" the emperor asks. "Three generations have passed since the Meiji charter took effect." There is no heat in his statement. It's as if he's enjoying a lively debate.

My father chimes in. "Traditions are important. But I believe they can unite as easily as they divide. You and mother have broken several traditions over the years. Raising your children in your own home . . ."

I nod, knowing what he's referring to. Mariko showed me news clippings. The emperor had been raised away from his parents, and the nation was shocked when he didn't follow in their footsteps. Too modern, they said. The end of the monarchy. I send my father a silent thanks.

The empress says softly, "A new tradition was born after that."

My grandfather pats his knee. "Whatever the answer, it is

not up to us to decide. The people will."

We all agree to that. Bigger things are at play here, and it isn't a decision one person will make. That's a part of being in an institution. I am my father's daughter, too. We all have our place.

It doesn't mean the story can't change. It just affects how it will.

Besides, I don't even know if I want to be empress. Being a princess is hard enough. Doesn't mean I wouldn't like to have the choice, though. That's what this is about. Choices.

The emperor stands, followed by the empress. The room springs to life. Chamberlains and attendants close in. My father rises from his chair. I stand too, keeping my gloves tucked in my hand.

The empress approaches me. "You will do well here," she says.

I feel like it's my obligation to be honest. I discard Mariko's advice. "My time here has not been without a few hiccups, Your Majesty."

"No. You will do well. Not only do I predict it, I deem it so."

Well, hard to argue with that. She leaves, trailing behind the emperor.

My father leans down and whispers, "You survived."

It's over. I breathe deeply, and it's like the first inhale after you dive to the bottom of the pool and swim frantically to the surface.

My father begins to walk. I stay behind, planning to follow in a minute and take my place in the rafters. But then, a murmur runs through the crowd. The empress has stopped at the door. She speaks earnestly to the emperor and he agrees with a solid nod. Hearing them, my father returns to my side. "Their Majesties request their entire family be present on the balcony." His smile is wide, proud, and contagious. "A new tradition."

My hands flutter at my sides. My heart lodges in my throat. Words are impossible.

The hall is lined with various officials, men in suits, guards in full regalia, and the rest of the imperial family. It's a commotion as they're informed of the new plan: all of the family will join on the balcony. The emperor and empress lead. My father and I fall in line behind them. Then my Uncle Nobuhito and his daughters, the Shining Twins. His wife, their mother, is absent. No one remarks on it. Then come Uncle Yasuhito and Auntie Asako, followed by their children: Sachiko, Masahito, and Yoshi, who winks at me. The imperial procession carries on.

A set of double doors are opened by imperial guards in dashing green uniforms, red ropes around their shoulders. They salute. Forty-five thousand people have gathered outside to wish the emperor well.

The emperor goes first, then the empress. We all take our places beside them: My father to his immediate left. Me next to him. All others on the empress's side. We're behind bullet-proof glass, but it does little to hinder the noise. It is deafening, alive, and charged. Thousands of Hinomaru flags wave in the air. The emperor speaks into two microphones. He gives a speech, thanking the people for coming to wish him well on his birthday. In turn, he wishes them health and happiness. This delights the spectators. He steps back and waves.

The crowd chants Tennō Heika. *Heavenly sovereign.* They

grow louder still, clapping, shouting, merrymaking. I wave along with my relatives. Together. As one. Joy bubbles in my chest. Pride, too. This is destiny. It cannot be any clearer. I am meant to be here. This is where I belong.

26

A celebratory luncheon is served in the banquet hall. I sit with my cousins minus the Shining Twins, whose seats are empty. Tables are draped in swaths of white linen and set with crystal and china. Low flower arrangements display golden chrysanthemums. Chandeliers cast a warm glow, and chilled, chrysanthemum-soaked sake is served. Toasts for longevity are made. The emperor sits at the head of the table, my father next to him. The prime minister is present as well; upon entering, I inclined my head to him, and he bowed. All is well. The mood is jolly.

"All I'm saying is"—Yoshi uses his fork to push a bit of pork with brown sauce around his plate—"you should consider releasing bald eagles instead of doves at your wedding. You know, as an homage to our fair American cousin here." My laugh spurs Yoshi on. "We'd have to have them imported from the States, but that shouldn't be a problem."

"I am one hundred percent sure Fish and Wildlife Services would not go for that," I pipe in.

"Chickens then, maybe? Wasn't that supposed to be the national bird?" Yoshi asks.

Masahito sighs, slumps back in his chair, and throws his napkin on top of his plate. "Turkey. The national bird for the United States was supposed to be the turkey."

"Well, that shouldn't be a problem," says Yoshi. "Turkey it

is. They don't fly and aren't nearly as magnificent, but I guess in a pinch, they'll do."

Sachiko rolls her eyes. "I'm not releasing doves, eagles, *or* turkeys at my wedding."

"Yes," Ryu chirps. "Save the idea for your own wedding, Yoshi. Whoever the very unfortunate girl may be."

Yoshi pouts and frowns at the same time. "Don't blame me when the wedding is a bore. You could've had turkeys."

I wipe the corners of my mouth, take a sip of sake, and let my eyes scan the room. The wall behind the emperor is papered in silk, the print a blazing sunset. White-gloved servers line the walls alongside imperial guards. I find *him*. Our eyes connect, then dart away.

Slowly, I stand. "Excuse me."

"Can't hold her sake," Yoshi announces at my departure.

The hall is quiet, but there are a few stragglers—a dignitary speaking on the phone, a couple of chamberlains squabbling over schedules, the Shining Twins' ladies-in-waiting . . . huh. They're blocking the bathroom, as if guarding it. Curious. One holds a glass of water in her hand and opens the door. I glimpse the Shining Twins bent over a woman. Their mother. Midori. Her hands are pressed against her head. She is dressed to the nines in a silk gown, but it is clear she is unraveling. Harsh words are muttered lowly and the lady-in-waiting retreats, water untouched. My steps slow. Pause. Then I'm turning. The ladies-in-waiting stand shoulder to shoulder as if to stop me from entering. Like there's a chance of that. I look sharply at them, let the weight of my stare settle on their shoulders. They part, gazes downcast.

I step forward, open the door and make sure it's closed

before I speak. "Is everything okay?" I ask softly.

Midori moans low and averts her head. The twins' eyes narrow at me. They step in front of their mother, hiding her. I shift, trying to peer around them. "Do you need me to get someone or something? Water? A doctor?"

Noriko steps forward. Her dress is a high-necked, sky blue number. It complements the angry gold flecks in her eyes. "You will not speak of this to anyone," she says.

"Of course, I won't—"

Akiko comes to her side. She's in pastel green. Her hands curl into fists at her sides. "You don't belong here."

I back up. "I won't tell anyone."

"You even think of it and we'll ruin you," Noriko promises.

"Like I said, I won't tell anyone. But this isn't the ideal place. If you can, you should try to move her."

The twins share a look. It's Noriko who speaks. "We will decide what's best for our mother. Now please go."

I take a beat, eyes flickering to each. It's really none of my business. Time to move on. I switch on a smile. "I hope you feel better," I say, voice rising to reach their mother. They watch me as I exit.

Back in the hallway, I resume my course. I walk away from the banquet hall, deeper and deeper down the rabbit hole. I turn right. This wide hallway is nearly empty. Two imperial guards positioned under bamboo lanterns stand at attention as I pass. The red carpet hushes my footsteps as they become more hurried, more frantic to match my beating heart.

Finally, I come to a set of doors. I slide them open and close them softly behind me. It's the same room where my photograph was taken earlier. Through the windows the sun is bright and light filters in, dust particles suspended.

The doors slide open. I whip around. Akio. I knew he'd follow. For a moment, he stands quietly, watching me with a tilt of his head. The sunlight catches him, lighting up all the hard planes in his face. He is beautiful. Cut from marble and glass. "You left the banquet," is all he says.

I smile gently. "You said we needed to talk."

He trudges forward. "Right."

I tip my chin up. "So?"

Silence stretches on. He shakes his head. "I'm not sure how to begin." I stare at him, transfixed. Heart lodged in my throat and all that. He reaches out, fingers skirting down my elbow to my palm, then catching mine. "Izumi. Princess. Radish." He pulls me close. "Will you dance with me?"

"I don't know," I hesitate. My head is spinning. "Last time didn't go so well."

"Last time, I was a fool."

When the man is right, he's right. I place a hand on his shoulder. "We don't have any music." He'd said the same to me before.

At last, he smiles. "I've come prepared." He slips his phone from his pocket, scrolls through the options, and chooses a song. "The Rose" starts playing. "I couldn't find the Gay Men's Chorus version. The original Bette Midler will have to do."

"I'll get over it." My body relaxes with a sigh. All is right with the world.

He rests his chin on my head. We start to sway together. "How did things go with the emperor and empress?"

"Good, I think." I snuggle into his chest. Briefly, I fill him in on the luncheon. Yoshi's jokes. The Shining Twins in the bathroom with their mother.

"Princess Midori has not been well for some time. The press will be hard on her for missing the emperor's birthday speech."

I stop. "That's unfair."

His gaze is tender, his voice fierce. "Better her than you."

"You shouldn't say things like that," I say, though it's always nice to have someone stand up for you.

"It's true."

I pat his chest. "Just try not to repeat it."

"I'll keep my thoughts to myself."

We resume dancing. The song ends, then starts again. "You put the song on loop?"

"I learned from the best."

"I didn't think you noticed."

"Of course I did." His voice drops, sounds a bit a hoarse. "There isn't a thing I don't notice when it comes to you."

We stop again. My breaths are shallow. His heart is pounding. "Are you going to tell me what you wanted to talk about now?"

"Isn't it obvious?" His hands move up my waist, fire burning in their wake.

"I'm the kind of girl who likes things spelled out for her."

His brown eyes shine suspiciously bright. "Kyoto was the best night of my life. The thought of never having it again, the thought of never having you . . ." His grip tightens. "Radish, I'm so heartsick for you." I shudder, racked with all the feelings. These are the sweetest words I've ever heard. All I ever needed to hear. I close my eyes, open them.

"Please, say something," he begs.

I tip my chin up and smile. Everything has come together, like fingers interlacing, or a key sliding into a lock. We fit and shouldn't be apart. "I definitely think you should kiss me now."

He exhales. "Best idea I ever heard." His head lowers. His lips brush mine, tentative at first, then he presses in. I do, too. Our bodies are flush. We break apart, stare at each other wonderingly, then come back together. Lips find lips. Hands touch hands. Here, in this room, in this building, on this soil, millennia of traditions come crumbling down.

Some rules are just made to be broken.

THE TOKYO TATTLER

Breaking News!
HIH Princess Izumi caught
with imperial guard

May 15, 2021

In an exclusive story, *The Tokyo Tattler* reveals
Her Imperial Highness Princess Izumi's affair
with imperial guard Akio Kobayashi! The two
have been secretly cavorting all over Tokyo
and Kyoto. Our sources reveal sparks flew the
moment they met.

It all started with a heated discussion between
the two when HIH Princess Izumi arrived in
Japan. HIH Princess Izumi had an unscheduled
stop in the airport to use a kitchen restroom.

Busboy Denji Kanroji remembers witnessing
a tense discussion between the princess and
her guard. "It was clear they did not like each
other," Kanroji says.

So how did these enemies turn to lovers? The
turning point happened one night in Tokyo.

The princess escaped for a night on the town and got into some trouble. In pictures obtained exclusively by *The Tokyo Tattler*, we see HIH Princess Izumi being carried, obviously inebriated, by her imperial guard out of a karaoke club. The two grew even closer while in Kyoto, our palace insider says.

Then, of course, who can forget the hospital incident a week ago? Here, Kobayashi appears to be covering HIH Princess Izumi after a cart was knocked over. "He held on to her for way too long," our palace insider says. "Even after the threat had passed, he hugged her tightly."

Lastly, at the emperor's luncheon, the two were caught dancing and kissing in an empty ballroom.

Who is this imperial guard who has caught the princess's eye? His name is Akio Kobayashi, and his father is a former highly decorated imperial guard. Despite his family legacy, Akio was set to enlist in the Air Self-Defense Force. "His father was devastated when Akio chose not to follow in his footsteps," an anonymous family friend says. "It wasn't until Akio's mother grew sick and his father retired that Akio begrudgingly decided to become an imperial guard. The boy has always had his head in the clouds. Wanting to be a pilot one day, now the princess's consort!"

"He's overreached," imperial blogger Himari Watanabe says. "I feel awful for the princess. It's clear she's been taken advantage of. Kobayashi should be fired, to say the least. It's such a shame. The princess deserves better."

Others don't see things as clearly as Watanabe. "Both are to blame," a source within the Imperial Household Agency says. "The princess courted the guard's attention. She's a romantic at heart—much too American. Brash, bold, and headstrong. Both overstepped their roles."

The Imperial Household Agency declined to comment.

27

The next morning, I wake to my phone thrashing about on my nightstand. I stretch and grab it. There is a slew of text messages from Noora and the girls. The last says: *Are you okay?* An article is attached. I click it open. Headlines flash before my eyes, words burning an imprint.

HIH Princess Izumi.

Affair.

Imperial guard.

My hand flies to my mouth. It's all very tawdry. Very salacious. Akio is the villain. I am the American upstart. Even worse are the photos—from the karaoke bar, outside the restaurant in Kyoto, the hospital, and, finally, from the emperor's birthday. Those photos are fuzzy, as if taken from far away. The angle tells me they were snapped from the doorway. Someone was spying on us.

Pieces click into place. *Palace insider. You don't belong here.*

The Shining Twins.

They must have orchestrated this, and have probably had me followed this whole time. I played along, practically handing them the story that would be my own downfall.

Immediately, I think of Akio. The thought that he might be hurting is more than I can bear.

I find his phone number and ring it. Disconnected. I text. *Call me.* It bounces back undelivered. I try again. Same thing.

WTF. The sounds of voices carry through the palace. I slip on a robe and wander to the living room. Mr. Fuchigami is there along with Mariko, two other chamberlains, and a gaggle of assorted imperial staff—secretaries, publicists, and guards. No Akio. No Crown Prince.

"Hey," I say. My voice is a bit shaky. My body, too, for that matter.

The room quiets. Eyes meet mine, then flicker away. I take stock of myself. Wild hair. Bathrobe. Tears fracturing my vision. This is bad. This is Death Star–exploding, Thanos's Infinity Gauntlet bad.

"Izumi-sama." Mariko says.

I go to Mr. Fuchigami. "I can't get hold of Akio."

Mr. Fuchigami ignores the ringing phone in his hand. "Your Highness, we have much to discuss. Perhaps you should dress for the day. We will sit down and strategize."

"We'll have to deny everything," Mariko says behind me.

Mr. Fuchigami's smile is placid. "Impossible. The damage is done. We'll be playing up the *Tokyo Tattler* article. The princess was taken advantage of."

"No," I blurt out, squeeze my hands into fists. "Just . . . no. Akio. Where is he? I need to speak with him."

Mr. Fuchigami looks at me, as if he's surprised I'm still standing here. *Didn't I tell you to go?* "Mr. Kobayashi is no longer employed by the Imperial Guard. You will be assigned a new guard who understands their position."

Fired. Akio's been fired. This is my fault.

My ears are ringing. It's hard to think. I might throw up. This looks so bad. What damage have I done? God, I'm mad at myself, but not as furious as others may be with me. "Then, my father? I'd like to speak to him."

Mr. Fuchigami says, "The Crown Prince is with His Majesty the Emperor. The events from yesterday exhausted your grandfather. I'm afraid they cannot be disturbed from official imperial business. However, your father has been apprised of the events and will see you for dinner this evening."

My stomach contracts. I've never been kicked in the gut, but I'm pretty this is what it would feel like. I don't want to look at Mr. Fuchigami. *I cannot imagine the consequences in the papers. As a member of the imperial family, we're expected to be beyond reproach,* my father had said after the prime minister's wedding.

"Okay." My voice cracks. Words are hard to form. Why even bother? I pivot and force myself from the room.

Conversations start up again behind me. I don't slow down. I find one thread of hope and hang from it. In my closet, I open drawers, pull out leggings and a T-shirt, and slip them on. Mariko appears, blocking me from leaving. "Where are you going?" she asks carefully.

"I need to see Akio."

"Izumi-sama," she says, full of pity.

"Let me by." My legs feel watery. I want to collapse. Curl up in bed until it all goes away. *Get it together.*

"You can't go see him."

"Please call the driver," I say unsteadily.

Mariko says, "This isn't wise."

I swipe under my nose. Tears flow unchecked. "You don't understand. I need to see him."

Mariko places a hand on each of my shoulders and squeezes. "If you go to his parents' house, you will only make it worse. The place is surrounded by paparazzi. The best thing you can do for yourself *and* for Akio is to let this die down."

I stand, numb. Mariko makes sense. No reason to add gasoline to the fire. But I don't want him to think I've abandoned him, either. I know what to do. "Will you take him something from me then?" A letter. I'll write him a letter.

Mariko's nostrils flare. "Mr. Fuchigami is still here. He has prohibited anyone from entering or leaving the palace." She twiddles her thumbs in thought. "But I happen to know your cousin Yoshi is in residence and doesn't have such restrictions. Perhaps you'd like to take a bath? With the window open? There is a lovely breeze right now. Of course, I'll alert security to clear the area."

I want to kiss her cheeks. I find a smile instead. It's bittersweet. "A bath does sound good. Would you mind getting my running shoes and some paper? You know how I usually like to bathe with those items."

"Yes, Your Highness," Mariko says, ever so wisely. "Might I also suggest a sweatshirt with a hood? Something dark that blends well with the trees on the properties? I think I know the perfect one. Very trendy for spring and secret romps through the forest."

28

Akio,

*Please do not strike me
from your memory, from the
perfect shape of your
heart. Please let us carry on
as we were, against the world*

*I'm so sorry for everything. Meet me by the highway 40
sign at 1 p.m. just outside of the imperial property?*

Izumi

Hood pulled up, I sprint across the property. I'm winded when I reach Yoshi's home. The architecture is very similar to Tōgū palace—modern with clean lines, but a touch smaller, not nearly as grand.

A crunch of gravel behind me, the sound of a gun cocking. "Kōgūkeisatsu no meirei de, te o agete kudasai." I never considered learning Japanese might save my life. Good thing I understand enough to do as ordered. *Hands up.*

I spin, hands in the air, letter clutched between two fingers. It's Reina, and her firearm is pointed right at the center of my chest. "Your Highness." Reina reholsters her weapon and bows deeply. "Forgive me. I mistook you for one of Yoshi's fangirls."

"Issokay," I say, hands still pointed to the sky.

Reina's gaze is hard. "You can put your hands down."

I lower them slowly. "Yoshi's home?" It's more of a statement than a question; where Yoshi goes, Reina follows. My pulse is still racing. I breathe in and out, brushing off the near-death experience.

She nods to the house. "He's in there and didn't get back until three in the morning. Might not even be awake yet. He probably has a bad headache. Talk loudly if you can. In fact, ring the bell, he hates that."

Wow, Reina, tell me how you really feel. "I'm not supposed to be here," I say, eyeing the earpiece in Reina's ear.

She shrugs. "You forget I pulled a gun on you, I forget you were here."

"Deal." We bow to each other. Reina melts back into the landscape. I knock on the door, then just for Reina, I ring the bell three times in rapid succession. Wake up. Wake up. WAKE UP.

After a few minutes, Yoshi answers. His hair is disheveled, standing up at odd angles. His V-neck T-shirt is white, and his velour track pants have a sequined gold stripe running up each side. He groans, loud, long, and pained. "I told Reina no visitors," he shouts to the trees. I'm not positive, but I'm pretty sure wherever Reina is, she's holding up a middle finger. "Oh, it's you." Yoshi focuses on me, eyes concerned. "How are you, darling? Holding in there? Is that the phrase? It doesn't sound right."

I push back my hood. "You know what happened?"

He scoffs. "Media ban or not, the whole family is aware. The Imperial Household sent a memo." He smirks, leaning against the door frame. "You dirty, dirty girl. I didn't know you had a thing for your imperial guard. Now, come in and tell cousin Yoshi all the details. I'll fix you a drink. What is it Americans say? It must be five o'clock somewhere. I'm sure I got that one right."

He turns and I fist his T-shirt, pulling him back toward me. "Hands off," he says with a horrified look. "This is Dior."

I let go. "Listen, I need you to deliver something to Akio for me."

Yoshi's chin goes up. "I'm intrigued. Tell me more."

"This." I press the letter into his hands. "Please, it's important." I tell him where he lives. "I can't reach him."

"Phone was probably confiscated by the Imperial Household Agency." He turns the letter over in his hands. "What does it say? I'm not sure how wrapped up in your sex scandal I want to be."

"It's just to arrange a meeting place. I need to speak with him."

His face softens. "Izumi. What are you doing? You know nothing good can come of this, right? You can't possibly think you can date a member of the working class."

"Sachiko is marrying a commoner."

"Sachiko is marrying an heir to a rice empire related to the Takamoris. Ryu can support the life she is accustomed to. Takai, takai, takai." The three words are a well-known cliché, playing off the meanings. Good income, good school, and tall. Ideal characteristics for potential male love interests. He tries to give the letter to me. I step back, refusing to take it.

"Please. For me."

His sigh is long, resigned. He folds his arms, letter tucked under an armpit. "What happens if he shows? You run away together?"

"*If* he shows. No running."

"What happens if he doesn't?"

Stars will explode. The earth will stop turning. I shuffle my feet, peering at the ground. "I don't know." The breath rushes out of me. Japan is Akio. Akio is Japan. I shut my eyes tight, then open them. "Just give him the note. I'm sure he'll show up."

Yoshi's tongue plays behind his cheek. "I'll take it to him."

I smile and go in for a hug. "Thank you. You don't know how much this means."

He wraps his arms around me. "I know, I know, I am the greatest." He squeezes, lets go. "And please, I beg you . . . do something with your hair. You're not going to win any hearts looking like that."

"You are the worst, Yoshi. Simply the worst." I say, but for the first time all day, I'm smiling.

He clutches the letter to his heart. "You'll never know how touched I am by your words."

I cross my arms. "I'm pretty sure Reina hates you."

"Untrue. Blasphemy. She is blinded by her love for me." He flicks under my chin with the letter. "Happily ever or not with the guard, you'll be all right. Take it from me. I've been in love half a dozen times. You'll get over him."

"Sure." I couldn't say it less convincingly.

I sprint back to the palace, leaving Yoshi with the letter in his hands. I think about Akio. His generous spirit. His kind eyes. Our kiss. This can't be the end.

I'm early. Mariko is covering me at the palace. In case anyone asks, I am napping. The sun is high and bright by highway sign 40. I'm wearing the same clothes as this morning. I did not take Yoshi's advice.

I slip my hands in my pockets, check the time. Almost one o'clock. A car switches lanes, slows at the curb, then comes to a stop, red lights flashing. The door opens. I hold my breath. It's not Akio, just a couple of girls. They giggle and walk off.

Twenty minutes pass. He's now officially late. That's okay. Traffic in Tokyo is a bitch. Maybe his mom needed something. Or he couldn't get through the crowd outside his house. Yeah. That's it. I cycle through excuses as more minutes, then an hour, ticks by. I watch cars fly past. Funny how life goes on when it seems mine has stopped. It's 2 p.m. I've found a bench a few feet down and curl up on it.

Noora is keeping vigil. She texts.

Noora

Anything?

Me

Nothing.

Me

Tell me the truth?

Noora

Always.

Me

**If someone you cared for got you
fired from your job, you'd forgive
them, right? Even if that job
was everything to you and your
family? Even if that job had been
passed down from generation to
generation and it meant honoring
hundreds of years of tradition?
And leaving it in shame would
cast your family in a shadow for
all time?**

Noora

Oh, honey.

Right. I breathe, barely. It's painful, like tiny icicles punctur-
ing my lungs. All my hope is gone. I've spent everything. I'm fresh
out of emotions to charge. Akio is never late. He isn't coming.

It's time to pack it up. My body feels heavy and hollow as
I walk back to the palace.

Inside my room, Mariko waits for me. She says, "He didn't
show?"

A single sad shake of my head. I don't want to talk about

it. Can't. I wander my room, touching the down comforter on the bed. I dreamed of so many things here. My eyes land on the gold chest. A bonsai tree has been left in place of the original iris flower arrangement. I study it. The branches are bent, disjointed. Like me. A bone wrenched from its socket may be set back in place, but it's never the same. That's what happens when Japanese Americans return to Japan. They bear the resemblance of the body they originated from, but they are different. Askew. *Foreign.* And that's the god-awful truth.

I don't belong here. So much separates me from Japan. I'll never fully understand the customs, the culture, the rules. My final lesson has been learned: princesses don't date bodyguards. Like pointing, or walking in front of the Crown Prince, or wearing sweats to the airport, or mentioning the prime minister's sister, it just isn't *done.*

"Izumi-sama?" Mariko says.

"I'm okay," I say, lifelessly. Or at least, I will be. The closet is my next stop. I bypass the racks of pastels and dig out my red duffel bag from the bottom shelf. The color is garish, a gash among all this finery. Oh, the irony. How could I think I'd ever fit in?

"What are you doing?" Mariko hovers, expression flickering between pained and gentle and reluctant.

"I'm going home." One fact is irrefutable. If I hadn't come to Japan, none of this would have ever happened. I was foolish to believe my roots could expand past all these walls built around me. Your life can only be as big as the container you're planted in, after all.

I stuff yoga pants, sweatshirts, Care Bear underwear into the bag. My phone buzzes. A crown lights up the screen—the emoji I'd designated for my father. He leaves a message, then follows with a text. *We need to talk. Leaving soon.* I clear the screen.

Mariko watches. "You're not telling him you're going?"

We need to talk. Last time he'd said those words, he'd been so angry. I can't imagine how mad he is now. I don't think I want to find out. Besides . . . "It's better this way," I say. Clean breaks always heal best, because the thing is. The thing *is.* Everyone will be fine once I'm gone, probably better off. Everything will go back to the way it was, except for Akio. I'll never forgive myself for that.

My packing frenzy continues. Mariko stands by, bearing witness to the absolute destruction. I dial my mom and stick the phone between my ear and shoulder.

"Zoom Zoom?" Her voice is sleepy.

"I want to come home. Can you help me book a flight?"

I hear shuffling, then the sound of a light clicking on. "What's going on?" I stay silent. My jaw is tight. "Izumi. Talk to me."

I breathe in. Breathe out. Sniffle. "Tokyo's a mess."

"What about your dad—"

"Please, Mom," I blurt. "Just help me get out of here. I'll tell you everything when I'm there." All that matters is getting home in one misshapen piece.

She takes a moment to respond, but her voice is level. "Okay. Give me a few minutes."

I hang up. She's on it. The duffel is full. I go to zip it.

"Wait," Mariko says. She fetches the file of my mother's family history from my nightstand. She thrusts it forward. I clamp my hands around it. She doesn't let go. We tug-of-war it out. "Please, rethink this."

"My mind is made up." She must see it in my eyes. I shall not be moved. Her hold loosens and I place the file in the duffel, closing it.

"So that's it?" Mariko asks flatly, but her eyes are glossy. "You're just going to leave?"

"That's it." Tears fall unchecked, hers and mine. "But you should know . . . you're the best lady-in-waiting I ever had."

A slight eye roll. "I'm the only lady-in-waiting you've ever had."

"Yeah, but I know. You're the greatest. To top it all off, you're a really awesome friend, too." Mariko should've been born a princess. "You're worth so much more than all the Akikos and Norikos and school bullies who made you feel so low. I won't ever forget you."

Mariko sniffles. She finds a handkerchief hidden in her sleeve and blows her nose. "What's the plan? How are you getting out of here?"

"I'm going to catch a cab out by the highway."

She shakes her head. "No. That won't do. I'll order you a car. It will meet you by the highway sign."

"You'd do that?"

"Of course," she says, all prim and proper again. "I'm your lady-in-waiting. It's my duty and honor."

30

In 1991, a study was conducted in Japan around the phenomenon of neurovegetative responses to psychological stress leading to LV dysfunction. This state is called Takotsubo cardiomyopathy.

So, hard evidence: *broken heart syndrome* is a real thing.

The flight home is uneventful. As I deplane, the flight attendant says, "Have a nice day." Her smile is bright and well meaning. It's a canned speech. I nod out of habit and reply, "Thanks, but I have other plans."

I am tired and mourning. Feelings are a real son of a bitch. First chance I get, I'm going to turn mine off. Unfortunately, I am positively grotesque with emotion. The movies on the plane made me cry. The couple on their way home from their honeymoon made me weep. When the flight attendant asked if I wanted the fish or salad with goat cheese and pickled radishes, I burst into tears.

It's a lonely walk through the airport. I'm used to Akio frowning, Mariko fussing, and Mr. Fuchigami pointing out historical landmarks. In keeping with my burn-it-all-to-the-ground vibe, I've blocked all international phone numbers. The only calls getting through are Mom's and the AGG's.

Down the escalators I go, the bag on my shoulder weighted down with all my deep emotional issues. Next time I get a hankering to search for my father only to find out I'm a princess, I'll do the smart thing and shut that shit down. Yeah. Next time.

Mom is waiting for me. I find my first smile when I see she's brought Tamagotchi. I scoop him up and he growls and squirms until I put him down. He hides behind my mom.

"Careful, I'm pretty sure he ate some deer pellets this morning," Mom says.

"He does love a pooh-pooh platter." I give him one last head rub and he nips at my hand. Then, I fall into her arms, find that soft spot in her neck, and cry. I'm so used to bowing and nodding that physical touch feels novel, but not unwelcome. She smells like incense and laundry detergent. Like home. All suddenly feels right with the world, or at least a little better.

She smooths my hair, cups my cheeks. "Oh, Zoom Zoom. Tell me everything in the car. Let's get your bags."

Arms slung over one another's shoulders, we make our way to the carousel. I lean into her and let my sadness show in the sag of my body. She carries the weight.

Luggage is already spinning around. I search for my bag and my eyes catch on a bright pink sign. *Welcome home from the hospital! The rash cleared up, yay!* Three girls are smiling and wave frantically—Noora, Hansani, and Glory.

"They insisted on coming," Mom says, resigned. She knows better than to try to keep us apart. What God has put together let no man (or woman) put asunder. "You're going to have to sit in the middle. It's going to be a tight fit."

I don't care. I run and hug each of them.

"I told them the sign was too much," Hansani whispers to me. In elementary school, Hansani was a bit of tattletale. She follows the rules and is unashamed.

I pull back, staring at each. "I hate you." I turn to Hansani. "Except for you, you're awesome." Then, I pull them back to me.

It's a five-hour drive home. I am the main entertainment, and I tell them everything. All the bitter details. Akio and me starting off as enemies. The developing relationship with my father. The Shining Twins sabotaging me at every turn, and their grand finale, selling my taboo romance to the tabloids. The landscape has changed from scrublands to pine forests. Hostess wrappers litter the car floor. The girls came equipped. Glory even brought a biscuit from Black Bear Diner.

"Did you tell your father?" Mom asks.

I stay silent. I did tell him. After the prime minister's wedding, I tried to explain about the twins setting me up, and he brushed it off. How'd that feel? Not good. Not good at all. "They make me feel stabby," I say instead, picturing the twins' stupid evil faces.

"I'm sure any jury would acquit you," Noora assures me.

In the rearview mirror, Mom smiles. Hansani is riding up front. She's an excellent copilot, cheery and bright, pointing out interesting landmarks. I'm sandwiched between Glory and Noora. I don't mind. It's nice, like a cocoon. With them, nothing can touch me. Or at least, I can forget for a while all the things that hurt.

"I don't even care about that anymore." I do, but there's much more to focus on, like my broken heart. "Akio hates me. I ruined his life." It's why he didn't meet me that day. How could he, after everything I'd done? Love can cut as easily as it can heal.

"Maybe," Glory carefully suggests, "you just need to give him some time to come around." Guess Glory is a bit of a closet romantic. I'm happy her parents' divorce hasn't jaded her too much. She'll make it back to the world of coupledom, but me . . .

Did I leave too soon? Give up too easily? "No," I say. Glory wasn't there. She wasn't waiting on the sidewalk, watching the sun inch through the sky with her heart in her hands and her soul bared then bludgeoned. "It doesn't matter anyway. I never was one of them. I don't belong in Japan."

Noora pats my leg. I lean my head back and close my eyes. There is no happily ever after. Fairy tales are bull.

The end.

31

An entire week passes. I hole up in my room. For a while, I kept up on the tabloids; they were still reporting on my affair, feasting on the body even though Akio had gone dark and I was on another continent. I couldn't take it anymore, so I switched to bad television, mostly reality shows. On day seven, I binge a show about some guy with five wives. I am making incredible advances in feeling sorry for myself. It's award-worthy. I convince myself it's a positive. Got to keep those goalposts moving. Also, I haven't showered. The weather is warm and there's no air conditioning. So yeah, it's bad all around.

Mom reluctantly supports my newfound hermit lifestyle. She brings food and drinks and makes sure my blinds are open, even when I hiss at the sunlight like a vampire. Jones has stopped by, bringing me a tincture for broken hearts and some aromatherapy—peppermint to improve my mood and increase my energy.

Noora prances in. She eyes my jammies. I've gone with a Christmas theme this morning. "Did someone forget it's afternoon?" she asks. Her hair is particularly glossy today. I hate it.

I give her a dead-eye stare, praying for the sweet release of death.

She sniffs the air. "Well, at least your shame cave smells a bit better this morning. Is that patchouli and peppermint?"

I roll onto my back. "Jones brought it."

"Have you been outside at all?"

"Mom opened the window this morning." I don't mention I haven't been outside this whole week. There really is no reason to be. The world is a cold place. Graduation is in a few days. My cap and gown hang in the closet. I suppose I'll have to make an appearance. Jones is planning a celebratory dinner. I am one thousand percent sure it's just to spend time with my mother. I see through him. All the way through to his unrequited love. Poor schmuck. I feel for him. I really do.

On-screen, the wives groan about being persecuted for their beliefs. Noora rolls her eyes and turns off the show.

"Hey!" I say, though there's no heat in it. "I was watching that."

"Zoom Zoom." She sits on the bed near my hips. "This is a new low."

I turn toward her. "I can't. I just can't. It's too painful." All I can think about is all I had. All I lost. How badly I'm fractured. "I thought Japan was the answer to everything. But I'm still me. Nothing has changed." I squeeze my eyes shut, tears leak from the corners. The big revelation over my seven-day reality show coma is that I don't feel much different.

She lays down beside me and snuggles in. We're almost nose-to-nose. "Why is that so bad?" Her dark eyes are pools of concern.

"Don't you ever feel like you don't belong anywhere? Like you're two discordant halves living in one body? I'm not American enough. I'm not Japanese enough." I thought moving to another country and getting to know my father would make me whole, give me a way to stitch together those parts.

A couple seconds tick by. "Ah. I see. You're having the whole born-a-different-race-in-white-America existentialist dilemma."

"There's a name for it?"

"Sure is."

"What's the antidote?" My heart expands with its last little bit of hope.

"I'm not really sure there is a cure. Some things are just meant to be felt."

"So no easy answers?"

"Sorry. I don't think so. We all have to figure out on our own who we are and where we fit in."

"Where do I fit in, then?"

"Well," Noora says. "I'm not sure, but I think you fit pretty well next to me . . . and Glory and Hansani, but mostly me, because I'm the best." She grins. "That's something, right?"

I sniffle and wipe my nose on my sheets. "That's a lot of something."

"Come back to the land of the living," Noora says, taking my hands in hers and placing them between us. "If there isn't an answer, at least we can be together in our perpetually confused states. We need you." Her face twitches. "Plus, you need to clean your sheets. Why do they smell so sour?"

Right. I spilled some milk a few days ago. I think about Noora's gentle prodding. She's right. This backward slide isn't me. My natural disposition walks on the sunny side of the street. Plus, I've got to get off the reality shows. I must do it for myself and the world. It's time to return to the land of the living and be a contributing, or at least semifunctioning, member of society.

We start by stripping my bed. Small steps. Noora makes a big deal of gagging when crumbs and wrappers fall out, even asking Mom if she has a hazmat suit on hand. No bother.

We're stuffing sheets into the washing machine when there's a knock on the door. I pour a generous amount of detergent in the barrel and slam down the lid. That should do it.

There's another knock. "Probably Jones," I say to Noora, skipping ahead of her. Yesterday, he promised fresh honey. Tamagotchi goes crazy and follows on my heels.

The door swings open. My jaw drops. I let out a little gasp.

Noora skids to a stop behind me. "He's here," she whisper-shouts. "Asian George Clooney. In the flesh."

I am speechless. Breathless. A fish washed ashore. There, framed in the doorway, as easy as you please, is my father—*the* Crown Prince of Japan.

32

His smile is easy, fond. He inclines his head. "Izumi-chan. I found you."

"What . . . what are you doing here?" Tamagotchi sniffs my father's shoes and tugs on one of his pant legs. I find a bone on the floor and throw it down the hall. Tamagotchi gives chase.

"You invited me," my father says simply.

"Oh my God," Noora says. "I'm FaceTiming the girls."

"Hello." My father cocks his head, peering at Noora over my shoulder. "I'm Makoto, Mak for short. Izumi-chan's father." He extends a hand.

Noora is quick to pocket her phone and push me out of the way, which is easy, since all my limbs-slash-defenses are null and void right now. She takes my father's hand. "Noora. Of the Farzads. No relation to the Farzad dry-cleaning family."

"Izumi's friend. She has told me much about you." Noora giggles. Actually giggles. She also hasn't let go of his hand. Right. Time to squash that. I pull them apart, then hip check her. Down, girl.

"I wasn't expecting you." Now is the time I notice my plaid pajamas are buttoned unevenly. I don't think my father has ever seen me dressed down. What do I look like? Good question. The only answer is garbage, slightly warmed . . . So, trash. Basic trash.

"You weren't?" He's perplexed, pretending nothing has happened. Like I haven't embarrassed him with my alleged torrid affair, then left without saying goodbye. "I guess I am a bit early for your graduation. Either way, here I am."

I have nothing. Words fail me.

Noora nudges me, saying through the corner of her mouth, "Here he is."

"You shouldn't, you can't—" My speech is rushed. What am I trying to say? "I didn't actually think you'd come—your schedule. You can't just take days off. You don't belong here." It feels just as bad to say it as it sounds, but I've compartmentalized my lives. There is a line down the center; one half is Japan, and the other, America. Never the two shall meet.

"Of course I belong here. You are here," he says, like it makes all the sense in the world. "I brought a gift." In his hand is a small, yellow box of Tokyo Bananas. The cream-filled cakes are all over the airport. He offers them to me with both hands.

Bringing an omiyage is tradition. I can't refuse. I accept the box with both hands and say, "Thank you." Then I step back, toss the box on the table, and close my fist around the doorknob. I might shut it in his face. He must sense this, because he places a foot on the threshold. "Izumi. You left without saying goodbye."

My chin dips down. "It was for the best. I thought . . ."

"What? That I'd be angry, that I'd turn my back on you?"

"Yes." To all of it. I feel Noora place her hand on my shoulder. "You said that, as a member of the imperial family, I was expected to be beyond reproach."

His brow scrunches. "I did say that, but it was in context

of the tabloids. The media holds the imperial family to such a high standard, an impossible standard. But nobody is without faults. I'd never blame you for making mistakes. Is that what you thought?"

"You were furious at the potential of a scandal." I cross my arms and uncross them.

"No," he says slowly. "I was furious on your behalf that the tabloids might hurt you with their vicious reporting. I was trying to protect you." His foot is still in the door. "This whole thing is my fault. I wanted you to come to Japan so you could know me and your family, but I didn't spend enough time with you. I didn't fully appreciate the gift I'd been given, what it meant to have you there. I've been too formal about keeping scheduled appointments. Our time together shouldn't have been so rigid." He splays his hands, smiling. "So, here I am. You spent weeks in Japan learning where I am from. Now, I will learn where you are from."

I stand, frozen, the weight on my heart lifting. My head spinning—he was trying to protect me . . . was angry for me . . .

Noora elbows me again. "What are you waiting for? Let the man in, Zoom Zoom. She's surprised." Noora addresses my father. Her default is covering for me. Years of parent shenanigans and it's what we automatically do. "She just needs a few minutes to adjust. You and I could go for a walk. I'd be happy to show you around Mount Shasta. You know, take you to all the local haunts. If you're interested in goat farming . . ."

Mom comes into the room. "Zoom Zoom, you overloaded the washer again—"

"Hanako," my father says and, *wow*, does his face light up.

It's the force of one thousand happy suns.

Mom stops short, grips the back of a chair. Her face drains of color. "Makoto."

He tries to move forward, but Noora and I are blocking him. He speaks over us. "I'm sorry to intrude like this . . ." He pauses, shakes his head as if in a daze. "Forgive me. You haven't changed."

As one, Noora and I swivel to assess my mom. She shuffles her feet, fluttering a hand over her hair. "Oh . . . I . . . um . . . I haven't even gotten dressed yet." She looks quite nice to me. She's wearing her usual weekend gear—jeans, bare feet, and one of her signature feminist T-shirts. Today's reads Believe Women. "I've been cleaning."

My father pushes through us. "You look lovely."

Noora squeezes my hand. "Are you seeing what I'm seeing? They are totally eye-boning each other."

"Shut it," I whisper back. "Adults are in the room."

My father stands in front of my mother. I can't see her. His tall form dwarfs hers. "What are you doing here?" she asks, the same as me.

"I'm here to make things right," is all he says.

A siren wails outside. The sound comes closer and closer, multiplying. Red and blue lights flash against our windowpanes. Mount Shasta Police, along with some dark cars, careen into the driveway and stop with a spray of gravel. My father pulls away from Mom. "Ah. I should probably inform you. I didn't tell anyone I was coming here. It appears the police have arrived. Guess I've been caught." He doesn't seem sorry. Not sorry at all. Then, he does something I've never seen him do, ever.

He laughs.

*

I force Noora to go home.

Then, it takes a good two hours to sort out my father's mess. There are police. The Japanese Ambassador. Even the president calls and invites my father to dinner at the White House. The Imperial Household Agency is on their way. My father's chamberlains and imperial guards will be here by tomorrow morning. Until then, there are four police cars and a smattering of secret service agents on loan outside our house. Because none of the local hotels have been vetted by security, we have no choice but to keep him.

My father seems pleased as punch. Completely unfazed. My mother is disheveled, vacillating between making surprised eyes at my father and a bad case of nerves. I've never seen her this way. She spills an entire cup of water while setting the table for dinner, burns the ravioli, then apologizes profusely. "I'm sure this isn't what you're used to . . ." Mom says, taking in the table—the pasta in a cracked bowl, the mismatched place settings, the flea market dining set. She's also slipped one of her work cardigans on over her T-shirt.

"This is wonderful." He seems genuinely happy. His movements are fluid as he undoes his cuffs and rolls up his sleeves. Just a man ready to dig in.

As for me, I'm still not sure how I'm handling all this. Things have certainly taken an interesting turn. "Would you like a beer? You still like beer, right?" Mom asks. "I don't have any, but I'm sure Jones does. Remember, he went through that whole brewing phase?" Mom says to me. Yikes. So much word vomit.

"Who is Jones?" my father asks, placing a paper napkin in his lap. I never saw a paper napkin at the palace. They were all cotton or linen, neatly pressed and folded. The silverware was either warmed or cooled for the dish we were eating. Ours is fresh out of the dishwasher, water stains and all.

"Mom's stalker."

My father chokes on his sip of water.

"Zoom Zoom," Mom chides. "He's our neighbor. Very kind."

"He's in love with Mom."

"He may have a little crush," Mom says. "It's not a big deal."

My father frowns into his plate. Does he not like the fork scratches he sees? "His feelings are unreturned?" he asks.

"I don't know," I say. "Mom and him grew pretty close while I was in Japan. You know, lonely spring nights by the fire . . ."

My father misses my mother's WTF wide-eyed stare. Trust me. I'm doing her a solid. In my romance novels, this always works. Everything you read in books is at least half-true.

After dinner, Mom does dishes and I give him a tour of the house. It lasts all of five minutes. We spend the most time in my room. The bed is still stripped.

He walks the perimeter. I did the same in Akio's childhood room, snooping and soaking up everything about him. Must stop thinking about Akio. I'd love to confide in him. *My father showed up. Is he here for me? My mom? Both of us? Didn't he get the memo when I left? Princess Izumi out.*

My father stops and takes in a *Hedwig and the Angry Inch* poster, courtesy of Noora. Fairy lights have been strung up around it. "Much different than your room at the palace," he remarks.

I'm picking up armloads of clothes and shoving them in my closet. I blow bangs out of my face. Does he remember asking about my room that first night in Japan? "Yeah. I'm sorry it's not very clean. I haven't had time"—or really, the will—"to tidy up."

He resumes course, then pauses at the framed pictures on my dresser. All of them feature Glory, Noora, Hansani, and me. The two most mortifying are: a photo Noora snapped of me where I'm laughing at the same time Tamagotchi is licking me so it looks like his tongue in my mouth and the entire AGG squad in the fifth grade wearing coordinated denim outfits. 'Nuff said.

I'm trying to read my father. Is he disappointed by what he's found? His focus shifts. Scratch the above. There's an even more mortifying photo. It's a picture of Forest—rather, what's left of a picture of Forest. I've blacked out his eyes and drawn devil horns on his head. Confession: Akio's photograph isn't the first I graffitied. I'm just thankful there aren't any penises on this one. This is Izzy's pre-penis earring phase, circa junior year—a lonely and angry time.

"That's Forest. Ex-boyfriend," I say.

He considers the photo then me. "We've never talked about boyfriends."

"Not much to talk about."

"The imperial guard . . ."

"It's over." Though, I'm still stuck on how much it hurts to love him. How much it hurts not loving him. Such a paradox.

My father comes to me. "That might be for the best."

"You wouldn't approve?" I ask grimly.

His forehead bunches up. "My approval doesn't matter. Though I hope you would choose someone who loves you as much as I love . . ." *Your mother.* He was totally going to say *your mother.* "Someone a bit braver, perhaps. If this guard couldn't weather the press storm, then perhaps it's better it ends now. It takes a certain sort of person to date a member of the imperial family."

"How do you know I didn't leave him?"

"You fled Japan. I have some experience with love and running from it." He winks at me. "Therefore, I must surmise a broken heart is the reason you left."

That, among other things. He might not be mad at me, but it doesn't change a whole lot. How can I explain? It's Akio, but also the press. The Shining Twins. The whole imperial family. I could spend a lifetime learning the customs, navigating the culture, but I'll never belong. I'm a Twinkie. Yellow on the outside, white on the inside. I hate that term. Does that mean I hate myself? No. I just hate the division.

"Even if he did want me, it would never work though, right? A commoner and a princess?" I repeat Yoshi's sentiment.

"Life is full of possibilities, Izumi. But things don't happen magically. Relationships are work. I was afraid of that when I met your mother. I was too focused on myself and my role. If I'm wrong, and this thing with the imperial guard is serious, then . . ."

"It's not," I cut in. "I wanted it to be. But he didn't feel the same way, I guess."

"It's as I figured." He grows thoughtful. "Would you like me to have him removed from the city? There are nine and a half million people in Tokyo, so the odds are very low you would run into him. But I could have him banned."

The corners of my lips turn up. "Can you really do that?"

"No." He grins. "I'm pretty sure it would violate all sorts of laws. But I would do anything in my power to ease your pain." My father's smile broadens. "Come back to Japan, Izumi-chan."

I instantly sober. "No. I can't." Even when I thought I was succeeding, I wasn't. There's just too much to know, more than a lifetime's worth. There's no use walking forward when someone is digging a pit right in front of you.

"All right." He looks at his gold watch. "Chamberlains will show up tomorrow. But I'll make it clear I'm staying through to your graduation. Looks like I have three days to convince you."

"Feel free to try." I smile to soften the blow. I've learned my lesson. The Land of the Rising Sun and I are not compatible.

Even so, I'm very glad a little part of Japan is here with me.

Day One.

The Imperial Household Agency descends on Mount Shasta. Chamberlains, secretaries, private chefs, and valets arrive. A private meeting is held in our kitchen. Mom and I are relegated to the driveway with the secret service agents, imperial guards and diplomatic vehicles designated for foreign state visitors. Furious voices filter through the windows. My father slams out of the house.

"Mak?" Mom says.

I hold Tamagotchi's leash while he digs into the gravel driveway.

My father's scowl lightens. "It's all right. We were just ironing out all the details. Some meetings had to be canceled and rescheduled. Bit of unfortunate news, though. It seems like a hotel can't be secured . . ." He scratches the back of his head.

I'm pretty sure I heard one of the chamberlains say the opposite.

"Oh," Mom says. "Well, you're more than welcome to stay here. I'm afraid I don't have room for all your staff, but maybe Jones . . ."

"Thank you for offering your hospitality. The chamberlains will camp if necessary." My father's smile is triumphant. What a sneak. The chamberlains have spilled out of the house, black and navy suits, briefcases, and all. "Now, I'm excited to get to know Mount Shasta." He holds out a hand. One of the chamberlains—or is it his secretary?—snaps open a briefcase. He awkwardly balances it in his hands while he fishes a Mount Shasta Visitor's Guide out. "What should we do first?" He flips through the pages. "Bike riding? Hiking? Exploring downtown?"

Mom swallows. "I suppose we could hike by Castle Lake? Maybe stop by Berryvale and get some picnic items."

My father flashes his teeth. "Sounds good to me."

"Zoom Zoom, you okay with hiking?" Mom asks, brow arched like a dare.

"Absolutely," I say with all the enthusiasm I don't feel. Mom casts me a suspicious look. She's sniffing me out. She knows hiking isn't really my thing. The last time she suggested it to me, I said something along the lines of *I'd rather give a gorilla an enema.*

"Excellent," he says. "I want to see everything that matters to you." My father is excited. Truth is, I kind of am, too.

Day Two.

My legs still ache from the hike yesterday. We made the mistake of bringing Tamagotchi. He quit about halfway and I had to carry him. Such a lazy dog.

"You're supposed to eat the whole thing?" My father stares at the dinner plate–sized biscuit in front of him.

"Yep." The Black Bear Diner is pretty empty. A couple of old dudes in the back play checkers. A trucker downs coffee and eats pie at the counter. The waitstaff wear suspenders and go about their day like there aren't secret service agents and imperial guards in the booths surrounding us and posted outside. Paparazzi have shown up, but they've been banned from nearly every establishment. Mount Shasta might hate monarchies, but they hate violations of privacy more. The town I never thought wanted me suddenly has my back.

My father sets to his biscuit with a fork and knife. My mom laughs behind her hand and he smiles like they're sharing a private joke. He dips his bite in the butter and warm jam, then eats it. "It's very sweet. I like it," he declares. He orders biscuits for everybody on the Crown Prince's tab.

After we've devoured our biscuits, fluffy pancakes, and greasy sausages, my father wipes his mouth. "This is where you come with your friends?" he asks.

"Yeah." I toy with the newspaper print menu.

A chamberlain stands, bowing to my father. "Excuse me, just one moment," he says, leaving the table.

Mom's foot slams down on mine. "Ow."

"You're acting weird," Mom accuses.

"No, I'm not," I say back. "You're the one acting weird. I mean, hearts are literally floating from your head."

Mom carefully places her balled-up napkin on the table. She cradles her head in her hands. "You're right. What am I thinking?"

Wow. The AGG and I follow this Twitter account called *Am I the Asshole?* People write in the scenarios and ask public opinion. You know, am I the asshole for asking my bridesmaid to lose twenty pounds before my wedding? Am I the asshole for asking my wife for a paternity test? I wouldn't need it now. I am totally the asshole. "I'm sorry. You're not acting like a lovesick fool." She frowns at me, disbelieving. "Well, you are, kind of, but so is he. It's disgusting. I hate it," I say, but there's no heat.

"After all these years . . . I never thought there would be a chance for us. But if you don't want . . ."

I reach over to pat her hand. Sometimes my mom is too much. "It's okay. You have my blessing. Just, you know, try to lock doors, or maybe hang a sock on the door handle."

"Izumi," she says, back in full Mom mode. My father is finishing up his conversation.

I stick my hands up. "I just don't want to see anything that might scar me for life."

She purses her lips. "I think we should discuss why you won't go back with him." On the hike, my father asked me to come back to Japan again. I dodged the question, pointing out a super interesting juniper tree.

"I don't know what you mean." I suddenly find a water spot on the wall fascinating.

"Sweetheart." She waits until I look at her. "You've got to let him in."

"Can we just enjoy lunch and our time together while he's here?"

She scowls. "Is it because you think he won't like what he hears? Because your job isn't to be likable."

My father returns. "What did I miss?" he asks, smile falling at the tension at the table.

Mom crosses her arms. She turns her ire on my father. "Centuries of pressuring women to be agreeable and conform to unrealistic emotional expectations."

"That doesn't seem fair." My father frowns.

"You're telling me," Mom huffs. Her jaw sets. I'm sure she's daydreaming about mutiny. Burning down the patriarchy. You know, little things.

I motion to the waitress. *Check, please.*

Day Three.

In the afternoon, Glory, Hansani, and Noora come over to officially meet my father. All said and done, introductions go well, even though Hansani curtsies. He seems impressed when he finds out Noora will be attending Columbia next year. I stay mute. The state college I got into is looking less and less glamorous. After, Mom shows my father the compost bin. Note to self: give Mom tips on romance.

"Do you think if we said we need some wood chopped, he'd do that?" Noora asks, fingers on the window ledge. We're totally spying now, all four of us crammed together, peeking through the blinds. My parents have brushed up against each other no less than three times already. She points something out and he nods.

"He'd probably need to take his shirt off. It's awfully warm out today," Glory remarks.

"Stop objectifying my father," I say to them. As usual, Hansani is quiet, but she's guilty by association. My mom and father have come to the compost pile. Flies buzz around it. "Don't stick your hand in it. Don't stick your hand it. Please don't stick your hand in it," I say.

"Gross," says Glory.

"She totally stuck her hand in it," Hansani says.

Yep. Mom has a fistful of compost and is showing my

father. To his credit, my father actually looks interested. He's dressed more casually today, in slacks and a polo shirt. Mom throws the dirt back into the pile, wiping her palms on her jeans. "She's going to show him the worm bin next. I can't watch." I cover my eyes and push away from the window.

Noora and Hansani fall away. Glory remains. "She's at the worm bin. You don't want to know what she's doing now."

Noora says to me, "We still on for movie night?"

"Yeah." My father has asked Mom to dinner. Mom thought Indian food would be a great idea, but I steered her away. Curry is something you pay for later, if you know what I mean. I booked them a table for two at the local Italian eatery.

"Hansani wanted to watch *The Bodyguard*, but I told her it was way too soon," Noora says.

Hansani is offended. "I did not."

Noora smirks.

I fall back on my bed. "No romance, please. Nothing with princesses either," I say.

"What about binge-watching a show? *Schitt's Creek*?"

"Too happy," I say.

Glory turns from the window. "Horror it is."

"Yes," I reply. "Preferably something where the cute guy is killed early."

34

In no time, it's graduation day. The day passes in a haze. Chairs and a stage are set up in the middle of Mount Shasta High's football field. Blue gowns flutter in the warm breeze. Noora gives the valedictorian speech. When I walk and receive my diploma, the cheers are extra loud—mostly from the AGG and the imperial guards, whom my father requested wear tie-dye for the occasion. They totally blend in with their tucked-in T-shirts and dress pants and earpieces. Totally.

After, Jones goes all out and prepares a GMO- and pesticide-free, farm-to-table, vegan, nothing-we-eat-has-a-mother feast. A huge buffet on a wooden table is set out under string lights. Mismatched chairs and even an old couch dot the lawn. The sun is setting, a watercolor of pinks and orange. The mood is merry. The Grateful Dead plays on an outdoor speaker. Noora, Glory, and Hansani are celebrating separately with their families, but will stop by soon. The company is still good: a mix of Jones's buddies, Mom's coworkers, officials from the Imperial Household Agency, and the guards. Everyone seems to be getting along.

I fix myself a plate of vegetable paella with brown rice and wander into the woods. Still wearing my scratchy blue gown, I settle down on a log, enjoying the quiet for a few moments. My father will be leaving soon.

Needles crack underfoot. "Mind if I join you?" Jones asks.

He's got a plate and is wearing a diarrhea-colored corduroy suit with burgundy tie and Birkenstocks. It's awful. Truly awful.

"Sure." I scoot over.

Across the lawn, through the gaps in the trees, I spy my mom and dad chatting animatedly, heads bent toward each other like magnets seeking their other half. "Hard to compete with a prince." He's positively glum. Almost crying into his paella.

"Is that what the suit is about?"

"Yeah." He sets his plate down. Yanks at his tie. "I hate these fucking things. They're not me." The tie slips over his head and he tosses it to the ground. He unbuttons his top two buttons. "You gotta own your shit, you know? I'm just glad I didn't shave my beard." He palms his jaw, running a hand over his glorious facial hair.

"I guess."

"You liking the dinner?"

I hold up my plate. "Yummy." I place it back in my lap, wishing I was alone again. "Thanks for doing this."

He pats my back. "You're a good kid, Izzy."

My father and mom make their way across the lawn, sights set on us. "Mr. Jones," my father says, sticking out a hand. "Thanks for hosting this. If you ever come to Japan, you're welcome at the palace."

Jones stands and clasps my father's hand in a handshake that quickly turns competitive. "Just Jones. No last name. Thanks for the invite, but I have strong feelings on the in- stitution of monarchies. They conflict with my fundamental egalitarian values."

They disengage. "Of course. I respect your position," says my father, unfazed.

Jones turns to Mom. "You need anything, Hanako, you know where to find me."

I'm next. Jones bends, squeezes my nose between his thumb and pointer finger. "Honk."

I bat him away. Effing weirdo. But he's ours. No choice but to keep him, I guess.

Then he's gone, trouncing over pine needles and yelling at one of his friends to break out the bongo drums. It's probably a good thing my father is leaving soon. First the bongos, then the clothes come off.

"Your neighbor is . . . interesting," my father says.

"You get used to him," Mom says. "He means well."

He nods sagely. "I have to go soon. Izumi-chan, one more walk?" Already, chamberlains are closing in. The imperial guards are buzzing, ready to be on the move.

"Sure." I stand, leaving my plate next to Jones's tie. Mom slips away, but stays close.

My father and I walk the perimeter of the woods, our steps meandering. "You ready to go home?"

"I miss my own bed." He grins. The futon he's been sleeping on is lumpy and dusty. "But no. I wish you were coming with me." It's his final plea. The question is there in his eyes. *Won't you reconsider?*

My gown flaps in the breeze. My hands ball into fists, and my stomach sours. "I can't." I'm staying here, summering with AGG and enrolling in College of the Siskiyous in the fall. It's a done deal.

"Is there something you're not telling me? Something else

that happened there? I don't understand why you're being so stubborn. This isn't like you." His voice is hard-edged with frustration.

Something inside me bursts, floodgates opening. I can't hold back. "I'm . . ." My voice shakes. "You don't even know me." My gaze is hard, fierce, determined. I don't know what I'm doing, what I'm saying, but I plow onward. "I don't keep my room clean. Mom has to force me to do laundry. My grades are mediocre at best. If I applied to Columbia or Harvard, their laughs would be heard around the world. For the last two years, my New Year's resolutions have been to eat things with more sprinkles on them. I read mostly romance novels, followed closely by middle grade fantasy. I love my friends, but we do stupid shit like see if we can fit in the fridge, or buy a single grape from the grocery store, or play The Floor Is Lava for an entire Saturday."

He blinks at me. "Lava?"

I flick a hand. "When you pretend the ground is hot lava and you can't touch it or you'll melt. It's dumb." But so fun. I peer at him. "You never played that when you were a kid?"

"I didn't have very many friends. I played *Go* with my brother." Right. Go—an abstract strategy board game. The object is to gain more territory than your opponent. In short, introductory war games for children.

"See. That's my point." My shoulders droop. Our childhood games are a perfect example of the distance between us, of our differences. We're worlds apart.

"What's the point?" He's confused.

"The point is . . . the point *is*, I'm American." He's dumbstruck. I'm on a truth roll. Might as well keep traveling downhill. "No matter how hard I try, I can't be who you—who Japan wants me to be." I take an unsteady breath.

He mulls it over and responds. "I don't want you to be something you're not. Why would you ever think that?"

"I'm not perfect." My chin is set.

"Me either." His chin is equally set.

"I'll never be good enough for Japan. I'll never belong there."

"You are my daughter," he says evenly, fiercely. "You belong with me." He exhales slowly, taking in the trees, the birds. "I'd like to tell you not to worry what anyone says, but it's much more difficult in practice. To tell you the truth, the worry never goes away. You'll screw up. The papers will report it. Your life won't feel like your own at times. That's the life as a member of the imperial family and the weight we must carry, Izumi-chan," he says, voice softening, eyes on me. "Come back to Japan. Let's figure this out together. Nothing is insurmountable."

I reach for *yes*. But the word is a wall I can't climb.

"Fine. I won't pressure you anymore." He sighs. "I invited your mother to Japan. She refused, too."

I shuffle my feet, stare at them. "You're welcome here anytime. We'll totally have you. I'm sorry." He plans to visit again in August.

"Don't be," he says easily. "Just don't cut me out of your life. Promise?"

"I promise," I say, then wait a beat. Not everything is perfect, but things between my father and I feel okay. I scrunch up my nose. "Do you think we should hug?"

"I think if there were ever a moment for two people to

embrace, it would be this one." He opens his arms. I slip into them. "Sprinkles, huh?" he says into my hair.

"Oh, yeah. They really jazz up whatever you're eating. Makes everything so much more festive." We pull apart.

"Makes perfect sense to me," my father says. He nods at me. "Daughter."

I nod back at him. "Dad."

Mom and I walk Dad to his car. It's as if the three of us are trying to slow time. I don't want this to end. Just Mom and me has always felt like enough. But now, the prospect of returning to our duo existence fills me with acute loneliness. The driveway comes too soon. An imperial guard holds open the door to a black town car.

"I'll see you at the end of August, then," Dad says. "Less than ninety days."

"Ninety days," I say back.

He hugs me and whispers, "I'm so proud of you." I get choked up.

He focuses on Mom, touches her cheek, bends forward, and kisses it. I avert my gaze from the intimate moment. "Until next time." There is a promise in his voice.

He fixes us with a final look, a single nod, then he gets in the car. Doors slam. Engines start. We watch the trail of red lights travel the driveway and disappear down the street.

My hand seeks out Mom's. "Well, that's it." Something rises in my throat. Sadness. Regret. Confusion. I'm slowly processing the last twenty minutes, all his words. *You belong with me.*

"There he goes," Mom says.

"He'll be back soon," I tell her.

"Yeah. No time at all." I'm not sure if she's reassuring me or herself.

"I mean, why would I go to Japan?" I ask airily.

"For love," she says wistfully.

What do I need to prove? So what if I'll never be accepted? I accept myself. The tears on my cheeks are cold. I'm crying, but it's happy and sad at the same time. The reality is razor-sharp. It's all so transparent—a revelation as bright and as clear as the sunset. I don't have an American half *or* a Japanese half. I am a whole person. Nobody gets to tell me if I am Japanese enough or too American.

I snap to attention. "Mom?"

"Yeah, honey." She's still watching the road, watching her second chance drift away.

"I think I made the wrong decision." I draw her attention.

"I think I made the wrong decision, too," she says.

I crack a grin.

We don't pack suitcases, and barely have enough time to figure out where Tamagotchi will stay. Jones agrees to take him, though he refuses to make him wear a leash. Noora shows up during the frenzy.

"We have to catch my father." I grip on to her.

Noora clutches her keys. "Please. I've been waiting my entire life for this."

Then, we're in Noora's car, speeding down the street and onto Mount Shasta Boulevard. Noora darts in and out of traffic.

"What are we doing? This is crazy!" Mom says. "Oh my

God, Noora, if I knew you were this terrible of a driver, I never would have let Izumi in the car with you. Headlights. Please turn on your headlights." It's getting darker. Noora laughs and flicks on her headlights. A car lays on the horn as she passes it.

I kind of blanked out what happens next. Somehow, we jumped from point A to B, ended up near the ramp to I-5, and caught up to the imperial cavalcade. Japanese flags wave on the hood. My dad's in there, in the middle car.

I reach over and press down on the horn. *Beep. Beeeep. Beeeeep.* Red and blue lights flash in Noora's rearview mirror. Traffic slows to a near stop because of the commotion.

"Pull over, Noora," Mom says. "We're not breaking any more laws."

"They're so close," Noora says, maneuvering the car to the shoulder. We're just a few cars behind them. I don't wait until Noora comes to a complete stop. I'm out the door and running into traffic, desperation in my steps. Arms out, I cry, "Wait!" A stitch forms in my side. I swear, if I make it back to the palace, I'll start a new jogging regimen. My graduation gown flaps, my hair flying behind me. The imperial cavalcade brakes. Then a door is flung open. My father steps out. "Izumi-chan."

I stop in front of him, put my hands on my knees. Traffic whizzes by. I hold up a finger. "Need a moment to catch my breath."

He barks something in Japanese. A bottle of water is shoved at me. "What's going on?" He helps me stand. "Hanako?" His attention turns to my mother, who's walking up.

"This is a touch more dramatic than I thought it was going to be," she says, folding a piece of hair behind her ear.

"We . . ." I gesture wildly between us. I say, between giant breaths, "We want to go to Japan."

"You do?" The speeding laws we've violated. The traffic we're holding up. Me nearly falling on my ass from exhaustion. Seeing my dad's face light with joy. It's all worth it.

"Do you have room for two more?" Mom is a little shy. We're totally causing a scene. Imperial guards are holding back Mount Shasta police. We've narrowly avoided a standoff and an international incident.

Dad doesn't seem to care. "Always," he says. "Always."

We decide to go home and pack a few things. Lock our doors, make sure Noora doesn't get a ticket or jailed, that kind of thing. Dad comes with us and delays his flight.

At Redding Airfield, a small municipal airport nearby, we board a private plane. The inside is plush—white leather seats with mahogany accents, warm lighting, and tabletops with sprays of bright floral arrangements. The chamberlains sit up front, the imperial guard in the back, our little family huddled in the middle.

"You know," Dad says as the jet ascends. "You could have just called."

Mom stares out the window. She's sitting next to him and hasn't said much. She's in a general state of shock, I think. Not sure what she's diving into, risking it all for love. Whether it will work out. We'll see. My own love story sure didn't, but I have high hopes for them. I'm a sucker for romance that way.

Once we've cleared ten thousand feet and hit cruising altitude, the chamberlains descend. There's much ado about our current situation. It's decided Mom will be snuck into the palace and her visit will be kept secret. It's what she wants. Then, I'm next on the agenda. What to do with me and how to clean up my mess are hot topics. The tabloids are still running the story of my affair. In the absence of new material, they've started to conjure all sorts of new outlandish stories: "Princess Izumi Pregnant with Bodyguard's Love Child." "Crown Prince Sent Daughter Away for Hiding Tattoos."

The chamberlains have lots of ideas. A press conference by the Crown Prince? A strict media shutout? Deny it all, because photos can be doctored?

"If I may." I clear my throat to be heard. There's a stutter of excitement to my heartbeat. "I have a suggestion on what I'd like to do."

It takes some convincing. My father is my biggest cheerleader. A plan is hatched and agreed upon. I inhale, staring out in the inky night. It's a little intoxicating, this power. When we hit the tarmac in Japan, I'm still smiling.

36

Tōgū Palace is exactly as it was before. Mariko is reinstalled, and it's as if I never left. God, I am blessed to have two places to call home. Mount Shasta, Tokyo—both are a part of me and not just separate pieces anymore. They're braided together, tangled up, inseparable.

Forty-eight hours after our arrival, I'm sitting in the living room. Dad is present, but Mom is on a walk. Don't want our visitors to see her. The room is abuzz. Chamberlains in their best suits are in varying states of worry. Imperial staff dart in and out, offering refreshments. My new guard is also present—a man with a wide jaw and a predilection for wearing sunglasses indoors, who looks as if he's chewing wasps. Then, there is the press—Yui Sato and her photographer. Yui is the executive editor of *Women Now!*, a small boutique magazine with a good circulation and known for being progressive on women's issues. This is my idea. There's a saying: if you can't beat them, join them. It's unprecedented. An exclusive interview with a member of the imperial family, by a reporter outside of the elite Imperial Press Club. Mr. Fuchigami came through with a selection of women's magazines for me to choose from, fanning them out on the dining table.

Mariko dusts a final coating of blush on my cheeks. The interview will appear in print, and pictures will accompany it. The photographer snaps a couple of warm-up shots. It's been agreed all pictures will be approved by the Imperial Household Agency. We'll have a chance to preview the article, but not for approval—whatever *Women Now!* says, goes. "Are you sure this is what you want to wear?" Mariko bites her lower lip. This is the fourth time she's checked my wardrobe choice.

I smooth a hand down my navy skirt and check the pearl buttons on my cardigan. Underneath, I'm sporting my Riots, Not Diets T-shirt, though it's hard to see the writing. That's okay. I know it's there.

Yui bows low. "Thank you for this honor, Your Highness."

I incline my head, then stick out a hand for her to shake. A beat passes before she takes it. Her grip is strong and self-assured. Self-doubt kicks in. I question my choices here. My sanity. What am I doing? What have I gotten myself into? Instead of pushing my fear away, I allow it in to roam free, sniff around, see there is no danger as long as I tell the truth.

Yui settles onto the couch. An assistant hands her notes. I haven't seen any of the questions ahead of time, and neither has Mr. Fuchigami. Mariko steps away. When we start, there won't be any interruptions—also agreed upon. The first half will be just me. In the next half, my father will join us.

The photographer raises his camera. I paste on a smile. My posture is strong. God grant me the confidence of someone having an entire conversation on speakerphone in public.

"Ready?" Yui asks, eyes shrewd. She won't go easy on me. I don't want her to. I'm up for it. I've stepped out of the Mount Shasta lane, skipped over the princess road, and on to a path of my own making. From here on out, I'll blaze my own trail. It won't be easy to balance imperial responsibilities, uphold traditions, and stay true to myself. But it can be done. I will it to be so.

I nod. "Let's begin."

The interview took most of the morning. Yui asked some hard questions. I think I answered well. We'll see when the magazine hits the stands in a few days. Summer has descended on Tokyo, sticky and sweet. Despite the afternoon heat, I decide to take a walk. Guess I'm not so adverse to using my two feet after all. A girl has a right to change her mind. Don't try to paint me into a corner. Evolving is part of life.

Mom and Dad are having lunch in the city. A restaurant has been shut down for them. NDAs were signed, it was a whole thing. I was invited to join them, but I declined.

Instead, I trudge through the property, new imperial guard behind me. I'm deep in exploration when footsteps pound behind me. The Shining Twins approach. They wear coordinated running gear. Their hair is slicked back into sleek ponytails. They glisten with sweat, and their cheeks are an appealing shade of pink. They brake in unison. Still so creepy. I'll never get used to it.

"Cousin," Noriko says.

"Heard you gave an interview this morning," Akiko says.

I know what's around the corner. A threat. Noriko runs a tongue over her teeth. "If you said anything about our mother . . ."

I'm kind of over the whole family feud thing. "Yeah, yeah,

you'll destroy me. Seems to me you've already done your worst, though."

They look at each other, then focus back on me. "What do you mean?" asks Noriko.

She must think I'm totally clueless. "I mean, snapping pictures of me and Akio. Giving them to the *Tattler* has got to be a new low for you."

Akiko's face screws up. "We didn't give pictures to the tabloids."

"Right." My voice is loaded with sarcasm. I cross my arms. My imperial guard stands by, hands folded in front of him. The Shining Twins also have a pair of guards close. Wonder what they would do if we threw down.

"Seriously," Noriko says.

"I totally believe you." I totally don't, and it's clear by my tone.

Akiko says. "Ugh. You think we'd actually talk to the tabloids? They've been horrible to our mother. To us. We'd never subject someone to the same treatment."

I cast an eye at both of them. Their posture is relaxed. They're certainly not acting shifty. Either they have a sociopathic level of dishonesty, or they're telling the truth. It does make sense. . . . I remember how protective they were of their mother on the emperor's birthday. Maybe they really do hate the tabloids.

After a while, Noriko speaks. "We almost felt sorry for you." She says it like she finds it very annoying. You know, being a human and all.

"Believe us or not, we didn't rat you out," Akiko says.

They trot off, bony shoulders bumping into me as they go.

Their imperial guards follow.

"If you didn't do it, then who did?" I holler after them, rubbing my shoulders.

Noriko turns, jogging backward. "No idea."

It's all the help I get from them. I watch until they disappear. I pop out my phone and text the AGG right away.

> Me
>
> Just ran into the Shining Twins.
> They say they didn't sell me out.

> Hansani
>
> What?

> Noora
>
> You believe them?

> Me
>
> Yeah, they were all like, we'd never
> do that. Have you seen what the
> tabloids have done to our mother?

> Glory
>
> Plot twist!

> Noora
>
> If they didn't do it, who did?

I think it over. The articles cited a palace insider. I'd naturally assumed it was the Shining Twins. But it could have been someone else in the family. . . . I flinch at the thought of a certain person. The only other person who had such unfettered access to me. It's as if I've been punched in the gut.

Twenty minutes later, I'm at my Auntie and Uncle's house. I circle around and, lo and behold, Yoshi is in the front yard sunning himself, ridiculous drink with an umbrella on a nearby table.

"Stay here," I tell my guard. "You're not going to want to see this." Reina is also on hand. I give her a jerky wave. As I approach, Yoshi smiles. I see through it.

"I heard you were back. Come, sit. Have a drink." He gestures to the chair beside him. His chest is covered in some type of oil and completely hairless.

"No, thanks. It's not even noon." At my harsh voice, his smile fades.

"You're in a mood," he says.

"Why'd you do it?" I ask, hands balling into fists.

"I'm not sure I know what you're talking about." He settles back on the lounger, tipping his chin to the sun.

"Why did you sell those photos to the tabloids?" I was supposed to be safe with him.

"Oh. That," he says softly. A long time passes. The sun heats my head. The air smells of pine and suntan oil. "Why does anybody do anything? Money." He shrugs. "I needed income besides that provided by the imperial family. Do you know that, as a prince, I really don't have any marketable skills?"

I release a long breath. It helps that he doesn't deny it. That

I won't have to strangle the truth out of him. "I thought you were my friend." The hurt is evident in my slouching shoulders, in my wavering voice, in my watering eyes.

Yoshi sits up, takes off his sunglasses. He hangs his head. "I am your friend. Or at least, I *was* your friend. I didn't plan to like you as much as I did. I wish things were different. But . . ." He shakes his head. "You don't know what it's like growing up here. What a burden it is—someone always telling you what to do, where to go. It's no life at all." He slips on the sunglasses again, shutting me out. Polished, carefree Yoshi is back. It's a neat trick, this mask he wears. I thought it was a cover for a soft inside. But now I see. He's just a sad, lost boy who will do anything to get what he wants. "Besides, I did you a favor. You said you wanted to go home."

My stomach turns with nausea. Absolutely sick. He hurt me. He hurt Akio. Lives were ruined in his quest for a payday. So he could afford—what, an apartment? A private chef? "That was my decision to make."

"Izumi." He *tsks.* "What's done is done. My valet is packing as we speak. I'll be moving out as soon as my new apartment can be cleaned and furnished." His eyebrows draw in. "For what it's worth, I am sorry. If the circumstances had been different . . ."

"Yeah, I'm sorry, too." It's for different reasons. I'm sorry I trusted him. I'm sorry he's such a spoiled brat. I start to walk away. I'm not letting him off the hook. I'm letting myself off the hook. He's the one who has to live with himself. My conscience is clear. I don't really want to be anywhere near him right now. Only . . . A question bubbles up. "The letter. Did you deliver it?"

I know the answer before he says anything. Yoshi shakes his head once. "But I didn't sell it to the tabloids either. I could've gotten a lot for it. You want it back?"

I swallow, feeling the empty space in my heart where I kept Yoshi. "Throw it away," I say. Delivered or undelivered, it doesn't matter. What would have changed if Akio had gotten my letter? Nothing. He lost his job, his legacy, and the pride of his family. I hurt him. Badly. I still have everything, and he has nothing.

Yoshi's jaw clenches. "Reina!" he yells. "I need you. Come lotion my back."

Reina's scowl is ferocious as she walks toward us. She's seen everything. Probably already knew all her boss's dirty little secrets, all the games he's played. I wonder if she's as disgusted by him as I am. I think she is. I think I know a way to punish Yoshi.

"Reina," I say loud and clear. She peers at me. "Have you ever thought of working for an aspiring self-actualized princess who makes lots of mistakes but keeps life interesting and would never sexually harass you?"

Reina swallows. Ever so carefully, she places the tube of lotion down. "Your Highness, are you offering me a job?"

I jut my chin out. "Think about it."

WOMEN NOW!

Her Imperial Highness Princess Izumi, The Iron Butterfly

June 21, 2021

Hounded by the tabloids until they exposed her alleged affair, HIH Princess Izumi fled Tokyo. Now, she's back, and she has something to say. In an unprecedented interview, HIH Princess Izumi sits down with executive editor Yui Sato to discuss her childhood, finding out she's a princess, discovering her culture, learning a second language, falling in love, and a future full of possibilities.

It began with a book about rare orchids, Her Imperial Highness Princess Izumi says. She sits straight, legs crossed at the ankles, hands folded in her lap. She cuts a regal profile, even though her upbringing was not. There are hints to her sun-drenched California roots—a smattering of freckles across the bridge of her nose, a reddish highlight in her hair, a genuine warmth radiating from within. She is grounded yet bubbly, almost effervescent, especially when describing her mother and friends back home. "My friend was the one who found the inscription in the book." It was a poem from her father, The Crown Prince of Japan. He penned it eighteen years ago to Princess Izumi's mother, Hanako Tanaka.

For over two decades, rumors have swirled about the Crown Prince's love life. An avid outdoorsman who enjoys skiing and mountaineering, he has had his fair share of high-profile romances, the most recent with Japanese British-born Hina Hirotomo, whose family can trace their lineage back to powerful daimyos and viscounts before the banishment of nobles in Japan. His love life is, and continues to be, of great concern to the Imperial Household Agency. There is pressure for Crown Prince Toshihito to provide a legitimate male heir. Though the imperial family recognizes Princess Izumi as a member, she is neither legitimate nor a male. Questions have arisen about the line of succession and altering the law to include women. Princess Izumi has a response to this, but more on that later.

At this point in the story, she's found her father, or who she believes to be her father. "My friend is an excellent detective, and through her skills, she was able to track him down. She started with the Harvard registrar, but a regular old Google search ended up being how she found him." Princess Izumi's mother is a Harvard alumni and distinguished college professor of biology, but the princess doesn't share her mother's passion for science. "I am afraid I am aggressively average," she shares enthusiastically.

"It was pretty obvious as soon as we saw the Crown Prince and my father's photos. I have been told I resemble him." She does. It's in her nose and her high cheekbones. "My mother gave me the email of a mutual friend they shared in college. I drafted a short letter . . ." She shrugs. The rest is history. A week later, press had gotten hold of the story, and Princess Izumi was on her way to Japan. What happened next was a series of follies.

"My transition to Japan wasn't seamless," the Princess says unabashedly. "Far from it, actually." Though she looked forward to reconnecting to Japan—she has a special fondness of dorayaki— the princess faced many hurdles. Chief among them was her decidedly American upbringing. "It felt like coming home but not at the same time. Growing up Japanese in the States wasn't easy. I struggled with my identity living in a mostly white town. So when I came to Japan, my expectations were high and not exactly reasonable. I may never achieve the knowledge and cultural awareness as someone born here [Japan]. I am a foreigner, but also not a foreigner. It's a bit of a paradox." Adding to her difficulties is a distinct language barrier. Princess Izumi's Japanese is improving, but when she first arrived, she had no grasp on the language at all. "After World War II [The Pacific War], my grandparents stopped speaking Japanese. They wanted to fully assimilate into America. They died before I was born. So much of my history was lost."

Tabloids were merciless in exposing the Princess's cultural faux pas. "It was hurtful to hear, but also useful. I am constantly learning, which means I will make more mistakes. All I ask is for people to be patient with me. I am working hard to be worthy of this institution and at the same time remain true to myself. It's a delicate balance," she says. "I am my mother and father's daughter."

Her biggest transgression was her relationship with imperial guard Akio Kobayashi. Leaked photos of them embracing and caught in a torrid kiss violated two norms—affection in public and a member of the imperial family dating far below her station. "Technically, the photographs were of private moments. I won't deny they happened. But I also won't go into any detail." So, are the guard and the princess still an item? "While I agree most of my life is public and will play out in the media, I am committed to keeping some moments to myself, in particular those regarding my love life, at least until I am ready to share. But I would like to apologize to Mr. Kobayashi and his family. It was never my intention for the press to find out, and I am sorry for any harm it caused. In addition, I'd like to set the record straight. The tabloids painted Mr. Kobayashi in a very bad light. The relationship progressed evenly on both sides. I was not taken advantage of. For a while, we made each other very happy." Her voice is wistful—the tone of someone who has loved and lost.

One person the princess doesn't speak much about is her mother, Hanako Tanaka. "My mother is very private," she says. "But I will tell you she is a wonderful parent—compassionate, kind, and giving." On a possible reconciliation between the Crown Prince and her mother, the princess stays silent, directing the conversation to the topic of her first meeting with the emperor and empress. "I was very nervous," she admits. "But honored at the same time. We made small talk at first and I think that was their way of putting me at ease."

When asked if the emperor and empress disapproved of their son's affair and child, imperial royal biographer and winner of the Osaragi Jiro Prize for his book, *Emperor Takehito: The Man and His People*, Terry Newman, said, "The empress is known for a desire to be progressive on women's issues, including children born out of wedlock, something frowned upon until the last three decades. She is also open-minded, having grown up in a similar situation to her new granddaughter. The empress was born in a poor village and didn't know a thing about court life until she accidentally met the then–Crown Prince at university. She was there on a scholarship. More than anything, the emperor and empress are extremely family-oriented. They made headlines when they decided to break tradition and raise their children in their own home. Admittedly, the stakes are a bit lower for the princess. If she'd been male, then there would be more concern on whether he could inherit the throne as an illegitimate child."

What about Princess Izumi? There have been discussions in the past about a female inheriting the Chrysanthemum throne. Could she picture herself as empress? "I don't know," she says, completely forthright. "I'm just trying to get a hang of being a princess for now."

Whatever the future holds for HIH Princess Izumi, one thing is sure: her father approves. But more importantly, it seems this Princess approves of herself. That's something we can all applaud.

Read next week for part two of the article, where HIH Crown Prince Toshihito joins the conversation.

37

Turns out, Tokyo is a city of romantics, forgiveness, and graciousness. Since the *Women Now!* article published, stuffed bears, lanterns, origami, plates of dorayaki, and notes have been placed outside the gates. The guards bring them in by the armload, sifting through to make sure there are no security risks—like a kawaii doll with laser beams for eyes—and bring them to me. It's mostly from teenage girls. Their notes are in the shape of hearts and express their undying support of my non-relationship with Akio. There are other letters, too, from Japanese born abroad who identify with my story and who want to share their own. The response is overwhelming. I never thought I'd ignite such a flame. I'm committed to writing back to everyone who has left an address. Mr. Fuchigami does not like it. But he has left time in my schedule for me to respond. So, there.

"Oh, this is an invitation to someone's wedding," Mariko says, holding up a piece of card stock with elegant writing. I've enlisted the aid of my lady-in-waiting to sort through the piles.

"Put it in the miscellaneous stack," I say.

"What about this one?" Mariko holds up a note tied to a bunch of flowers. "It's an actual marriage proposal to you." She flips it open. "He states his income is more than five million yen per year. Oh! He's left a picture. He's not completely unfortunate-looking." She flashes me the photo. He's twice my age with a lump of dark hair in bad need of a cut.

"Miscellaneous," I say rubbing my temples. I may have bitten off more than I could chew. Mom offered to stay to help, but I could tell she was anxious to return to the States. All the media surrounding me had given her a serious case of the hermits (i.e., an undeniable urge to stow away in your home, shut all the blinds and drink unfiltered bathwater). Dad is going to visit her soon. I'll be going with him. The two are giving the term *baby steps* a new definition. It is *beyond*.

"Things keep getting stranger and stranger," Mariko remarks. She's opened a small box. The remnants of gold wrapping paper cling to it—the imperial guards most likely unwrapped it first.

"What is it?" I keep working on the note I'm writing. "If it's more dorayaki, it has to be donated. We don't have room to store it all."

"It's a key chain with your name on it."

Slowly, I raise my head, peering at the item dangling from Mariko's blunt fingers.

She digs around in the box. "There's a note."

I'm out of my chair. "Let me see." I take the key chain and piece of paper from her. It's wooden, and a rainbow has been painted on it. My name has been carved into it as well. Clearly homemade. Personal. I'd told Akio about this in Kyoto the night of our walk, our first kiss. What had he said? *I wish I could take your sorrows and bury them deep.* I turn it around in my hands, then read the note.

Now I understand
It is all so clear to me

Against, wind, rain, sleet
I stopped believing in love
Until I saw the leaves fall

It's from *him*. As sure as the earth rotates around the sun, I know Akio's hands have touched this. My heart beats fast, climbing up in my throat. "When was this delivered?" I don't wait for her to answer. I'm already walking, slipping on a pair of shoes and leaving out the front door. Reina is there. She accepted my position as my new head guard. She's been dragging boxes of notes from the gates every hour to me.

She bows to me outside. "Your Highness."

I don't stop. Can't stop. There is fire nipping at my heels. I'm racing to the gates. Reina is behind me. Then she's beside me. You know, because I'm a slow runner and all.

"Not really dressed for a jog," she says.

I'm wearing a pair of slacks and a silk blouse. I finally convinced Mariko about the merits of pants, which are pockets, comfort, and the ability to get out of the car like a person. More guards form in my wake. The closer we get to the gate, the more the security presence intensifies. The key chain is in my hand. It's silly to be racing off like this. I'm sure I'm bound to walk the disappointment plank again. Akio couldn't possibly be waiting for me. But he might be. The stitches I closed up my heart with are bursting. There's still room in there for him. There will always be room in there for him.

I slow down when the gates are in sight. It's nearly evening. The crowd has dispersed. Imperial guards have no choice but to open the gate lest I crash into it.

"No. No. No," Reina is adamant.

"I'm sorry," I call back. "Don't be angry with me. It's for love!"

All at once, I'm on the sidewalk, and I'm noticed. Momentary surprise keeps the stragglers from growing into a crowd. Imperial guards form a barrier around me. Time stills and slows. I walk along the gate, smile and nod at the people. Pretend this is all part of a plan. I clutch the key chain in my palm, searching for a tall, dark-haired former guard with emotive eyebrows.

"The prince never tried to outrun me. This is a first," Reina says through her teeth. Poor Reina. I promise to make it up to her.

My eyes scan the sidewalk, the bushes, even the trees. They land on a figure twenty feet away. Tall. Dark. Out of uniform. My heart pounds hard. Akio is there, body framed in shadow, the setting sun behind him. I continue to approach slowly. I might be floating. Who knows. He sees me, too. His eyes are hooded, fond. A murmur of recognition runs through the crowd. A picture is snapped.

"Hi," I say when I'm close enough for him to hear me.

"Hi." He bows with a flourish.

I'm a little out of breath. "Did you leave this for me?" I open my hand, show him the key chain.

"I did," he says. His voice is rich and warm, fills me up.

"Thank you." It's the best, most perfect gift I've ever received.

"You're welcome." We stand and stare at each other dumbly.

"As much as I'm enjoying this reunion, so is everyone else," Reina pipes in.

Akio rocks back on his heels. His hair is a little longer. He brushes it from his eyes.

"Would you like to come in?" I nod toward the palace. "That is, if you're not busy."

"Not busy at all," he says. "In fact, I'd cleared my next few days. Had to wait outside a palace, planned on taking as long as it needed to see a princess."

"Well, then . . ." I smile like a dummy.

Side by side, we walk to the gate. "New guard?" Akio nods to Reina.

Reina is whispering into her earpiece. "Stole her from Yoshi," I say.

His eyes crinkle with a smile. "Bet he hated that." He doesn't know my cousin was responsible for leaking the story. I'll tell him later. There are more important things to focus on now.

"She knows how to snap someone's neck using only her own body weight. She's going to teach me later," I say.

Akio addresses Reina. "Please don't show her that."

"I already told her no," Reina says, gaze directly ahead.

My hand is so close to his. I could hold it. Instead, I fold mine into a fist. Too many witnesses. We're nearly to the gate, our progress slow because of the growing crowd. My name is called. Pictures are snapped. But it's like we're in our own private bubble, and I am light as air. My limbs tingle. Akio is here. He came for me.

We pass a palace map. There is a red arrow and it says 現在地. Genzaichi. *You Are Here.* Then the gate is in view. It opens, and we're through. We keep going up the driveway until the path bends and we're out of sight. The guards have fallen away, too. Only Reina remains, keeping a respectful distance.

"I saw the magazine article," says Akio.

"You did? What did you think?" I don't wait for him to answer. "I'm so sorry, Akio. I never meant for you or your family to be hurt."

He shakes his head. "I should be apologizing to you. You left Japan because of the *Tattler* article . . . because of me."

"You were fired," I say.

He grimaces. "I wasn't fired."

My thoughts freeze. Time slows and stretches. "Mr. Fuchigami said . . ." *He's gone. He couldn't possibly stay,* is what Mr. Fuchigami had said. "I thought you'd been fired."

"What? *No.* I quit," Akio says. "As soon as the story broke, I turned in my resignation. It didn't seem like a big deal. I was going to leave soon anyway." He says it all so nonchalantly. My brows dart in. He hurries to explain. "I was planning to quit the guard. I was going to tell you at the luncheon, but then we started dancing, and then . . ." He blushes. Then, we were kissing, he means. Full-on making out.

I feel myself blush, too. "I don't understand. Your parents, the media . . ."

He nods. "It was rough at first. Definitely not how I wanted to break the news to my father. But he understands, or at least he's trying to. It helps that he likes you so much."

My frown is fierce. "I thought I ruined your life."

"And I thought I ruined *your* life," he says. "That's why I didn't come around. I thought you didn't want to see me. But then I read the article and the reporter intimated you might still have feelings for me. . . . Was she—is she wrong? Is there any hope for us?" He stops and turns fully toward me. "I know I'm not the man you or your family need me to be. But I'm on my way. I promise if you give me this chance, I'll spend my lifetime being worthy of you. I've enlisted in the Air Self-Defense Force. In a few years, I'll be an officer and can make a good income. It will be difficult, but—"

I cut him off with my lips on his. No more talking. Just kissing. His hands land on either side of my neck, thumbs stroking my jaw. We pull away from each other. He wipes a tear from under my eye. "Radish," he says. "Don't cry."

"They're happy tears," I say. Only happy tears from now on. Orange light filters through the trees. The sun is setting. Reina has turned her back. We kiss again softly and let it linger. "I just never thought I'd belong anywhere," I whisper.

He strokes my jaw with his thumbs again. "Izumi, you are a world unto yourself. Build your own space. One meant uniquely for you." My thoughts exactly.

Another kiss, deep and long. Akio's eyes are melting chocolate with a silver ring, awash in the rising moon. Even though there is no music, we dance, swaying back and forth. I lay my cheek on his chest, probably getting makeup on his white T-shirt. We can't bear to let go, so we don't. We stay. Linger. Let the night come.

What happens next? Where do we go from here? Is this happily ever after? I don't know. What I do know is this moment is pretty damn good. That's got to be worthy of some sort of pyrotechnic display.

Cue fireworks.

ACKNOWLEDGMENTS

During the copyediting stage of this manuscript, I learned that a friend died. She was one of the inspirations for the AGG. We went our separate ways in high school and didn't keep in touch much. But she was a formative presence in my life—confident and so comfortable in her own skin. I'm sorry she's gone. The world will miss you.

There are so many people who make a book into a book. There are people, like my friend mentioned above, who are inspirations. I'd like to add to that list by thanking my husband, Craig, and my twins. Thanks to my parents, who instilled in me a love of reading, which led to a love of writing. Thanks to my siblings, my extended family and friends.

Then there are those people who get their hands dirty and work on the book with you. Thanks to my agent, Erin Harris, who has believed in my writing from the beginning. Thanks to Joelle Hobeika, who is fearless in her edits but also so kind it's a little suspicious; Sara Shandler; and Josh Bank, all at Alloy. Thanks to Sarah Barley, an amazing editor who believed in this book and saw its heart. Thanks to John Ed de Vera for his wonderful work on the cover. Thanks to the entire team at Flatiron—Sydney Jeon, Megan Lynch, Cristina Gilbert, Malati Chavali, Bob Miller, Claire McLaughlin, Chrisinda Lynch, Vincent Stanley, Jordan Forney, Katherine Turro, Nancy Trypuc, Erin Gordon, Amelia Possanza, Kelly

Gatesman, Keith Hayes, Anna Gorovoy, and Jennifer Edwards. And thanks to anyone I've forgotten. For those of you who don't know, author acknowledgments are written far before the book is published. I am writing this in August 2020. In the following months this book will pass through many hands at Flatiron, people I will come to know and respect and wish I could've named and thanked formally on paper. I'm thinking of you all now.

Also, thanks to Carrie, a friend and a fabulous reader in Japan who helped with fact-checking. I cannot say enough about what a wonderful person you are—intelligent and thoughtful. I'm so glad we met. There isn't anyone else I'd like to discuss imperial naming conventions with. Thanks to Naohiro and Ruta, as well, who also read this book and offered feedback.

And finally, thanks to all the readers. I'm so damn lucky that I get to share words with you. My heart is full.

© Susan Doupé

Before Emiko Jean became a writer, she was an entomologist, a candlemaker, a florist, and most recently, a teacher. She lives in Washington with her husband and unruly twins. Emiko is also the author of *Empress of All Seasons* and *We'll Never Be Apart*. When she isn't writing, she's reading.

www.emikojean.com

 @emikojeanbooks